GILDED
CROWN

GILDED
CROWN

PRAISE FOR GILDED CROWN

"*Gilded Crown* is a captivating story full of twists and turns. Deep bonds of friendship have equal time to shine along with the sweet romance that builds while the characters navigate political intrigue, the looming threat of war, and fast-paced action... all interspersed with the perfect sprinkle of humor. With themes of duty, love, friendship, and loyalty mixed with the complexities of trauma, this story is perfect for readers who love action/adventure fantasy with a deeper current running through."

—**R. M. Scheller, author of the *Extension Squad* series**

"The stakes are high, the characters are engaging, and there are royal shenanigans as far as the eye can see. It has everything I like to see in a fantasy adventure! I'm fully invested in the world of Kalmyra and I cannot wait to explore it further as the series continues."

—**Laura Hollingsworth, creator of the webcomic, *The Silver Eye***

BOOK ONE IN THE KINGDOMS OF
KALMYRA SERIES

GILDED CROWN

Natalie Nordby

Elerya Publishing

To God,
who first gave me the gift and passion to write.
I would never have come this far without Him.

THE WORLD OF
KALMYRA

CHAPTER 1

Leo

POLITICS IS A GLOBAL GAME OF CHESS.

My aunt's words rang all too true in the halls of the palace. Even when studying chess, I couldn't keep my mind off blasted politics. I flipped to the next page of the chess strategy book, scanned over the contents, and scratched a note into my paper on the side table.

Peaceful silence reigned in the royal library—a place where my uncle and the tutors never thought to look for me. "Even when I try hard, I'll never be as good as you, Dez," I murmured to my sister's quill, absently running a thumb over the sleek feather.

My sister had always known how to find the best solution, and she never let people dictate what she did. I wished I had learned her trick to that kind of confidence before she'd passed.

Muffled footsteps on carpet drew near. I looked up and immediately returned to my chess strategy. "What do you want?"

Lord Thompson tsked. "So this is where you are."

I kept my gaze focused on my task, doing my best to ignore him. The Parliament member was only five years my senior, yet his condescending air grew by the month. "Don't you have better things to do?"

His finger tapped the open page of my book. "That's quite a statement, coming from you of all people, Prince Leonidas. Is this where you always run off to and waste your time?"

My grip on the quill tightened. "I'm not the one wasting my time right now. Then again, you don't do much in Parliament. A kitchen maid could do better."

"Remind me, when was the last time you even attended a Parliament meeting?" He remarked, "Daystra just trades one worthless royal sibling for another."

"Leave my sister out of this."

"It's not like she's here to hear it."

I jumped to my feet, the book on my lap falling to the ground with a soft thud. Anger flared in my chest. He'd never left my sister alone, even after she outright rejected him, and now he used her to make jabs at me.

"How dare you speak so irreverently," I said through gritted teeth.

"What? Do you intend to solve all your problems with reckless action, just like Princess Dezaray? It didn't get her very far in the end."

My fingers twitched, and I curled my free hand into a fist.

Lord Thompson's smirk grated on my nerves. It made me want to pound that smug look off his face.

"You should speak with more caution when it comes to my sister, unless you want to be associated with the scum that killed her."

"Harsh words." Lord Thompson leaned an inch closer, a taunt lacing his words. "You almost speak as though you have authority as crown prince. If you wanted such power, you shouldn't act as you do. Even now, you shirk your duties."

"What do you mean?" I gritted out.

"The meeting with Lady Catania, of course."

Blasted crimson! I had lost track of time. Shoving past Lord Thompson, I snatched up my book and notes. I took no pleasure in those arranged marriage meetings, but I had wanted to make up for the problems I'd caused the day prior with the last one.

"You will never make it there at this rate."

I stormed past the Parliament member and took the winding library steps two at a time. As the grand wooden doors shut behind me, the sweet floral fragrances of the palace overpowered the smell of books, parchment, and ink.

"Don't see how it's supposed to make things smell *nice*," I muttered to myself. "Good for sneezing, though."

I darted through the marble-floored halls before a commanding voice stopped me in my tracks.

"Prince Leonidas Cassander!"

I cringed at the all too familiar voice calling—or rather shouting—my full name from somewhere behind me down the long palace hall. *He has perfect timing, as always.*

"Don't walk away when I'm speaking to you!" His voice had taken on a sterner tone.

With a repressed sigh, I turned to face him. The scrutiny of his gaze banished the slouch from my shoulders, and I stood straighter. I was tempted to focus on the silver embellishments on his blue jacket, but I met his eyes instead.

"Yes, Rueben—I mean, Uncle Rueben?"

He frowned, as if he already knew the thoughts going through my head. "Use proper titles. Are you aware that you missed the meeting with Lady Catania? She waited for an hour before her patience waned, and she left."

Before I could open my mouth to reply, he added, "Don't act like you forgot. I cannot understand you when it comes to this. First yesterday's disaster, now this? Do you know how close you came to ruining a very important relationship? She was the heiress to one of the largest dukedoms in Daystra! They've helped sustain the economy for decades. You, of course, had to be so much like yourself."

I clenched my hand. "You pin everything on me, but I didn't plan on missing this meeting. And yesterday wasn't my fault—she was so stuck up! She got offended by most of what I said."

"Come now, Leo. I know how you are. You're especially gifted in the ways of putting people off with your behavior."

Once again, Rueben had so much trust in me.

"I wasn't trying to ruin anything."

If he heard me, he pretended like I hadn't said anything. "Don't make any more messes. I have enough to clean up because of you. Now hurry on to an additional two hours I scheduled with one of your tutors to go over etiquette."

I did my best to keep the irritation out of my voice, but some still slipped in. "Fine, but don't expect it to fix me."

His dull brown eyes looked over me with the disapproval I was all too accustomed to. I could predict the lecture before he even spoke.

"How many times do I have to remind you? You will be eighteen in two weeks. This is the time when such matters should be addressed."

It was hard to stay calm when it came to such a frustrating matter. "Why do I have to get married anyway? There aren't even political reasons for this!"

"Every king needs a queen at his side. Keep an open mind, and give it a chance. You can't avoid it forever."

"Want to bet?" I muttered under my breath before meeting his stare. Our eyes were nearly level. He folded his arms across his chest and looked at me expectantly. Despite my height, Rueben still made me feel like a small child being reprimanded. Maybe it just went with being the steward of Daystra.

I broke my gaze away first. It was pointless. This wasn't the first time we'd had this argument, and it wouldn't be the last. There was no way I could avoid the extra tutoring.

"I should go. I have a lesson to attend."

I turned and walked away, hearing his exasperated sigh in response.

✿ ✿ ✿

After a tutoring lesson that dragged on, I escaped into the halls.

I had barely turned the corner when Symon strode over. At least it was his shift now.

"How did it go?"

"How do you think?" I stretched my shoulders, tense from sitting ramrod straight.

Who made that carpenter angry enough to make such a horrid chair?

He looked over me, his neutral bodyguard expression softening. "Did you get enough sleep last night?"

"Who needs sleep?" I stalked down the hall.

"Leo—"

"Just another thing I'm not good enough at. I should be used to that by now."

My remark made Symon fall into silence for the remainder of the walk.

Relief washed over me as we arrived at my room, one of the few sanctuaries I had in the palace. It was nothing overly lavish or luxurious. There was a large bed at one end, a desk near the corner, an armoire on the other end, and a rectangular table in the center. It was the way I liked it, simple as I could get, being who I was.

I crossed over to the table. All of a sudden, water splashed the back of my head and down my neck. It dripped from my hair and into my eyes. I blinked in surprise and wiped at my face.

"Hey!" I spun to face him.

Symon smirked with a glass of water still half full in his hand. "What? You needed something to snap out of it."

"Uh huh. I see." I lunged for the glass, but he ducked. "You coward!"

"I'm not the coward here." He tossed the water at me again.

"Why you!" I pulled out a chair to slow him down as he chased me around the table. "This could be seen as an attempt on the crown prince's life. You could be hauled off to the royal dungeons for this!"

He raised a questioning brow. "Are you saying Daystran princes melt when they get wet?"

With as straight of a face as I could muster, I said, "Yes. Yes, they do. It's a state secret, so you must take it to the grave."

Symon nodded back, just as serious. "Of course. I swear on my honor as a royal guard."

I chuckled, unable to hold back my wry grin any longer. He relented and set the glass of water back down on the table, seeming satisfied with that.

"You certainly are the most mischievous prince of the kingdoms."

"Not everyone would determine that to be a good thing..."

Wandering to one of the tall windows in my room, I gripped the windowsill and looked out. From here, I could see over the gates of the palace and into the city below. The view of the familiar buildings filled me with a longing to slip through a passageway and disappear in its streets.

Instead of the open city, I was surrounded by cold, restricting walls. The walls that had trapped me all my life.

Maybe one of these days, I would finally work up the courage to leave the palace for good.

The tantalizing possibility of freedom made my brain run through a list of everything that still had to be done today, including the never-ending meetings and lectures. Exhaustion weighed down on me from just thinking about it.

Exhaling, I slouched now that I was alone with Symon. I rubbed at a tight muscle in my right shoulder. Every time I spoke with Rueben, that blasted knot got worse. "I think he's going to drive me mad one of these days."

"I'm pretty sure you're going to drive him to an early grave before that happens."

I twisted around to make a face at him. "Don't be ridiculous. His ghost will come back to haunt me until I follow him to the grave."

He pushed his strawberry blond hair out of his eyes. "Maybe if you cooperated more, he wouldn't get so frustrated. Your reputation isn't exactly the pinnacle of responsibility and respect, you know."

"What's the point of trying? He'll never be satisfied, no matter how much I do." I leaned back against the window. "All he—all everyone—wants is for me to be their good little prince and do exactly as they say, as if I'm some sort of pawn. I just..." I trailed off, unsure of where I had been going with that sentence. "I'm so sick of it. I can already imagine how it will go when I sit on that lunarium throne, and it turns black and proves them all right."

"You are the heir. It will remain white."

"Yeah, well according to the legends, if you're the wrong ruler, bloodline or not, the lunarium will condemn you by turning dark as night."

"Which hasn't happened in over fifty years," he countered.

I heaved a sigh. Symon met my stare, and something in his brown eyes made me think he knew what thoughts lurked in my mind. "Leo."

I cleared my throat, not wanting that conversation right now. I didn't have the mental energy for it. "Forget I said anything. It's useless to complain about things that will never change."

"Why do you always do that?"

"Do what?" I asked, averting my gaze back to the window.

"I know things can be rough here, but don't forget that I have your back. And...I know Lord Rueben can be hard on you, but that doesn't necessarily mean he doesn't care."

I scoffed. "I find that hard to believe. I've always been the annoying burden he has to clean up after and nothing more."

"Don't be so negative."

Lord Thompson's taunting words still churned in my mind. His one particular comment still grated at me. *"Do you intend to solve all your problems with reckless action, just like Princess Dezaray? It didn't get her very far in the end."*

My hand clenched around the window sill. *They can play their politics. There are more important things to do.*

"I wasted enough time in this dreary palace. Let's go." I stomped over to the armoire in the corner of my room and rummaged through my small collection of disguises for venturing out into the city.

When Symon saw the clothes, he gave me a knowing look. "Brantley said he would handle things."

"He's a resourceful spy, but he hasn't followed up on it yet.

I'm not going to sit back and watch this lead slip away like all the others." I couldn't mess up my only real chance at finding any valid trails to the assassin after all this time.

Once I had changed into my disguise, I ran a hand through my black hair and attempted to tame a few spots that stuck out at odd angles. Mother's comments in the past about my unruly hair drew my thoughts to her. I wondered how much news about me and the possibility of an arranged marriage had reached the northern palace. I hadn't seen her in a while...

Symon came up behind me and lifted a brown wig toward my head. I whipped around to block his attempt. "What in Kalmyra are you doing?!"

"We already discussed this. You need to better disguise yourself after you were almost recognized last time. Oh, and here." He handed me a pair of eyeglasses.

I glared at the itchy wig and eyeglasses. "That's why I have multiple disguises now."

"You can never be too careful. Besides, the eyeglasses are something you could actually use to read things easier. You said before—"

"Who cares what I said before? I can read fine. I don't need them."

Symon shot me an unamused glare. "It's this, or don't go out at all."

With a sigh, I gave in and wore the wig and eyeglasses. "Fine."

The fact that he let me go out as long as he came along was enough for me to cooperate with almost any of his requests— even *this*, as annoying as it was.

He opened his mouth to say something more, but I spoke first. "You're about to say 'Leo, don't do anything stupid, and don't get into any fights. Don't forget your sword, and we have to be back before it gets dark out.' Just because you're two years older than me doesn't mean you get to mother me!"

He rolled his eyes. "I was only going to say avoid trouble."

"Hah! See?"

Symon waved me off. "Let's go already before it interferes with your schedule."

A knock on the door made me stop and turn around. "Who is it?"

"I have a message for Symon Caddel from Lieutenant Blaine."

I yanked the wig off and held it behind my back. With my go ahead, the messenger entered. Symon straightened and slipped back into bodyguard mode.

"The lieutenant wanted to notify you that you are lacking the necessary reports for yesterday."

"Oh, right. Thank you for delivering the message."

Oops. I shifted. I had been extra anxious to get out of the palace for as long as possible after yesterday's disaster. If I'd realized it would give Symon extra work, I would have gone back sooner.

"Sir Gruffud will temporarily take over your duties in your absence." The messenger bowed to me with a mildly surprised look at my commoner clothing before he left.

"You stay put, Leo. I'll be right back, and then we can go." Symon gave me an apologetic look before he hurried off to handle the forgotten report.

I groaned internally at the aforementioned bodyguard. *Gruffud? Seriously?* That guy was too perceptive. I'd never be able to go outside the palace with him hovering.

I grabbed my unmarked sword and headed for the wall perpendicular to my bed. Symon knew where I was going. He could catch up. I pulled on the nearest lighting fixture, causing a passageway to open. As I took the lantern from the wall, I closed the passage behind me. The familiar graveling sounds of stone grating on stone filled the near darkness.

I breathed a sigh of relief when I came to the other end of the passageway and made it past the outer walls of the palace and into the city of Maldenia unnoticed.

Freedom. Finally.

CHAPTER 2

Leo

INKY WATER FROM THE INLAND BAY REFLECTED THE moonlight and shimmered freely in the lapping waves. Wooden docks stretched out into the water, all with ships of various shapes and sizes moored there. Each ship had a unique style. I read the names of the vessels as I scanned the area.

Despite it being so late at night, the docks were oddly crowded. A seagull's screech made me jump, and I sidestepped the bird as it dived past me and right to the water. What was it doing out so unusually late? Everyone and everything there seemed busy and intent with their purpose, even the birds.

The assassin known as Devrim had last been seen in the neighboring country of Zuren, albeit that was a while ago. Emerald green letters painted on a sleek ship anchored at the end of the pier caught my eye. *Wanderlust.* The sails and structure of the ship weren't Daystran.

Could this be the ship Devrim came on?

A child's high-pitched scream shook me from my thoughts. I looked up to see three small children scrambling away from an older sailor. Terror filled their faces as the man backed them into a corner.

"Hey!" I darted in their direction, but a young woman beat me there. Her wavy brown hair wildly framed her face as she planted herself in the middle of things. The boldness in which she argued with the man surprised me.

I rushed over and stepped in front of the children. "What's going on here?"

"Scum." The young woman glared at the sailor. "Get away from those children."

The sailor scoffed. "Not that it's any of your business, but my lil' niece and nephews are tryin' to run away again."

"He's not our uncle!" one of the children wailed from behind me. "We were minding our own business a-and he cornered us and tried to take us somewhere—he threatened to beat us if we didn't go along with him!"

"Why, you little urchins!"

When he lunged at them, the young woman twisted his arm behind his back. "Leave them alone."

The man grunted and yanked free. "Get out of my way, lass." He shoved her to the ground.

I shifted my stance and rested my hand on the smooth hilt of my sheathed sword. Indignation flared within me at his roughness toward her. "I think you should leave. These children certainly don't belong with you."

Scrambling to her feet, the young woman shot the sailor a fiery glare from behind. She seemed ready to go off on him. I shook my head once, hoping she got the silent message that I had it handled.

The gruff sailor eyed the children once more before glancing at my sword. "Fine then," he said brusquely. "But if I see 'em round these docks again, I ain't gonna let 'em go!"

Once he left, I crouched down to speak to the children. "Are you three all right?"

The eldest nodded, her curly brown hair bouncing with the movement. "We are now. Thank you, sir. I don't know what we would've done."

"It's no problem. Maybe avoid the docks in the future? Sailors aren't always the best, most honest company, especially at this hour."

One of the younger boys blurted out, "We were looking for our father, and he was a very nice sailor!"

I smiled. "I'm sure he was. Do you need me to take you back to where you live?"

"That's okay, sir," the girl said. "I know the way to the orphanage. We won't trouble you further."

"It's all right. I want to make sure you three get back safely." I put a hand on the little girl's shoulder and gripped it firmly. "Take good care of your brothers. They need their sister; they always will." As I spoke, a tightness formed in my chest, along with a knot in my throat.

I turned to make sure the young woman was also all right. I picked up her satchel that had been strewn to the side. "I believe this is yours."

"Oh, thank you." She took it from me and smoothed out her dark green skirt. Her clothing looked more suited for traversing a ship than anything else.

"Quite admirable of you to jump into that. I can escort the children to their orphanage from this point."

The distrustful side-eye she sent my way caught me off guard. "I will go as well. For all I know, you could be worse than that lowlife."

"Have it your way."

One thing in particular caught my attention about the young woman—she had a Zurinian accent. *Was she on that ship from Zuren?*

As we walked together with the children, I attempted to get what information I could from her. "Where are you from?"

She narrowed her eyes. "What do you want? Everybody wants something."

If being a prince had taught me one thing, it was that she wasn't wrong—everyone was after something. Figuring out what they wanted and what they were after before it caught you by surprise was the trick. I couldn't say I blamed her caginess. If I were her, I would be suspicious of me too.

When I didn't immediately answer, she asked, "Who are you exactly?"

Her question caught me off guard. It took me a moment to come up with a reply. "I am many things, but I guess you could say I'm part of an importing-exporting business." Technically, this was true. The Crown had many businesses.

One of the little boys with curly light blond hair piped up then. "So the mister's a smuggler!"

"Huh?" I glanced at the children who had dissolved into amused giggling. "What would make you think such a thing?"

"Look, I don't need any trouble from some smuggler. I'm just trying to go about my business, so go swindle or recruit someone else, or whatever you're trying to do."

I didn't correct the young woman. I didn't know anything about her. What did it matter if she thought I was a smuggler?

"I'm just out to run a few errands."

"Sure you are." The disbelief in her voice was evident. "People like you always want something, and I don't want any part of whatever it is."

We might be more alike than you realize.

"That's unfortunate. I think you would have found me to be quite...interesting." If she found being the crown prince interesting, that is.

The little girl peeked back at us curiously as we rounded the corner. "You're trying to flirt with her!" She pointed at me.

"What? No, no. I don't flirt with strange ladies."

"I think he just likes to talk," the young woman stage-whispered to her, causing the three children to giggle more.

"If he's a smuggler, then what do you do, miss?" one of the boys wondered.

"I'm a ship captain."

Ship captain? I glanced at her from the corner of my eye. She could have seen Devrim.

We arrived at the orphanage and watched the three children wave goodbye as they scurried inside safely. A beat of silence passed before I turned to her. I introduced myself with the shortened version of my surname I always used when going somewhere in disguise. "I'm Cass."

She paused for a moment. "Zandra." Before I had a chance

to say anything more, she glanced down at her pocket watch. "Tides, I'm going to be late, thanks to that louse."

"Wait," I said. "Where are you heading? It would make me feel better if you allowed me to escort you there."

"That's not necessary. I can handle myself just fine."

"I can see that, but I'd still feel more at ease if I went with you." I couldn't miss the chance to find out more about the ships that had come to Maldenia recently.

Zandra threw a glance over her shoulder. She returned her gaze to me, crossing her arms. "What do you want, smuggler?"

I decided to take the opportunity. "Information. You said you were a ship captain. I'm looking for someone that came here on one of the ships from Zuren."

"Give me a reason why I should help you."

"You can name what you want in return. I honor my deals."

She shot me a suspicious look. "You're an odd one for a smuggler." The young woman walked away without another word, and I didn't follow. I guess that was that. Then, without looking back at me, she added, "I'll be around the docks tomorrow night at nine."

"I'll be there!" I called back.

"Good for you."

A faint smile tugged at the corners of my mouth as I watched her disappear down the street. Six long years had gone by, but now I finally had a potential source for information that could lead me to Devrim.

One step closer to making my sister's murderers pay.

A voice snapped me out of my thoughts in an instant. "So

the black sheep's been wanderin' again."

I whipped around to face the young man a few years older than me with curly auburn hair. "Brantley, don't sneak up on me like that."

"You wouldn't have to worry about bein' sneaked up on if you'd taken Symon with you." He lightly jabbed me in the ribs.

I pushed his hand aside. "He got caught up with a report. I knew he could catch up—but how did you find me here?"

"I have my ways. Now come on."

I crossed my arms. "I'm not done at the docks. I'm going to find Devrim."

"The docks are dangerous this late at night. We both know Devrim wouldn't be openly waltzin' around there. You'll only get yourself killed like this." Brantley dragged me along down the street, and I didn't argue with him. My spy friend had a point, frustratingly enough.

When would leads quit turning into walls?

"Where are we going then?" I asked.

"To come up with a real plan—preferably one that's less idiotic."

CHAPTER 3

Leo

THE SMELL OF LEATHER AND BURNING COAL GREETED me as the door to the blacksmith's shop closed with a thud. I lingered at the entrance for a moment. I hadn't come to this place in a while; instead, Brantley had been meeting with me elsewhere. Everything was the same, though.

One large wooden table dominated the middle of the room with the anvil and forge in the back right corner. A soft glow emanated from the smoldering coals warming the shop. Various swords hung from the wall opposite of the forge, all clean and polished, while tools hung on the adjacent wall.

Brantley crossed over to the table and started polishing a leather saddle. The glow from the forge behind him lit up his auburn hair like fiery red coals.

"So what's your brilliant plan?" I said. "Or was this just your excuse to get me to help with chores?"

"Ha!" Brantley flashed me a grin. "Well, puttin' you to work *is* the highlight of my day."

I grabbed a scrap of leather off the table and aimed to smack him with it. He dodged and ruffled my hair.

"Hey, quit that! We're not kids anymore. Not to mention, you'll mess up my hair with those greasy hands of yours and make me look like a lunatic."

"Oh, aren't ya one of those already?" He chuckled, wiping the tallow off his hands on his leather apron.

Brantley picked up the saddle and carried it to the other side of the room. I followed.

Why was he intentionally subverting the conversation?

"You said you'd look into the lead on Devrim and report back right away. Why didn't you?"

He didn't respond as he set the saddle in its place and made sure it was situated properly.

"Brantley, you promised to tell me things even if the rest of the palace lied to my face—unless something has changed in the last four years?" I knew it wasn't fair to play that card, but he was acting strange.

"It's not that. My father had some complications with the smithy, so I needed to take care of those affairs." He shifted and wouldn't look me in the eye. There was something more.

"You once told me spies still had to be able to trust at least one person in their life."

Brantley shot me a scolding look that could have rivaled Symon's. "Way to just say it out loud like that! Are you *tryin'* to blow my cover? Who knows who might be eavesdroppin'?"

Despite the conversation, I couldn't help a faint laugh. "Always so paranoid." After a beat of silence, I asked, "What did you find out then?"

"There probably won't be much new information these days. Devrim is long gone, or maybe even dead, given the line of work he was in. I don't think it's likely we're going to find 'im, that's all I'm sayin.' He's like a ghost."

I heaved a sigh. Brantley's point made sense. And yet...I couldn't let it go that easily. The assassin had killed my sister, for Kalmyra's sake.

"I still have to try. I understand if you can't spare any more time searching for me."

"That's not what this is about. I'm always gonna help you, with this and anythin' else you ask of me. I just don't want you to get your hopes up."

"I didn't know I had any hope left."

"Leo." Brantley met my gaze. "You said you wouldn't go back to bein' the way you were after your father and sister passed. You promised—"

"I remember. I'm not that thirteen-year-old kid anymore."

Silence settled over us, save for the din of the forge and the crackling fire. I stared into the flames. The sputtering of red and oranges lured me into a trance. Memories of a younger me helping my father in the forge when he had free time from his kingly duties flickered through my mind. An eternity might as well have passed since those days.

After several minutes, my friend broke the quiet reverie.

"I *did* recently overhear a rumor that could prove to be somethin'—or nothin' at all."

At that, he had my full attention. "What is it? Why didn't you mention this right away? Or leave a message about it?"

"Like I said, I don't want to get your hopes up. Give me some time to look into it, to make sure it's legitimate. I'll let you know when I find out more."

I crossed my arms. Brantley never avoided telling me things in the past. I didn't like the idea that he was starting to do so now. He was the only royal investigator that actually listened to me. "I find your 'plans' to be very lacking as of late. You know I don't like waiting and being in the dark."

"Believe me, my friend, I'm well aware that you're the most impatient person in all of Kalmyra."

I rolled my eyes. "Psh, am not."

"Are too."

A small bell jingled above the door followed by a rush of cold air seeping into the shop. I glanced up. A man dressed in cobalt garments with ivory embroidery took one look around at the blacksmith's shop and crinkled his nose. "Boys, where is your master?"

Brantley crossed over to him. "My father's busy makin' a delivery and runnin' some errands, but I can help ya."

The noble took one look at him and frowned. "Well, I suppose. It's not as if I have a choice."

Brantley pasted on a smile, though I could imagine the few choice words he already must have been thinking of for the noble. "What can I help ya with?"

"I am looking for a short sword of the highest quality."

Brantley went through and showed him various swords. Each one the noble seemed to find unsatisfactory. The longer it went on, the more forced Brantley's words became and the tighter his smile grew. I just leaned against a wall and watched their exchange.

Finally, the nobleman said, "On second thought, I shall return when the master blacksmith is present so that I may see the entire selection, not just the measly few you have shown me."

The moment he left and the shop door swung shut, Brantley slammed a hand down on the table. "Oh, blasted crimson! Now there's a perfect example of a classic noble. They all think they're so much better because they have 'noble blood' like some kind of well-bred horse—not like you, of course. I know you're not like that—but this man. He acted like speakin' to me for too long would make 'im dirty. I mean, honestly! How ridiculous is that? Because 'us commoners' are *so* different. I don't know why I'm tellin' you this. You deal with these idiots more often than I do."

"They really are something else." I had always found the distinction people made between commoners and nobility to be rather pointless. As if the blood in your veins affected the kind of person you were—although it did for many, just not in a positive way.

I pushed off the wall. "Since I'm here, I hope you're not going to rant the whole time while I stand around."

"Ha! Nice try." Brantley gave me a slap on the back. "You and idle hands don't mix—I've seen that firsthand."

Grinning wryly, I put on one of the brown leather aprons hanging from a hook on the wall.

Helping Brantley forge blades from steel was hot and sweaty work, but it was worth it when I could hold the tangible results of my effort in my hands. During those hours, I was able to lose myself in the work and forget about the tedious things waiting for me back at the palace. I often wondered if that was why my father liked forging so much for a hobby.

"So..." I traced a hand over a chisel lying on the table, contemplating whether or not to ask him about the matter. "There might be someone I was hoping you could look into for me."

Brantley paused to look at me, his curly auburn hair falling into his eyes. "What are ya gettin' yourself into now?" He heated a horseshoe in the forge, then stepped over and quenched it in a barrel of water. The hot metal hissed and steamed as it cooled, making a cloud in the air. "Pass me that hammer, will ya?"

I reached over the table and handed him the hammer. "It's nothing to worry about."

A knowing look gleamed in his blue eyes. By his expression, he seemed ready to lecture me, but instead, he only said, "Don't ya have enough to do, bein' prince and all?"

"You know I don't do much around the palace besides being their pawn."

"Aren't you melodramatic?"

"If you don't want to, just say so."

"Fine," he relented while starting to hammer at the horseshoe. "Who is it?"

"Her name's Zandra. She has long brown hair, blue eyes, and is a ship captain with a Zurinian accent. Rather paranoid too—you two would get along well."

"So am I lookin' for information about her for business purposes, or because it's some charmin' girl you met on the streets?" Brantley raised an eyebrow, pausing his hammering.

"Oh, shut up."

He smirked. "I see. So it's the latter."

"Why, you—"

I moved to jab him in the ribs, but stopped short when Johann entered from the back door, carrying several bags from his errands. The master blacksmith was his usual tall, intimidating self. Of course, Johann wasn't as unapproachable as he appeared, despite his deep, booming voice.

"Brantley!" he barked. "What're you doing puttin' the prince to work? We've talked about this before. He ain't a blacksmith."

"No need to scold him too badly," I chimed in. "I came to check in with him about other things. Your son is good at what he does."

"Yeah, good at bein' nosy and eavesdroppin' on others' business." Johann set the bags down and began putting away jars of fresh tallow, leather pieces, and iron ingots for the smithy. "Shouldn't you be gettin' back to the palace?"

"Yeah, I figured as much." I returned the tools I'd been using to their places and hung up the leather apron. "Let me know right away about those things, Brantley."

My friend waved absently, absorbed in his task. "I will."

I left the blacksmith's shop and headed back to the palace. However reluctant I was to go, I had to sooner or later. As I strolled through streets now illuminated by orange lamplight, the intriguing young woman kept coming to mind. I wondered where she was now...

Symon wouldn't let me out of his sight after I left without

waiting for him. I'd have to convince him to sneak out next time. Knowing he'd have my back was reassuring—even if it meant I'd have to endure his bodyguard lecture. Again.

I arrived at an access point for one of the secret passageways and slipped inside the tunnel.

Brantley worried too much about me getting directly involved in the search, but I had seen the darker side of the world. I was not so easily fooled. I was familiar with assassins at this point.

There had already been four assassination attempts over my years of being the sole remaining heir to the throne. It was nothing new to me, not after my sister—

I cut the thought short and slammed the passageway entrance closed, refusing to remember that night six years ago. Now wasn't the time to get dragged into the past. I could never escape the cruel twist of fate that left me as the crown prince of Daystra.

As my sister used to say, I would just have to soldier on.

CHAPTER 4

Leo

"IT'S YOUR MOVE, LEO."

I studied the chess board, contemplating several possible moves. I reached for one of my knights but changed my mind and retracted my hand. I did this several times.

"You're indecisive today." Cyra eyed me from her place across the table. "Is something on your mind?"

"What do you think?"

When I had arrived back at the palace after visiting Brantley last night, Rueben had not been happy. He had rescheduled half of the meetings I had missed, a few of which had been with more possible marriage contenders—*solely as punishment*, I thought sourly, although I knew he usually wasn't that petty. Maybe he was finally fed up with me and my reluctance to cooperate.

Regardless of how frustrated my uncle and others might be, I would not budge on my position about the arranged marriage.

As she so often did, my aunt remained silent and simply waited for me to elaborate, giving me time to work through my thoughts and figure out exactly what I wanted to say.

"I don't want to marry someone because of politics."

It was a relief to actually say the words. The admission had long been in the back of my mind, but I had never dared to voice it before now.

Leaning back in my chair, I said, "Enough of my life is tangled up with politics as it is. It's the reason why I have to do this, or can't do that, and why I have to think of the *Crown's image* when I do anything—even when I take a breath. I just...for once, I want my life to have nothing to do with Parliament's game of politics. For once, I want the choice to be up to me. It's my life. Why don't I get to decide what I want to do with it and who I want to spend it with?" I threw up my hands. "And besides all of that, if I can never do anything right according to the people around me, how in all of Kalmyra will I do any better with a *wife*?"

When I finally met her gaze, I found understanding and sympathy in her light blue eyes. There were few others who would have this reaction to me voicing my frustrations.

I had always felt closer to Cyra than my mother; in fact, she might as well have been my mother. But she was more than that. She was also my mentor and friend. Someone who shared a similar way of thinking as me, one that others usually found to be unorthodox.

Even my appearance was more like my aunt's. We both had the same dark hair and tan complexion. My green eyes were the only physical trait that I'd inherited from my mother.

"I wish for your own sake politics and marriage would be kept separate; however, you know as well as I do that taking such a path wouldn't be easy. Politics is a global game of chess." Cyra tapped the king piece on the chess board as she repeated the saying she'd made up long ago. "And unfortunately, Rueben and most of Parliament are not as forward thinking."

"Hardly." They were all stuck in tradition and how things had been done for centuries. *Heaven forbid* we change something for the better.

"So you're aware that the Zurinian envoy is arriving at the palace today?"

I shifted, avoiding her gaze. "Oh, that's today?"

She gave me a look. "You may have others fooled, Leo, but I know you didn't forget."

I shrugged a shoulder in response. Cyra was the only one who knew that, in reality, I did glance at my schedule every now and then and knew what I was supposed to be doing. I simply chose to disregard much of the useless activities. And today, I was not in the mood to entertain guests.

"You'll have to let them know I won't be able to attend."

"I don't need to remind you how vital it is that Daystra gains a better alliance with Zuren, do I? Our countries have had enough bloodshed between each other, and the Zurinian princess has come in an effort to secure a stronger, more lasting peace."

"That's exactly why I don't want to be involved. It'll be one tense and awkward meeting after another." I knew the chances of getting out of this were next to nothing, but I had to try at least once.

"Prince Leonidas!" the annoyingly familiar, wheezy voice of one of my tutors called from somewhere out in the hall.

Blasted crimson, how had he found me so fast? Usually it took at least an hour before they found me again when I took refuge in my aunt's study.

Cyra raised an eyebrow. "Still dodging your tutors I see?"

"You know, if you would just officially tutor me, then Rueben would get off my back, and things would actually be interesting."

"As enjoyable as that would be, you need to know how to work with others who don't share your mindset."

That was always what she said whenever I brought this up. I fiddled with one of the smooth chess pieces I'd captured from her. "Even if I'd rather drink a cup of poison than listen to those tutors drone on?"

She laughed and shook her head. "Go on now."

"Fine, I'll go." I sighed and dragged my feet over to the door, speaking in an over-exaggerated tone. "But when you hear of my passing, you'll know what killed me."

I waited a moment to make sure my tutor had passed before I stepped out into the hallway. The door clicked shut, and I threw a glance around. Symon was no longer stationed just outside Cyra's study where I'd left him waiting. *That's unusual.*

"Where did he go off to without a word...?" I murmured to myself.

Something poked me in between the shoulder blades as a voice right behind me said, "I didn't go anywhere."

I jumped. "Blasted crimson!" I whisper-hissed, spinning around to face him. "Where did you come from?!"

A flicker of amusement crossed over him. "I've been right here the whole time. I didn't leave my post."

"Humph, you bodyguards."

All of a sudden, Symon shifted to a more upright posture and let a neutral expression slide into place. I groaned internally, wondering which tutor had found me.

"So this is where you have been. I should have known."

Oh, great. Even worse than a tutor.

I turned to face Rueben. "What of it? Am I not allowed to play a game of chess with my aunt when I feel like it?"

"Spending time with *her* will not do you any favors, especially with Parliament. Don't let her unorthodox political views influence you. There are other more productive things you should be doing with your time than talking about who-knows-what with her."

I clenched my jaw. Rueben had always disliked Cyra, without valid reason. One time I'd asked him, and his response had been, "*She's illegitimate. Being involved with her will only bring issues for you, both now and in the future.*"

Why it mattered to anyone that Cyra was illegitimate, I'd never understand. She was still the daughter of a king and my father's sister—a part of the royal lineage.

He eyed the door for a moment with dissatisfaction before returning his gaze to me. "You avoided your studies. Again."

Crossing my arms, I stared back. There was something else. "Why did you really come looking for me?"

"The Zurinian envoy has arrived in Maldenia and will be at

the palace within the hour. I advise you to make yourself presentable and come down and join the rest of us in welcoming them, if you have any interest in forming a lasting peace with one of Daystra's neighboring countries."

I scowled at my feet. "Understood." When Rueben turned to leave, I said, "What I want to know is—why send an envoy now?"

"What do you mean?"

"Forget it. I was just thinking out loud." I'd have to speak with Cyra about it later.

After changing into more formal—and therefore more uncomfortable—clothing, I paused on my way out of my room to glance at myself in the mirror. Dressed like this, I certainly looked the part of a crown prince. A convincing illusion. Deep down, I'd never once felt like a prince in my entire life.

In a moment of rebelliousness, I tipped my crown at a slight angle, making my reflection feel a little more like me. It was one small thing I could do that was my own choice, even if others thought it immature.

As I joined Rueben, Symon, Cyra, and several other dignitaries and ambassadors, I sucked in a breath. If there was one thing I hated more than anything, it was dealing with other countries and their envoys.

I stood rigidly with my shoulders back, as so many all my life growing up had criticized my posture. I hated standing this straight; it always made my back and shoulders ache later.

The envoy arrived with a total of ten ornate carriages. Servants began the tedious process of escorting the diplomats out of the carriages and unloading all of their luggage. The moment the Zurinians stepped out from their carriages, I could sense the change in the atmosphere. The guards around us were more alert and discreetly checking weapons, and even the diplomats that always seemed so comfortable in situations like these went rigid.

They don't look that different from us, save for their tanner complexions. Do we even have reason to hate each other so long after the wars?

There had been little communication between the Zurinian and Daystran monarchies. Their current king had ascended the throne of Zuren seven years ago, but beyond that, I only knew that he had a younger brother and sister.

From the middle carriage, a young woman emerged wearing a vibrant purple dress. Despite the simple design, the fabric and rich color announced her status without being ostentatious. Even her crown was a mere circlet of silver set with a single emerald. A female servant and several guards followed her.

I eyed the Zurinian princess as she glided toward us. She wore her brown hair twisted up into a braided bun. Cool blue eyes and a regally blank expression masked whatever her thoughts on Daystra might be.

She dipped a light curtsey. "Prince Leonidas Cassander, it is a pleasure to meet you."

For a terrifying second, my mind blanked, and I couldn't remember her name for the life of me.

From behind me, Symon hissed, "Alexandrina Veridian."

I cleared my throat and bowed in return. "It is a pleasure as well, Princess Alexandrina Veridian."

The princess gestured to two men on her right. One was taller and wore finer attire while the other had a bulkier build and a simpler uniform. "This is Rowan de Luca, my chief advisor, and Galen Eros, my chief bodyguard."

The others bowed before Cyra smiled warmly. "Welcome to Daystra. I hope this visit may bring about satisfactory results for both our countries."

The other diplomats on each side introduced themselves, although I wasn't paying attention to that. I was too distracted by the expressions on some of the Zurinian guards' faces. While some appeared impassive, others downright glared. Daystran guards glared right back at them, adding to the mounting tension.

I tugged on the collar of my constricting shirt, already feeling as if this blasted outfit was going to suffocate me.

Tense silence followed the introductions until Rueben jumped in. "Shall we have lunch then and perhaps hold official negotiations tomorrow morning? I'm sure you all are worn out after your long journey here."

Princess Alexandrina didn't have as thick of an accent like I'd assumed she would. Her silvery voice and refined tone made her words sound pleasant; however, the tautness in her expression negated it. "If you do not mind, I would rather commence the negotiations now and settle in afterwards."

Despite the unexpected answer, Rueben nodded, as if this had been the plan all along. "Of course. Right this way."

I exchanged a look with Symon before we followed. This was going to be a disaster, and I wanted nothing to do with it.

✿ ✿ ✿

Princess Alexandrina and the Zurinians sat on one side of the large, circular table while Rueben and Cyra sat on either side of me, along with the other Daystran diplomats.

The Zurinian diplomats opposite of us all wore green uniforms with gold embellishments. It was a stark contrast from the cold blues and silvers of Daystra's colors.

As the steward of Daystra, Rueben officially commenced the meeting. He stood and addressed the Zurinians. "We are pleased to host these negotiations for the sake of developing a lasting peace with Zuren."

I fidgeted with the silver-grey ring on my forefinger, zoning out while the diplomats went over the standing treaty in detail. I hadn't taken the time to read it before now, but Rueben and Parliament could handle it without me.

Princess Alexandrina shifted and exchanged a look with her chief advisor. Her movement caught my attention. I wondered what she was about to say.

Since the first White Sand War broke out eight decades ago, Daystra and Zuren's relationship had been strained. Why had they chosen to approach us now in an attempt to broker a more stable peace? No skirmishes had broken out at the border we shared lately. So...what had changed?

Her chief advisor, whose name escaped me, nodded once and whispered something to her before she addressed Rueben. Her even, calm tone sounded a little forced, as if she wasn't ready for whatever she was about to say. "Our countries have had unstable and temporary alliances for far too long. It is time we secured a stronger alliance with a country that shares a border with us."

"Do you have a suggestion?"

She hesitated for half a second. "I do, in fact. A marriage alliance."

The room went silent. Even the other Zurinians seemed shocked.

My jaw nearly dropped. *What?* Why would she want a *marriage alliance* of all things?

And just like that, the whole issue I had been so meticulously avoiding for the last few years came right back to slap me in the face. But surely Rueben wouldn't consider this...

I flicked a glance at him. His posture stiffened, but he kept his surprise better hidden than the others. A calculating glint flashed in his gaze.

Don't tell me you're actually thinking this could be a good idea?

"A marriage alliance?" one of the Daystran diplomats repeated, as if unsure he had heard it right.

"Yes, between me, the youngest of the Zurinian royal family, and Prince Leonidas."

I held my breath and looked to Rueben.

"This is quite...unexpected. I do not think anyone here expected Zuren to bring this up as an option." Tense silence hung over the room when he paused. "However, Daystra is not opposed to discussing it further."

My hands clenched into fists under the table. What did he mean we weren't opposed to discussing it further?

What if *I* was opposed?

Cyra, being on my other side, subtly reached over and patted my hand under the table. Her silent comfort made me unclench my hand and not say half of what I'd been tempted to say.

The rest of the negotiations were a blur to me, my mind too hung up on the possible marriage alliance to focus on anything else.

The luncheon following—or rather dinner after how long the negotiations had taken—was the most boring meal in all of Kalmyra. I sat across from the Zurinian princess. I risked a glance up at her. Our eyes met, and I quickly looked away. She hadn't seemed very pleased, if her expression was any indication. She seemed annoyed, almost.

I tightened my grip on my butter knife. *Great, she already doesn't like me, and we've hardly spoken to each other. What did I do wrong so soon?*

From that point forward, I kept my eyes down and focused on the meal, deciding it would be better if I didn't try to say anything. We both were content to eat in awkward silence.

The moment I could leave, I did so without hesitation, not caring if Rueben had wanted to speak with me afterwards. I was too frustrated with him.

On returning to my room, I came across an envelope left on my desk. I scanned the contents of the message. Brantley had found out information on Zandra. She had arrived in the capital city about four days ago on a ship called the *Wanderlust* and hadn't done anything questionable or gone anywhere overly suspicious.

I fingered the edge of the paper. Tonight was my chance to find out what I could from her about that ship from Zuren.

So I did what I do best—I sneaked out.

CHAPTER 5

Leo

THE AIR CARRIED THE SALTY TANG OF THE OCEAN, AN entirely different world from the stuffy palace—not only the air, but the colors, too. The tips of the leaves were beginning to turn a mix of vibrant reds and yellows.

The fading sky contrasted against the jagged buildings of pale sandstone that rose above on either side of the wide cobblestone streets. The capital city of Maldenia was renowned for its complex, stunning architecture out of all the cities in Daystra. It always felt so liberating when I explored the intricately connected streets.

However, for all the beauty and freedom of the city, it wasn't all great. Poverty lurked in the darker corners if one dared to look. On my way to the docks, I caught sight of a young boy who couldn't be more than five that huddled on a corner of a back street. He held out his hands to anyone who passed, begging for money and food. In his threadbare clothes with its tattered patches, he would freeze to death on the streets when it turned to winter.

Several people walked past the boy and brushed him aside. Some even shot disdainful looks his way as they hurried on.

I stuck my hands in my pockets. Three gold coins clinked together. It was all I had on me at the moment, but I wished I'd brought more along.

I crossed the street and slipped off my jacket. "Here, you need to stay warm."

The boy's eyes brightened as I pulled the grey jacket on him. He had to roll the sleeves up several times just to wear it. I left the three gold coins, the equivalent of sixty dineras, in one of the pockets for the boy to find later.

"Thank you, sir!"

I nodded, wishing I could do more, before heading back down the street.

It had bothered me before, and it still bothered me now. How could Parliament and Rueben let there be such grime and poverty in the capital city of all places? Couldn't they see the conditions right in front of them? Not that they ever listened to me when I tried to raise the issue with them.

I threw a glance back at Symon following from a distance. He really meant it about not letting me out of his sight. When I turned the corner, I nearly ran into someone in the shadowed alley. The unexpected sight of another sent my heart pounding faster. I scrambled back and tripped over an uneven spot of cobblestone. Throbbing pain tore through my palm as the sharp stone bit into my skin.

"Oh, blast it," I muttered, wincing as I pushed myself up. I fisted my hand and clutched it to my chest to try to stem the bleeding.

I glanced up to see who I'd bumped into and jumped to my feet. "Zandra? You're here."

"So I am." Her gaze drifted to my scraped-up hand. "You should check that there's no dirt or debris in that and get it bandaged."

"It's really not a big deal," I said, attempting to ignore the stinging pain. I was out on my own without the constant fussing for once. I wasn't about to let a little scrape ruin that.

"That's a nasty gash. We're close to my ship, and I have bandages on board."

Her offer threw me off, but I didn't object. "Okay then."

Did that mean she wanted to talk and make a deal like I'd hinted at before?

We walked down one of the piers, the commotion of the docks filling the silence. The midnight blue sky melted into the dark waters, and a breeze blew off the ocean, mingling with the smell of fish, tar, and smoke.

"What exactly do you want to know?" Zandra asked.

"I'm trying to find someone who came to Daystra on a ship from Zuren. They might have taken passage on your ship."

"Who is this person?"

"I don't actually know his name, but he's taller and would likely keep to himself as much as possible."

"That's not much to go on. I have a small crew, and we didn't have many others onboard for the voyage."

I repressed a sigh. I shouldn't have gotten my hopes up.

She continued, "We aren't the only ship that came from that area, though. If I were you, I'd check the ships' manifests. It's worth a try."

"That might be difficult to obtain, but thank you." That would have to be a task for Brantley to look into. I glanced down at the gash on my hand and pressed my other hand into it. The bleeding hadn't slowed much. "What do you want in return?"

"I'm considering this an exchange of information. So, tell me. What do people here say about the crown prince?"

I raised an eyebrow. "That's a rather strange thing to want to know."

"It's a trade of information. This is what I want to know. Hearing from a native is the easiest way to discern what the ruler of a country is really like."

"Okay then..." I let my gaze drift up to the evening sky and the few stars already twinkling above. "He was never suited for the crown, and the crown was never meant for him. It's only through the death of his elder sister that thrust him into the role. No one prepared him very well, and he gave up putting effort in when he seemed unable to catch up or be what was needed and expected. He's little more than a pathetic pawn."

"That is a rather harsh view of the prince."

I shrugged a shoulder, even though it stung deep down. I wouldn't attempt to make myself sound good. I knew what others said and thought of me. "It's the unfortunate reality of Daystra's situation."

None of them care, not even Adonai.

"And what do *you* think about the prince?"

Her question caught me off guard. "I...I'm not sure. I think he tries, but his efforts get snuffed out. He starts to lose hope, and that results in his irresponsible behavior he's infamous for. Almost like he begins to give up on being anything else besides what others have already determined him to be, for better or for worse. What do I know, though? I'm a nobody."

"On the contrary, your perspective was helpful and intriguing. Thank you, Cass."

Silence followed until I glanced at her, wanting to move onto a different topic. "How long have you been a ship captain?"

"For about a year, but I've been sailing for much longer than that."

I wanted to ask what made her take up sailing, but I wasn't sure if that would be too personal. Besides, it felt nice to have a conversation that didn't include diplomacy.

"How long have you been in the smuggling business?"

Her question caught me off guard, and I mentally scrambled to come up with a response that wouldn't count as lying. "You mean imports and exports? Well, it's sort of the family trade, so to speak. My father and grandfather were both in the business, and I'm expected to follow in their footsteps." A sigh escaped me despite myself as I stared at the dark, rippling water. "But...it's never been what I wanted." I clenched my bleeding hand tighter to myself. "It doesn't matter though. I don't get a choice, so what's the point in thinking about it as if I did?"

"Some of us don't get a choice." The melancholy tone in Zandra's voice made it sound like she knew how it felt.

In an instant, she tensed, muttering, "I think we're being followed." I glanced behind us, and she stomped on my foot. "Don't look back, you idiot! You'll tip him off!"

I shot her a glare, even though my sturdy boots had spared my foot. "It's fine. That's just my friend. There's nothing to worry about."

"Oh?" Her expression eased, but her shoulders remained rigid. "And why exactly is he following you from a distance like this?"

"He worries too much about my inclination to find trouble." I couldn't help my chuckle.

"Then your friend has good common sense."

We veered left down the pier to Zandra's ship. At the gangplank, she hesitated, her brow crinkling as she debated something with herself. I cocked a questioning eyebrow her way but said nothing. Then she glanced up at her ship before looking back at me. "Um." She rubbed the back of her neck. "You'll inevitably meet my crew since the bandages are below deck."

"I can wait here if you'd rather. Either way, I don't mind."

"It's fine. Come on."

When we came aboard, her crew stopped their work and wandered closer.

"Eh? Who's this?" an older man asked, lifting up his eye patch to get a better look at me. I resisted the urge to ask why he was wearing an eye patch when his other eye seemed to be working just fine.

"I'm Cass."

"He causin' ye trouble, Captain? Should we just toss 'im

overboard now?"

"No, we should at least commandeer his valuables first!" another disagreed, his shadowed form bouncing up on the rigging.

One of them poked his head out from the crow's nest, his dark hair falling into his face. "You think this guy has any money? Look at him—he's clearly got nothing worthwhile to his name!"

"Ahem." Zandra shot them all a scolding look. "He helped me out the other day, so be nice."

Another one of her crew who looked to be about thirteen remarked, "Ohh, so the captain's got a suitor now? Shall we feed him to the sharks if he breaks her heart?"

I stared in surprise, caught off guard by his remark.

"He is *not!*" she protested, a little too strongly.

Her crew member laughed in response. "I don't know. You sort of look like you might like him."

"Takeo!" A young woman came and grabbed him by the ear. "Stop teasing the captain. Are you trying to get yourself thrown overboard? Because at this rate, I'll be the one to kick your sorry hide over the edge!" She whipped back around to face me and smiled. "Hi, nice to meet you. I'm Sade. Ignore this imp; he rarely knows what he's saying."

"Hey!" Takeo tried to wiggle free. "What're you going on about?"

She sent him a look that could have withered flowers. "Below deck. Now. I believe there were some pots in need of a scrubbing."

While the crew members were distracted with the topic of

chores, Zandra led me below deck and had me sit down on a bench near the wooden stairs. After rifling through a small box, she came back with a roll of bandages and a cloth. I tensed as Zandra sat next to me and took my hand, expecting her to be rough. I flinched but made no other outward reaction while she dabbed at the stinging gash on my palm.

"You get hurt a lot, don't you? You seem like the reckless type."

"Hey, I'm not reckless. I'm just...free spirited."

"If that's what you want to call it." She set the cloth aside and wrapped my hand. Her touch was so gentle. It took me by surprise.

The subtle aroma of jasmine permeated the air when she was this close to me. I found myself staring. I hadn't noticed the freckles that dotted her cheeks until now, or the flecks of teal in her blue eyes.

"There."

I dropped my gaze to my hand. I slowly opened and closed my fist, testing how it felt with the coarse bandage. "Thanks."

"You're welcome."

An odd dazedness came over me as Zandra stood. She took a few steps toward the stairs and paused, noticing I was still sitting there. "Are you coming?"

"Oh, uh, right." I shook myself out of it and followed her back up on deck, trying to fully rid myself of that funny feeling. A fresh wave of salty air greeted me as my eyes adjusted to the brighter light of the lanterns flickering.

A man with dark blond hair came up to me. "You'll have to excuse the crew. They all get a little rowdy whenever someone new shows up."

"He's not staying," Zandra cut in. "He just fell and hurt himself like an idiot and needed a bandage."

"I hope you don't let the captain's grumpiness scare you. She rarely feeds people to the sharks. She just needs a little time to get used to strangers, is all."

I smirked. "Don't worry. I'm not scared that easily. And I'll have you know, I'm rather good friends with the sharks in this place."

Zandra snort-laughed and covered it with a cough.

He glanced at both of us and smiled. "Glad to hear it."

"*Okay*, it's time for him to go now." Before I could respond, Zandra grabbed my good hand and dragged me off her ship and back down the gangplank. "Er, sorry about all of that. They can get obnoxious sometimes." She shot an annoyed glare back at the ship.

My gaze drifted to her hand still holding mine. She quickly yanked her hand away, taking the warm sensation with her.

I managed to recover enough from the feeling of her hand in mine to say, "It was nice meeting your crew though. They seem very...*dynamic*."

Zandra huffed. "They're an absolute handful when they want to be. Anyway, it's late. I'm going to bed."

"You're going to bed this early?" I questioned.

"Unlike you, I don't stay up until the unholy hours of the morning causing trouble and doing who knows what."

I clutched my chest. "That's what you think of me? After all the quality time we spent together today?"

She rolled her eyes. "Goodnight."

I realized in that moment that if she wanted, she could sail away, and I'd never be able to find her again.

"Wait," I said. "Don't tell me you're going to leave now, and I'll never see you again?"

She didn't even look my way as she trudged up the gangplank. "I'll be in town for the next week or two. I'm sure I'll see you around."

"I look forward to it. Goodnight!"

Grinning, I turned and headed back down the pier.

Zandra was surprising, to say the least. I wasn't quite sure what to make of the ship captain, but I wanted to see her again. She had all but invited me back...in her own way.

I rejoined Symon who'd been waiting at the side of the harbor master's shop, and we returned to the palace. Once back in my room, I recounted our conversation and how I'd met her crew.

He just shook his head. "You really are so much trouble sometimes. It's unbelievable."

I shrugged. "Feel free to separate yourself from trouble then."

"I have trouble's back, whether he likes it or not." After a long pause, Symon asked, "Have you figured out what you're going to do about the Zurinians and the potential marriage alliance?"

"Ugh, it's too late to talk about *that* right now." I grabbed a pillow from my bed and threw it at him. I'd rather be distracted by the other topic. "I'm going to bed. You can leave. I know it's way past your shift."

Symon caught the pillow. "Is that a royal command?"

"If you vex me, yes."

"Pfft, as if. I'll only let you sleep in peace if you promise not to meet Zandra again—or go anywhere in Maldenia—without me."

"Fine, I promise." I threw another pillow at him on his way out. "You stubborn bodyguard."

Crashing back onto my bed, I blew out a breath. Zandra had seemed less suspicious of me than before. Her question about what I thought of the crown prince still puzzled me. Why would she want to know that of all things?

Curiosity kept drawing my thoughts back to the intriguing ship captain. A tiny voice in the back of my mind warned me not to get too involved with her—that it could possibly cause issues if I was forced to go through with the arranged marriage in the end.

I doubted that would be a problem, though. Zandra would leave in a few weeks, or I would discover something less than honest about her.

I settled further under the soft blankets as sleep overtook me, bringing me somewhere far away from all my current problems and muddled thoughts.

CHAPTER 6

Zandra

I LEANED AGAINST THE MAST AND LET THE SOUNDS OF lapping waves fill my mind in an attempt to drown out my thoughts.

Why had I said anything more to him? Why had I impulsively invited that smuggler to come back? I had already gotten the information I wanted.

Why did I have to listen to Milo?

Furthermore, there was something about Cass that I found... I didn't know what it was—but I couldn't afford such distractions.

Milo's boots tapped across the deck. I crossed my arms. "Why do you have to be so persuasive?"

His mouth quirked upwards. "I take it that means you invited him back?"

"Unfortunately, yes."

Even now, the peculiar smuggler occupied my mind. I

shook my head in an attempt to dislodge the thoughts.

"I'm going to explore the city. Is anybody else coming along?"

"Ooh, I'll go with you!" The cabin boy darted over, a mischievous look flitting across his face.

I raised an eyebrow. "Avoiding chores again, Takeo?"

"Don't give me that look. Chores will always be there, but this" —he gestured to the Daystran capital stretching out before us— "is something I don't want to miss. Besides, we all came along on this trip to have your back with all these Daystrans around. Sade and Soapy can handle the chores!" Without another word, Takeo raced down the gangplank. I followed him, struggling to keep the amused smile off my face.

The Daystran capital, Maldenia, bustled with more people than I'd ever seen at once, even for the evening time. It had so much *life*.

The unusual Daystran accents floated through the air and, though foreign to my ears, it wasn't unpleasant.

Several people wore clothing with shades of blue mixed in, which was an unexpected surprise itself. Wearing blue in Zuren was reserved for only special occasions, such as coronations and holidays, but in Daystra, it appeared to be a common color.

The more I watched, the more I noticed. I marveled at the way the classes mixed in the streets. It was so different from Zuren's strict social barriers that penetrated into the city's very layout.

"Ooh, I bet the stuffy traditionalists would cringe at all of this!" Takeo laughed.

"They would have a fit over it," I agreed.

Why do they all hate it so much? I'd never understand the traditionalists.

A crash drew my attention to a wooden cart that tipped over. When I stepped in that direction, Takeo grabbed my arm.

"Hey, where you going? Galen told us to make sure you stayed out of trouble this time."

"He's being overprotective. I can handle myself, just as I do in Zuren." I brushed off his hand and glanced back at the cart. Three men were already working on getting it upright and had it taken care of.

We wandered around the city, going from one interesting thing to the next. Thankfully, Takeo stayed out of trouble while we explored—or rather, he did until we came to the Daystran marketplace.

I snatched his wrist, eyeing the shimmering crystal in his hand. Of course it was something shiny. Again.

"What do you think you're doing with that?"

"Looking at it." He tried to pull free.

"Put it back. I told you *not to steal*."

"It's only a tiny souvenir."

I gave him a firm look, and the boy sighed in exasperation.

Before he could respond, a vendor from behind us exclaimed, "Thief! Get that boy!"

I turned, intending to set things right with the vendor, but Takeo bolted away. "Takeo!" I dashed after him. *Not again!*

He zigzagged through the streets, and I lagged behind a few paces. How was the kid always so fast?

Shouts from behind made him speed up. Zipping around a

corner and down an alley, he ran straight into the most rundown part of the city.

"Just give it back to them, and they'll stop chasing!"

He threw a glance over his shoulder. "No! What if they decide to cut off my hand?!"

"They won't—you aren't in Rin!"

"You know what those Daystrans are like! Can't trust 'em."

I caught up to him and grabbed his shoulder, slowing him and ducking into an alley. "It hasn't even been two hours, and you're already getting...into trouble..." I trailed off as a blur caught the corner of my eye.

Hushed voices carried down the narrow street. I crept closer and peered around the corner. A man in a dark cloak spoke with another figure, but a hood concealed his face.

"Understood. We will follow your directive, Byron."

"This is time sensitive. I won't tolerate mistakes. If there are, ensure they're aware that one of you will take the fall for it."

The one that seemed to be his subordinate nodded. "I'll relay the message and make sure the others do their part."

"Good. Daystra won't be the same after this."

I furrowed my brow. What did he mean by that?

Behind me, Takeo whispered, "Why are we eavesdropping on people now?"

I clamped a hand over his mouth and dragged him flat against the wall with me.

A voice hissed, "What was that?"

"Street scum, most likely. They're all over these parts."

"Then get your scum under control."

I held my breath, pressing further back into the rough stone. Takeo squirmed, but I kept him still.

Don't run. They'll see us.

Shuffling followed. As footsteps grew distant, I dragged my friend away from that street. My racing heart began to slow once we returned to a less conspicuous part of the city.

"Be more careful. You almost got us caught!"

He crossed his arms. "Caught by who?"

"I don't know who they were. They seemed like trouble." I glanced back at the street we'd come from. Something about them had felt...sinister.

"This isn't Zuren. You can't do anything about it here, Zandra."

"But still..." It bothered me. The way those men had spoken—whatever it had been about—gave me a bad feeling.

Takeo tugged on my arm. "Let's head back before any more Daystrans decide to give us trouble."

I returned to the ship with him, mulling over all that I'd seen and heard. The comforting click of our steps up the gangplank filled my ears. The security of being back on the familiar ship calmed the unease knotted in my middle. I slipped over to the bow and rested my arms on the railing. I watched the lapping waves and let everything else fade into the background.

My hands clenched as my brother's words echoed in my mind. *Daystra has problems just as Zuren does. When you are there, you will see plenty you want to fix—but you can't fix everything. That is true both here and there.*

A hand touched my shoulder, startling me out of my

thoughts. I lashed back and twisted his arm, ready to punch.

"Hey, it's only me!"

"Oh. Milo." I let go and wrung my hand to loosen the tension. "Sorry. I got lost in thought."

"Don't worry about it." He offered a small smile. "Galen wanted me to remind you not to be late."

Right. The part of this trip that I was less than thrilled about. Tomorrow would be a long day.

"Of course. Thank you." I eased around him to snag my satchel.

"Be careful, Captain."

"You know I will be."

"Yes, but this isn't Zuren. Daystra is more dangerous for us."

"Zuren was never that safe for us either." Not when the traditionalists shunned me in everything but name as one of the outcasts.

I crossed the deck and announced, "Milo's in charge while I'm gone—and if you burn anything down, it's coming out of your salaries."

"What salaries?" Soapy joked, causing the others to erupt in laughter.

"Aw, you're no fun, Captain!" Takeo complained. "Keilani and I were looking forward to causing a little bit of mischief here in Daystra."

Sade rolled her eyes. "Ignore the imp. I won't let him get out of hand and do anything stupid."

He scoffed. "Well, *excuse me*. If I remember right, you enjoy picking locks as much as I do."

"Not the point."

I interrupted them before a full argument could start yet again. "The point is that we're trying to lie low. We don't need what happened in Lyren to happen here. We all agree on that much, right?"

The crew nodded unanimously in response.

"Good. I'll see the lot of you tomorrow then."

I headed into the city, slowing my pace when I caught sight of the blue spires that pierced the sky.

Will the palace be better or worse than the city itself?

I shook my head and broke my gaze away. "Not now, Zandra," I muttered to myself. "Too many things to fix."

I gripped the strap of my satchel. That strange conversation had put me on edge. I continued on, not wanting my lateness to raise any suspicion.

✡✡✡

The cover of nightfall aided my trek to the palace. I made my way to the secluded servant's door located in the back. Orange light flickered from a hanging lantern, outlining two figures. One of the two came up to me.

"Your Highness." Marianne gave my hands a squeeze. "What was it like exploring the city as a commoner?"

"Interesting," I answered. "I'll tell you more about it later."

"You have five minutes," the other figure, shrouded in darkness, stated.

"Oh, then in that case I have plenty of time."

At my remark, he snorted before the three of us slipped

inside. "Don't you think you're cutting it a little close? I thought we agreed you wouldn't go out this late at night, even if it was just the ship." His tone edged on irritation, or as irritated as he ever allowed himself to be around me.

"It will be fine. No one is excited about my presence anyway. They'd probably be happier if I disappeared and never showed up again."

"Your—"

Footsteps scuffling across the pristine marble floors made us stop. Galen pulled me behind him, and we stayed still, waiting to see if whoever it was came down our path. I dared not even breathe when the footsteps stopped. After another moment, they continued down the adjacent hall until we could no longer hear them.

I released the breath I had been holding. Using the servant's halls was the safest option, but the risk of running into someone else and getting caught still put me on edge.

"Your Highness."

I looked up at him in the flickering candlelight. "Yes, Galen?"

Silence followed until he shook his head. "Never mind. I do not like your sneaking in and out, even if Lady Marianne acts in your stead as the princess. An assassin could infiltrate this place and come after you."

I knew worrying about my safety was his job, but still... "Do you really think anyone here would try to harm me? Even if they did, Peter and Airion would find out. Everyone would immediately suspect the Daystrans as being behind it, and the Daystrans know that too."

"Regardless, I do not like it, or Daystra. I wish you would let the ambassador and the rest of the envoy handle everything. It was not necessary to have Zurinian royalty come along for the negotiations." Galen added in a mutter, "I still wish the king had locked you in your room instead of letting you convince him and Prince Airion to send you along."

"You know why I came here, despite my brothers' initial objections. We don't have time for this conversation, especially right here and now."

"Of course, Your Highness."

When we came into the guest servants' quarters, Galen stood watch outside the door while I changed with Marianne's help. After she tied my hair up, I tugged on the slim waist of the purple dress. "Do I look okay?"

"Stunning as the princess you are." She picked a few stray threads off the skirt. "I will do your makeup in the morning."

The sound of a soft thump on the door interrupted our conversation, and I sighed. "Yes, Galen, I know I have to go now." I glanced back at Marianne, at times still unable to believe how similar we looked. "Do you have anything to report while you stood in for me?"

"No, it was rather uneventful. I can fill you in on more of the specifics later."

"Yes, let's talk about the details later."

I stepped out into the hallway and headed deeper into the foreign palace with Galen. After checking my room, he announced, "All clear."

With a sigh, I entered the unfamiliar room that was mine for the duration of the envoy's stay. Filled with luxury—but how much of it was a façade?

The men back in the alley still nagged my mind, despite the plethora of other things I ought to be focusing on.

"Daystra won't be the same after this."

CHAPTER 7

Leo

THE CREAK OF THE DOOR ROUSED ME FROM SLEEP.
I rolled onto my side, grumbling to myself.

"Symon, that you?" I mumbled. "Why are you awake at this hour? The sun's not even up."

Do bodyguards ever sleep?

No answer. I cracked an eye open and peered over the footboard. In the dim moonlight filtering through my window, I discerned the outline of the closed door.

"Is this revenge for that glass of water I splashed you with in retaliation?"

The ticking clock in the corner of my room felt unnerving in the silence. I sat up and huffed. Who in all of Kalmyra was waltzing around at this hour? Couldn't I at least sleep in peace? I swung my legs over the edge of the bed and got to my feet, leaving the comfortable warmth of the blankets behind.

"Who's there?" I asked groggily.

My voice echoed in the eerie stillness.

"If this is a joke, I'm *not* in the mood, Symon."

Was he hiding outside my door now that he'd heard me?

Still half asleep, I shuffled over to the door, quickening my pace as my bare feet registered the cold floor. I eased it open and poked my head out, glancing down the empty hall. I furrowed my brow. *Strange...* Where were the guards?

An arm wrapped around my neck and dragged me back. Terror from the crushing force drove me into action. I struggled against my attacker, managing to twist enough to relieve the pressure on my neck before I slammed my elbow into his gut.

In the blink of an eye, he yanked me to the ground. I kicked his leg out from underneath him, and he toppled. I sprang to my feet and darted away, putting distance between us.

I snapped my gaze to the wall next to my bed. My sword— where was my sword?

This is not happe—

The lean figure dressed in all black slammed me into the side of the table, knocking the wind out of me. I gasped for breath and shoved him away.

I stalled as I backed toward the door. "Am I finally meeting Devrim after all these years?"

"Sorry to disappoint, but I'm no Devrim." His voice, slick as oil, sent a shiver through me.

Before I could find a makeshift weapon or yell for help, he rushed forward and landed a solid kick to my chest. The force knocked me backwards, the back of my head slamming against the wall. Everything blurred and shifted in and out of focus.

I staggered and collided with a small table that held a vase. Both the table and vase crashed to the ground. Shattering glass rang in my ears. For a moment, I could only stand hunched over the table, stunned from the impact.

Come on, get it together—

The assassin crunched across the broken glass and pinned me to the wall. "You're a slippery one, aren't you?"

No matter what I tried, I couldn't get him off me. I clawed at his hands squeezing my neck. Dizziness set in from the lack of air. If I didn't do something soon, I would die just like my sister had.

As the assassin increased the pressure on my neck, the edges of my vision dimmed. The world turned blurry. My lungs burned with no relief. The remaining strength drained from my arms, and they dropped uselessly.

So this is how I die? Strangled by an assassin in the middle of the night? I haven't even found Devrim yet...

Things happened faster than I could process. Movement blurred behind the assassin before something came crashing down on his head with a cacophony of splintering wood. I rasped in a breath as the hands choking me fell away and the assassin crumpled to the ground.

My chest heaving, I stumbled and looked up.

A familiar face stared back at me, wide-eyed and breathing heavily. Symon.

I tried to speak, but my throat burned, and I only managed a strangled cough. I slumped against the wall like a tossed rag, shaking. Adrenaline pounded through me.

"Leo!" He gripped my shoulders. "Leo, are you okay?"

Instead of attempting to speak again, I nodded. I rubbed my throat gently and winced.

"Hold on, I'll get some water."

He was back right away with a glass of water. I took it from him, wishing my hands would stop trembling as I raised the glass to my lips and took a sip. When the water hit the back of my throat, it made me cough.

Symon clasped my shoulder. "Easy. Don't rush it. Take your time."

He crossed over to the open door and yelled for the guards. While they came and apprehended the assassin, I leaned my head back against the wall and closed my eyes, still focusing on getting air into my aching lungs.

"Why don't you sit?" he suggested as he returned to my side.

After a second, I opened my eyes and nodded. He steadied me while I stumbled to the other side of the room and lowered myself onto the edge of my bed.

Symon's gaze shot to my neck. "Are you hurt anywhere else?"

I shook my head.

"All right. I sent a guard for the physician. He should be here shortly."

"Thanks," I croaked out. I took several sips of water before I spoke again. "How—" My voice came out hoarse and strained, but I continued. "How did you know...I was in trouble?"

"I couldn't sleep, so I decided to volunteer for an early shift. Then I heard glass shattering and came as fast as I could."

My gaze drifted to the wooden chair in pieces on the floor.

"And you decided—a chair was your best option—to combat an assassin?"

"Hey, it was in the heat of the moment. I improvised."

"I guess—your quick thinking saved me."

Symon frowned. "You shouldn't be talking this much. Catch your breath and rest. I have four guards posted outside your room, and I'll stand guard inside until morning."

Always a royal guard. I gave him a look. When would he sleep then?

"I told you already, I couldn't sleep before, and I definitely won't be able to sleep now." I was well acquainted with the look in his eyes and that tone of voice. Symon wouldn't change his mind. It would be pointless to try.

"Fine," I rasped. "Doubt I'll sleep, though..."

"Then at least close your eyes and let your body rest—and *stop talking*."

"Yes, sir." I weakly saluted him before easing back onto my bed.

Symon rolled his eyes. "Nice to know assassination attempts never take away your sense of humor. If you keep trying to talk instead of rest, I'll make sure you don't miss tomorrow's studies and lectures you're supposed to attend."

"That a threat?" I mumbled.

He shrugged. "Call it motivation to listen to me."

I exhaled slowly. It still felt hard to breathe. I tried to rest like Symon wanted me to, but the miserable headache pounding in my skull didn't help. I clutched my chest with a shaky hand. My heart still beat too hard and fast, to the point that it ached.

After the royal physician checked on me and determined I would recover with rest, I sat against the headboard of my bed, leaned my head back, and closed my eyes. A minute later, I cracked an eye open to check that nobody else had sneaked into my room to attack me. Symon still stood near the door with his sword sheathed. I shuddered at the nightmares lurking in the back of my mind, waiting to pounce the moment sleep pulled me into a deeper darkness.

Letting out a sigh at the lack of sunlight, I closed my eyes again. It still wasn't morning. I gingerly rubbed my sore throat. The vivid feeling of the assassin's hands choking me lingered and made my throat tighten. I didn't want to be in this palace any longer. I wanted to go somewhere I didn't feel so trapped.

At dawn, a knock on the door made me sit up straighter. Symon spoke with the person briefly before he allowed them in.

Cyra rushed over to my side. "Oh, Leo, I was so worried when I heard what happened." She gave my shoulder a gentle squeeze, frowning at the bruise on my neck. "Are you okay?"

"Just shaken up." I roughed a hand over my face. My scratchy voice sounded as if I had a cold, but it didn't hurt as much after a few hours of rest. "Sometimes I still don't understand why there are so many assassination attempts... It's not like I'm doing much politically."

"I'm afraid there are many who disliked your father's rule, and they assume you will be the same and carry on his legacy."

"But I'm not the same. What's so hard to understand about that?" I flopped back with a suppressed sigh, then winced as I bonked my head. "Ugh, I'm so sick of this stuffy palace and its politics."

"Sounds like you're planning a little outing into the city soon?" Cyra guessed by my tone. "As long as the physician cleared you and you feel well enough, your secret is safe with me."

When she winked, I gave her a relieved smile. Cyra never tried to stop me from going out when I needed a break or time to myself. "Thank you. I wish I could." My gaze drifted to Symon. There was no chance he'd let me go anywhere in this state.

"What about the meeting with the Zurinian princess this morning?"

I suppressed a groan at the very idea. "Oh, that. You'll have to let her know I won't be able to attend. We will have to reschedule it for another time."

"You must be absolutely heartbroken about that."

I nodded gravely. "Heartbroken indeed."

With a shake of her head, she tried to hide her smile. "Get some rest, Leo. I will check on you again later."

I didn't remember hearing the doors shut as she left. A deep weariness dragged me into blissful ignorance as a dreamless sleep finally overtook me.

The faint murmuring of soft voices made me stir. I rubbed at my forehead. It felt as though I'd gotten dragged behind a horse down a rocky hillside.

Symon's low whisper drifted over to me. "Do you think the

Zurinians had anything to do with it?"

"Everybody would immediately suspect them—even more so with the Zurinian envoy here in Daystra. It would be too suspicious. Someone else is takin' advantage of their visit to divert suspicion from themselves."

Brantley?

I opened my eyes and grimaced at the bright morning light streaming into my room. I thought I'd slept longer than a few hours. I pushed myself onto my side to see Brantley and Symon talking in a corner.

Brantley's gaze flicked to me. "He's awake." They came over to me. My friend's eyes narrowed at the red marks on my neck, but he said nothing about it. "Glad to see ya got some rest, Leo."

"You slept for an entire day," Symon added, as if knowing what I was thinking.

I furrowed my brow. *An entire day?*

"What brings you here then?" Brantley only came to the palace when it was necessary or work related.

"Checkin' on you after what happened, and I needed to inform ya of a recent development." He threw a glance around the room before he took a step closer, lowering his voice. "You know that thing I mentioned earlier that I wanted to look into more? Well, turns out it wasn't just a rumor."

I sat up straighter. "What did you find?"

In the following silence, Brantley looked between the two of us, a flicker of unease in his gaze. "It's confirmed that Devrim's back in Daystra—and he was sighted in Maldenia."

CHAPTER 8

Leo

IT TOOK A MOMENT FOR IT TO FULLY SINK IN.

Not only was the person who had been hired to kill my sister no longer a ghost of whispered rumors, but he had been seen in Maldenia. Six years of searching for him without any luck—until now.

"Where was he last seen?"

"He was sighted in the assassins' guild in the city of Kayda, then sighted in Maldenia."

Kayda. That's only a three days' ride. Now the capital itself...

"Hey." Brantley gripped my shoulder. "I know you want to catch Devrim once and for all—believe me, I want the same—but this guy... He's one of the most infamous assassins this side of the Halcyon Sea."

"I'm aware." My hands clenched into fists. He made the mistake of coming back to Daystra. I won't let him get away."

"He'd kill ya without a second thought. That's not someone

to mess with unless ya have a solid plan, and even then, it would still be risky. We need to be careful and take our time."

"That scoundrel murdered my sister! And—and you want me to sit in the palace for who knows how long while he's this close?"

"Leo—"

"No, I can't—I *won't* do that." I jerked free of his hand and stood, ignoring the ill feelings that still clung to me from the attack.

Brantley blocked my path to the door. "Don't be rash. What if this is our only opportunity?"

"Exactly. What if this is my only chance? I can't waste it."

We stared each other down. Neither of us wavered. Pain twinged in my jaw from clenching it so hard. Impatience spurred me, and I stepped around Brantley and stalked over to the window.

"Leo." Symon caught up to me.

"If you're about to tell me how bad of an idea it is, just like Brantley, then don't bother."

"I'm not. You're right. We can't waste the opportunity, but Brantley's also right. We can't be rash with it." He rested a hand on my shoulder. "Take a deep breath, Leo."

I inhaled sharply and turned to face Symon. "I thought you'd tell me it's too dangerous."

"I have your back, even when you're determined to do risky stunts that might not be in the realm of common sense."

A rueful laugh escaped me. "Are you implying that I lack common sense?"

"Only some of the time."

I leaned against the wall, roughing a hand over my face. "Symon, I..." I trailed off, at a loss for words. My mind swirled at a dizzying rate, too fast to string together anything coherent.

"I know."

He said it so simply, as if he really understood.

"Thank you."

"We'll need more information before we move on Devrim," he reasoned, "and currently, there's an assassin with a possible link to Devrim sitting in the dungeons."

"Then it sounds like it's time to pay him a little visit," Brantley said as he came up behind us. "When Leo is ready."

I glanced at him. "You still want to be a part of this?"

"Aye, I'm with ya to see it through."

"Then let's not waste any more time. We have an assassin to interrogate."

The walk down the winding stairs to the dungeon felt eternally long, as was the connecting hall with the individual cells. Each step echoed, growing louder along with my pounding heart. In a matter of minutes, we could find out information that would bring me face to face with my sister's murderer.

I glanced at Brantley and Symon on either side of me. Right now, they were the only ones I trusted implicitly with this matter. Regardless of their own doubts, they had stuck with me. Over the years while I searched for Devrim, they had never stopped helping me.

We reached the prisoner's cell. Across the bars, the man in

question huddled in a shadowed corner. He lifted his head and laughed bitterly. "Well, well, the *Prince of Daystra*. Surprising that you would drag your royal self all the way down here, let alone so soon. To what do I owe the pleasure of you gracing me with your presence?"

The recent memories of his hands clenching around my throat tried to resurface. I shook my head and shoved those thoughts away. *Focus. This is for Dezaray.*

"Where's Devrim?" I demanded.

He tilted his head. "We parted ways weeks ago. Even if I did know, I would never tell you. Assassin's honor and all that."

I clenched my jaw. *If I could have just five minutes alone with him...*

"Who hired you?" Brantley took a threatening step toward the cell.

"Someone with enough power that I won't be intimidated by anything you do to me." His tone was light and carefree— even a little amused.

I narrowed my eyes. Was he implying one of the Daystran nobility was involved in this? Or... *Was he hired by the same people who sent Devrim after my sister?* The idea sent a chill down my spine.

Lying or not, I doubted we'd pry anything out of him about the identity of his employer. Captain Tesfira had questioned him for several hours already without giving him a break, and he hadn't answered anything.

The prisoner came as close to me as the iron bars allowed. "Just you wait, Prince. This isn't the last you'll see of me, and when we do meet again, I won't be behind bars. I'll be sure to make the end of your story plenty dramatic." His mouth curled in a disturbing smile.

Symon took a partial step in front of me, hand planted on the hilt of his sword.

I lightly rubbed at my neck. He couldn't get to me now.

"You'll be charged for high treason and hanged, unless you tell me what's going on. If you do, then I'll spare your life."

"You're as ludicrous as your father," the assassin spat. "He was nothing but a wall of false pretenses to hide his selfish agenda."

I lunged and grabbed the collar of his shirt, yanking him against the cold bars. "Don't slander my father's name," I snapped. "He was nothing like that."

"Are you sure about that?"

The taunting smirk on his face made my free hand curl into a fist. "If you received rougher treatment, I imagine that you wouldn't speak so much nonsense."

He laughed. "You don't have the nerve to do it."

"Want to try me? I'd be happy to wipe that smirk off your face." My fist clenched so tight my nails dug into my palm. If he was what stood between me and tracking down Devrim and those behind him, I'd do what was necessary.

"Leo." Symon's voice held a cautionary note.

For a brief moment, I glanced at him. He shook his head, the look on his face conveying his silent message: *"Don't take the bait."*

With a frustrated sigh, I let go of the assassin with a shove. Blast it all.

Brantley cleared his throat and continued the questioning.

"What's your name?"

The prisoner drummed his fingers on the bars, as though contemplating whether to answer.

Thoroughly fed up with his reticence, I turned to leave. "This is a waste of time. He'd rather hang than talk."

"Gabriel," the assassin decidedly answered. "My name is Gabriel Lemar."

I spun back around, but he had retreated into the darkest corner of his cell. The sound of our footsteps on the metal stairs echoed off the walls as we left.

"I'm surprised he even told you his name," Symon said. "I wonder why he did all of a sudden."

"Do you think it's a trick?"

Brantley stopped on the stairs, checking to make sure no one else was around before he moved in closer, lowering his voice. "I know it's not the best place to talk about this, but I feel I ought to say somethin.' To be honest, his mention of workin' for someone in a higher position isn't that surprisin.' I've always been suspicious of some of the people in this palace. I don't trust those nobles, and I don't trust Parliament."

I stared at him. "You suspected the person behind this could be a member of Parliament, and you waited until now to bring it up as a possibility?"

"I don't have any proof. Just a theory of mine. Sorry for not mentionin' it before. I didn't want to alarm ya when it was only my paranoia."

How long had Brantley been suspicious of people within these very walls being involved in my sister's death? To think that the entire time I'd been searching for Devrim and the people who had hired him, I hadn't considered looking *within* the palace.

"If you find anything, come straight to me or Symon. No one else—no matter whom your proof might be against."

Determination flickered in his eyes as he nodded. "Aye, I will. I'd best be gettin' on my way now." At the top of the stairs, Brantley took his leave.

Symon turned when it was just the two of us in the empty hall, his expression dead serious. I recognized that look of duty. He wasn't seeing me as his friend, but as his crown prince.

"When I became your bodyguard, I made a vow to protect you. I will keep that vow no matter who or what stands in my way. Whatever happens, I will remain by your side."

I rubbed the back of my neck in the silence that followed. The way he talked about protecting me at all costs made me uneasy. When Symon said things like this, I was never sure how to respond to the loyalty I doubted I deserved. I'd never been a model crown prince.

"Thank you. I know you're not saying that only because you're a royal guard. You're more than that. You're...like a brother, Symon, and I don't want to lose my brother—so no dying for me, all right? No matter what happens, please stay alive."

If Symon died protecting me, I could never forgive myself.

"Don't make me promise something like that, Leo." He crossed his arms, his eyes pinching with suspicion. "You're worrying me. It sounds like one of your stupid plans, like track down Devrim on your own and confront him—you aren't, are you? You promised not to do anything without me."

"Hey, you're the one who started talking like this." I raised my hands in surrender. "When I confront Devrim, I will make sure you're with me. There's no need to worry."

Running a hand through his strawberry blond hair, he muttered, "There's always a reason to worry with you. You can be so reckless sometimes."

Footsteps approaching made me turn. My mood soured further at Rueben's presence. His gaze passed over me and landed on Symon. "Sir Caddel, Captain Tesfira requested your presence."

"Understood." He nodded once to me before leaving to meet with the captain of the royal guards.

Rueben glanced over me, his gaze lingering on my neck. He didn't mention the bruises, even though he had clearly noticed them. "I notified Parliament about the incident. They agreed that it is best to keep this assassination attempt a secret. If it became public knowledge while the envoy is still here, it would be a political nightmare and endanger the new treaty we are trying to form. We don't need the public jumping to conclusions, blaming the Zurinians, and causing strife."

Right to business, as usual.

Although it was the first time he had seen me since the assassination attempt, he showed no concern for me, not even asking if I was all right. He never had after the last attempts on my life, so why would now be any different? What had I been expecting?

"I take it you didn't find out anything from the prisoner?"

Surprised he even cared enough to ask, I said, "I know his name, and that he has at least met with Devrim recently."

Rueben arched an eyebrow at me in that disapproving manner he so often did. "You're still fixated on Devrim? Do you really expect to find anything after all this time? You will likely just get yourself killed. Stop using this as an excuse to neglect your duties as crown prince."

No, I just care more about my duty to bring justice to my sister's murderers. But Rueben and I would never see eye to eye on this matter, like so many other things.

"I'm not arguing about this again. We'll never agree." I stalked past him, and he didn't stop me.

I gripped the hilt of my sheathed sword as I walked down the long hallway alone. Brantley's words from earlier echoed in my mind. It was beginning to feel like every corner and shadow in the palace held some kind of secret, something hidden and waiting for the right moment to strike.

It was only a question of when.

CHAPTER 9

Zandra

I PLACED THE LAST PIN IN MY HAIR, SATISFIED WITH the braids that I'd coiled around my head. I had always found styling my own hair to be an enjoyable task.

"Oh, Your Highness, that's a beautiful style." Marianne glided over to where I sat before the dressing table. "You always do lovely things with your hair."

"Thank you." I smoothed out the wrinkles in my lavender dress with white lace. Most of my outfits tied into the colors of Zuren—purples, greens, and golds—but after seeing some of the Daystran's blue dresses, I wished I could wear one of those.

A sly smirk crept up my face. The Zurinian traditionalists would abhor such a sight.

"What are you scheming now?"

I flashed an innocent smile. "Oh, nothing."

"Good then." Marianne picked up the powder and brush. "Hold still please."

I held still while she covered my freckles with makeup. My governess and the ladies of the court always remarked that freckles were unbecoming, but I didn't care. "I still don't see the problem with freckles."

"You want to make a good impression on the Daystrans, and I will help you do that."

"You mean you'll help me act like the subdued prim and proper princess expected of me," I countered.

Marianne set the makeup down. "I am not the one who makes the rules or expectations. I want you to succeed. This is important for you."

"It is." My gaze drifted to the door. "Did Galen return yet?"

"Not yet. Why?"

I jumped to my feet. "Because I have important things to look into. I'll be back soon. Don't tell Galen." I winked then ducked out into the hall before Marianne could try to dissuade me. This was the opportunity I'd been looking for since we had arrived.

I darted through the long halls of the Daystran palace, keeping to the quieter, more secluded areas. Spiraling pillars converged up into arched ceilings that stretched far above my head. They certainly didn't hold back on their architectural designs.

As I wound through the halls, it grew more difficult to avoid being seen, but I was beginning to grasp the general layout of the place. I'd just turned the corner when a voice made me stop in my tracks.

"Are you lost?"

Startled, I whipped around and pasted on a smile while

internally groaning. *Great. The prince.*

"Hm?"

Prince Leonidas raised an eyebrow. "I asked if you were lost."

"Oh, well, yes. I...suppose I got turned around. It's not at all like the Zurinian palace."

"Where were you trying to go? I can point you in the right direction." The annoyance in his tone only made my irritation grow on the inside.

I know exactly where I'm trying to get—if this tides-blasted prince would go away so I can continue!

Smothering a sigh of exasperation, I thought of the first excuse that came to mind. "I'd like to know where the morning meeting is taking place."

"I thought someone had informed you that the meeting was rescheduled?"

"What? Why?" My eyes strayed to his bruised neck and the two bodyguards behind him who had particularly paranoid and alert expressions. "What happened to you?" As soon as the words left my mouth, I pressed my lips together. Maybe that had been too forward.

"An attempt on my life."

"Oh. I'm sorry to hear that. Are you all right?"

"I am fine."

Prince Leonidas studied me for a moment, and I stared back. Did he think we were involved? Would the Daystrans blame Zuren for it?

"Right then." Prince Leonidas shifted and fidgeted with the silver ring on his pointer finger. He glanced down the hallway.

Before the prince of Daystra could escape, I blurted out the half-formed idea. "Instead of having a formal meeting as planned, we could do ourselves a favor and make it less awkward."

"How so?"

I continued before I had a chance to change my mind. "Well, instead, we could discuss things in the palace's gardens? Just the two of us—with the appropriate amount of guards, of course," I added hastily.

"I...actually like that idea," he agreed with a faint smile.

"Would tomorrow at midday work?"

Prince Leonidas tilted his head. From the look on his face, it seemed more likely he was running through a mental list of excuses rather than a list of responsibilities.

Finally, he nodded. "Why not? I guess it's better than the alternative."

Not exactly reassuring; however, it was the most positive response I had gotten from him thus far. Awkward silence followed. I racked my brain for something more to say. "I look forward to it then, Prince Leonidas."

He turned to leave but halted. "One other thing—I go by Leo, not Leonidas."

"All right. Thank you for letting me know...Prince Leo." I forced a stiff smile. His nickname was strange on my lips. It had to be a good sign, though, if he preferred I call him by the name he used on a regular basis.

When he disappeared down a corridor, I let my masked expression drop and rubbed my forehead. Tomorrow would be challenging.

This was the second time we had met, and the first time we'd had an actual conversation. I didn't know much about Prince Leonidas, but what I did know came from rumors, and those weren't the most flattering. I was willing to give him the chance to reveal his own self before I made up my mind.

I wondered what rumors circulated about me on Daystra's end...

"I don't appreciate you going off alone like this when in foreign territory."

"Galen!" I spun around with a yelp. Why was everyone deciding to sneak up on me today? "Tides, where did you come from?"

He folded his arms, his eyes burning with one of those chiding bodyguard looks.

"I go out alone all the time in Zuren. You taught me how to handle myself."

"And you know Zuren. Daystra is different." Galen lowered his voice. "They're the equivalent of enemy territory."

"You all keep saying that, but the longer I'm here, the less the Daystrans seem like the enemies the elders painted them out to be." I smoothed the skirt of my dress and continued back the way I'd come. "Regardless, I need to speak with Lord Rowan."

"Whatever keeps you from getting into more trouble." He trailed me.

"You make me sound as bad as the Daystran prince."

"No, he is worse. I pity his poor bodyguards." Galen's voice held sincere empathy, as if he understood their woes.

I glanced back at him. "Don't act like I am such a handful."

"Fine, then you are...a challenge. Is that better?"

Even as I rolled my eyes, I couldn't hide the laugh that slipped out. "Fair enough. Maybe I do give you more work, and the traditionalists shunning me do not help matters, but you haven't gone begging to Peter to resign yet."

"Oh, I can never resign, Your Highness. I couldn't put that on the next poor bodyguard that would take my place."

"Ha, ha. You never lose your sense of humor, Galen."

"I don't have time for one of those in my line of work."

As we returned to my quarters, I said, "I will get you to loosen up one of these days."

"Now that would be a sight."

I turned to face the voice. "Lord Rowan! Perfect timing. I wanted to speak with you—and yes, I do think Galen needs a day off."

"I'll take a day off when you finally do, Your Highness," he murmured.

Rowan chuckled, running a hand through his walnut brown hair. "Well, you heard the man. Shall we go in to discuss matters then?"

"Let's."

Once we found a more secluded place to sit and talk, he updated me on the development of the treaty. I rubbed a finger over the lace on my skirt. "I'm not surprised they're making the negotiations difficult. We knew that would happen when we were the first to approach."

"Indeed, but the Daystrans need this alliance as much as Zuren does. They won't refuse it outright." Rowan studied me with his perceptive gaze. "How are things on your end?"

I suppressed a sigh. "I haven't made as much progress as I'd like."

"Your disappointment is understandable, but be careful, especially of Parliament. Their web goes deep, and they are the ones who have the control here rather than the prince."

"Are you saying I should focus on them?"

"Politically, it's still best to focus on getting the prince in agreement with the alliance. For your ulterior purposes—perhaps."

I looked down at my hands in my lap while I mulled it over. In that case, I'd make more headway looking into the members of Parliament and other related nobles who might have been involved. The Daystran prince would have been too young to know anything himself, but that wasn't the case for his uncle...

"What do you make of the Steward of Daystra?"

"He's in a significant position of power, one he might very well lose soon with the prince's upcoming coronation. That would make me wary of anyone." Rowan cleared his throat to get my attention. "Either way, your position can only go so far in protecting you, even more so here."

"As long as it seems like I'm only focused on getting the prince to cooperate, no one will pay attention to what else I'm doing." I met his gaze. "This may be my only opportunity to find out the truth. I will be careful. We don't need another war igniting when a bigger one is already looming. Which reminds me..."

I continued on to explain what I'd overheard in the city street between the two men.

Rowan frowned. "Byron? The name is not familiar to me. It is likely nothing related to the palace, but I will look into it. It sounds ominous, and one can never be too careful."

Knowing he would look into it lifted a weight off my shoulders. "Thank you."

"Of course. Now if you will excuse me, I have a meeting with our ambassadors." Standing and bowing to me, he added, "I wish you luck with the Daystran prince, though I believe you will be able to handle him just fine."

Rowan left, and I sighed and rubbed my temples. All this talk of alliances and politics made me tired.

"Galen, what do you say we get a little fresh air? My schedule is open until the meeting with the prince tomorrow."

"You will do what you want, with or without my consent, so I do not know why you bother asking me."

I gave him my best angelic smile. "Because I'm nice and don't give you as much trouble as the prince of Daystra gives his bodyguards?"

"That I am grateful for," he agreed with a snort.

"I will switch places with Marianne and then we can go."

I had been itching to leave the palace. I wanted the ocean breeze across my skin and to smell the salty air again, even though it hadn't been that long. Time near the ocean always cleared my head. I'd be able to think more objectively and plan my next course of action.

I'll get to the bottom of your secrets, Daystra.

CHAPTER 10

Leo

SKIDDING AROUND A CORNER, I TOOK A LEFT AND RAN down the hall. My two recently assigned bodyguards struggled to catch up.

"Your Highness, please wait for us!"

"How is he so fast?! Is he a speed nymph or something?"

I laughed. At least the two newer bodyguards Cyra had assigned from the royal guard had a sense of humor.

When I came to a winding staircase, I sat on the railing and slid all the way down. At the bottom, I jumped off but stumbled to a stop on seeing the person standing there. He crossed his arms.

"What?" I said, a sheepish grin coming over me. "I'm testing them. If they can't keep up with me, how do you expect them to do a good job?"

Symon gave me a look. "Leo, I'm one of the few who can keep up with you, and half the time that's hard even for me."

"That just proves what an exceptional bodyguard you are. You should get a raise."

My two new bodyguards caught up, and Symon dismissed them. "I'll take over for the next few hours. You two can take a break. Don't forget to report to Captain Tesfira." As they left, he turned down the hall. "Come on."

"Where are we going?"

"To the Parliament meeting. You said you wanted to attend the next one after what happened."

"Right." I hurried to catch up to him. "I forgot that was today."

Symon opened a tunnel to take a shortcut to Parliament and pulled me in. As much as I held no fondness for Parliament and their meetings, it gave the best opportunity to figure out what was really going on.

All too soon, we reached the end of the passageway. I smoothed out my navy and black jacket framed with silver embroidery. I'd be going unannounced and without notifying anyone ahead of time. What kind of mess would I walk into?

Going from the dim tunnel to bright daylight momentarily blinded me. I shielded my eyes as we stepped out into a well-lit foyer.

The meeting had already begun when we entered through the large doors inlaid with gold carvings. All eyes turned to me. A hushed silence fell over the room. Murmured whispers circulated among the Parliament members as I went to my seat and sat down, Symon standing behind me. I might as well have waltzed right into the lion's den.

Lord Thompson had been speaking when I'd entered.

"Prince Leonidas. To what do we owe the rare pleasure of your presence?" He spoke with that same annoying smoothness he always did.

I refrained from rolling my eyes. Instead, I let a neutral expression slide in place. "You may carry on. I am only here to observe."

Rueben sat to the right of me. He kept his gaze forward as he said, "It's about time you began showing up again."

I had only attended a handful of Parliament meetings, which was a peculiarity in regards to custom. Most Daystran monarchs attended at least once every month. And of course, Rueben attended both meetings in a month, despite it not being required of him as steward.

"These things are pointless when everyone goes around in the same circles," I muttered.

He sent me a reprimanding look. "Do not speak like that in this building, unless you want these people to respect you even less."

I repressed a sigh and focused on studying each member closely. With the way the political parties were splintered, it wouldn't be hard to imagine schemes abounding. Some were in support of the royal line and Rueben, while others were only for the common people. Then there was a majority eager to steal as much power away from the monarchy as possible and grant it to themselves instead.

One of these fourteen members could be orchestrating the assassination attempts, and even the one who hired Devrim to kill my sister.

Now which one of you would commit regicide?

Lord Wellington, the spokesperson of the House, presided over the meeting as it commenced. The topic of debate that snagged my attention was the alliance.

To everyone's surprise, Lord Bradford, the Leader of the Common People's Party, spoke up first. "While an alliance like this always carries risk, we cannot neglect this crucial opportunity."

"What about Zuren's demands for the disputed land at our border?" Lord Thompson countered. "Is Daystra to bow to the conditions of the Zurinians like a docile mutt?"

"Compromise must be necessary somewhere to achieve a balanced alliance."

"And what happens when we cave, and they continue pushing for more land?" Lord Thompson gestured to one of the maps hanging on the wall. "Some of the most agriculturally rich soil is in that area. Daystra relies on it. Is that worth sacrificing in exchange for Zuren's forces and ships?"

I hated to even remotely agree with Lord Thompson, but he had a point about protecting Daystra's resources within the treaty.

"I'm quite surprised you, Bradford, of all people, favor this proposition—unless your values have been compromised." Lord Thompson quirked a questioning eyebrow, a challenge in his words.

"You are one to talk, given your affinity with the war-mongers."

"Gentlemen, let's keep the trifling talk out of the meeting," Lord Wellington chided.

"Of course." Lord Bradford straightened and smoothed out

the front of his coat. "In any case, I remain for the common people, Lord Thompson. This is the best course of action for the men and women of Daystra and their futures."

My gaze darted to the faces of the Parliament members, searching for any indication in their expressions that would give them away.

Rueben cleared his throat and added, "Then again, we must remember other hindrances that must be worked out for the alliance to fall into place."

I clenched my jaw and dropped my gaze to the floor as I felt several eyes on me. The Parliament members radiated silent judgment. Disapproving whispers spread throughout the room. I shifted in the rigid seat. Rueben just had to make unhelpful comments like that while I was here in person.

What had I thought I'd find out at this meeting? Most held distaste for me. *Any* of these nobles could be involved.

The meeting resumed, and I held my peace in order to not draw further attention to myself.

✵ ✵ ✵

After the tedious three hours were over, I didn't linger to socialize. Parliament would go on disliking me regardless of what I did. They preferred to criticize me behind my back.

Eavesdropping later would get me further with the information I needed. Rubbing the blasted knot in my shoulder, I quickly trotted down the marble steps leading outside the Parliament building.

A voice stopped me on the steps. "Prince Leo."

I spun around and relaxed at the sight of the two members approaching. They were some of the few nobles I respected among the aristocracy. "Hello, Lord Alan, Lord Bradford."

"You certainly surprised everyone with your impromptu appearance," Lord Alan commented with a chuckle.

"It's more interesting when you don't know what to expect," I countered.

"Many assume you've no interest in the country's future."

"I can assure you that is not the case. Just because I don't like politics doesn't mean I'm not aware of how the game is played."

Out of the fourteen members of Parliament, only Lord Alan and Lord Bradford had tried to help me navigate the complexities of Daystra's politics after my life had been turned upside down six years ago.

"How are you doing after the attempt on your life?" Lord Bradford inquired.

"I am fine. Thank you for your concern," I said, refusing to let my mind go back to the panic of being unable to breathe.

"I suppose such things are bound to happen every now and then," he mused. "Still, others may try to take advantage of the situation."

Take advantage...?

"What do you mean?" I threw a glance over my shoulder. No one except Symon was within hearing distance.

The two exchanged a look before Lord Bradford shook his head. "My apologies. You have plenty to deal with as is. You do not need my unwarranted concerns burdening you."

I stared at him for a long moment. What was happening

behind the scenes among those fourteen nobles? Did they suspect one of their colleagues of being involved?

The bell of the tall clock tower, an icon of the Parliament building, toiled as it announced the passing of another hour.

"Ah well, I should be on my way. My wife won't be pleased if I miss lunch again."

Lord Alan added, "I must be going as well, but I hope this is not the last time we will see you at a Parliament meeting. Who knows? Maybe you will even attend the Founding Day's Ball this year. I think it does much for your reputation for others to see you participating." His expression, however, held a deeper admonition—a caution, almost.

A crawling sensation like spiders prickled up my spine. I became hyperaware of my surroundings. "I will...keep that in mind."

The two Parliament members bowed. "Good day, Prince Leo."

"Good day to you too."

I watched them walk away, the creeping sensation moving to my stomach. I had never been fond of Parliament and their inner politics, and I disliked their circle of lords now more than ever. Someone was plotting against the crown.

Behind me, Symon cleared his throat. "You all right, Leo?"

"I will be once I know what's really going on." I headed toward a passage that would take us back to the palace. "It's time to get to the bottom of this."

CHAPTER 11

Leo

THE PALACE GUARD, FIONN, SAT ACROSS FROM ME, ramrod straight and tapping his fingers on his leg. Between Symon and me, we had interviewed most of the guards who had been on shift that night. We didn't know who we could trust, and we wanted the information directly. So far, there had been nothing out of the ordinary.

"Did you see anything suspicious when you switched off with the two guards at the end of the hall?" I questioned.

"Right after I finished my rounds and got off patrol, I thought I spotted someone on my way back to the barracks. I told him to stay there so I could check his identification, but when I crossed the courtyard, there wasn't a soul in sight. I notified Lieutenant Blaine, but I'd had a long, exhausting few weeks; I thought I was seeing things. I—I thought the shadows were playing tricks on my eyes." He lowered his head, his blond curls falling into his face. "Please forgive me, Your

Highness. I made a grave error and allowed an assassin to slip past our defenses and get to you."

"It's all right, Fionn. The assassin was stopped. What's important now is finding out who hired him."

Symon added, "If there's anything else you can recall about that night, let me or the prince know right away."

I stood. "You should take some time off and rest if you've had such a hard time. Be with your wife and daughters."

"Yes, Your Highness." He rose and bowed. "Thank you for being so understanding."

Symon and I left to go meet up with Brantley; however, Fionn jogged after me. "Your Highness!"

I stopped and turned to face him. "Yes?"

"Well, it's just that..." He trailed off, and I nodded for him to continue. "I think I might have seen a figure pass by the stables the night before, but with the way he was walking, I thought he was just another guard. Now with everything that's happened, I'm not so sure."

"And this was the night before the assassination attempt?"

"Yes."

The night before? Had the assassin been skulking around the palace for an entire day before making his move? Or had it been somebody else?

Pulling myself out of my thoughts, I nodded to the waiting guard. "Thank you. I will look into it."

"Glad to be of service, Your Highness."

From there, we took a detour to the stables to speak with the stable master, Heath. He was in the middle of cleaning and polishing several of the saddles when I approached him.

"Do you have a moment to spare?"

"I'm sort of in the mi—" He cut off abruptly when he caught sight of me. "Oh, Prince Leo! What can I help you with?"

"Well." I threw a glance over my shoulder. "On the night before the assassination attempt, a guard said he saw an unfamiliar person on the palace grounds heading in the direction of the stables. I was wondering if you might have seen something that night."

"O-oh, that day?" He turned around and returned a scrubbing brush to a basket. "Well...I don't recall anything unusual here."

"Are you sure?" I pressed. "Think about it carefully."

I waited for his answer while he kept pointedly not looking at me. In all the years Heath had been the royal stable master, he had always been an amiable man who'd yet to meet a person he didn't like. Heath wasn't the kind to be involved in conspiracies, but he was withholding something.

"O-okay, I...might have seen someone." He checked behind him several times as he spoke in a hushed voice. "They told me not to say anything. They threatened to slit my throat and kill my family i-if I said anything." His voice had a slight tremble to it, and fear filled his eyes.

Just who exactly are these guys?

"Nothing will happen to you or your family," I reassured him. "I will make sure of it."

After another moment of hesitation, he continued. "The night before the incident, I—I saw two guards meeting with two people—exchanging money, I think. It was hard to hear what they were saying, but I did hear one of them mention your name."

My name?

"Do you know the guardsmen's identities? Or have any idea about who they were meeting?" I stopped myself and gave him time to answer.

"I think from what I overheard, one was called Aycill and the other Ruell. But I don't know either of the men they were meetin' with. One was the burly, intimidating sort with a large scar running down the side of his face. The other was tall and lanky—the ugly sort—and he moved without making a sound."

"I...see."

Tall, lanky, and silent had to be Gabriel Lemar. So the night before the assassination attempt, the assassin had met with two of my guards, and the other man had paid them for information, I assumed. Maybe the guards had told him the best way to get into my room without being seen.

The question remained...who was the other man? A burly guy with a noticeable scar running down his face—there couldn't be too many people like that in the capital.

Realizing Heath was staring at me, waiting for me to either ask something further or dismiss him, I said, "You have been very helpful. Thank you, Heath. And you don't have to worry. Nothing will happen to you or your family. I will make sure of it."

He dipped a quick bow. "Thank you, Your Highness."

Symon and I slipped out to visit Brantley and fill him in on what we had learned. When we arrived, he wasn't at the blacksmith's shop.

"He went out," Johann said, busy pounding away at a new sword in the making. "I'll let him know ya dropped by, though."

"That would be appreciated. Thanks."

As we ducked out of the shop, Symon's brow knit together in contemplation. "I wonder what Brantley's finding out."

"Hopefully something significant."

"I want to speak with Captain Tesfira and learn if there were any irregularities with the patrols, check the royal guard records, and see if I can look up this Aycill and Ruell that Lemar supposedly colluded with."

"And I should see if I can find out anything more on that other guy with a scar—"

Symon stepped in front of me, and we halted. He crossed his arms. "Hey, don't try to go looking into things like that by yourself. Not unless I'm with you. I don't need you ending up dead in some street."

"You and Brantley are already both busy looking into things. I'm not going to sit around and be useless while you're off being productive." I stepped around him.

"No, you're going to sit around being safe." Symon shot me his scary royal guard look, the one that said, if-you-disregard-this-I-will-kill-you-myself. Or rather, find a devious way to trap me in my room.

I rolled my eyes. "Fine. I'll wait for you and be languishing in wasted time while you two frolic around the country."

"If you're so determined to do something, why don't you go see if Lord Rueben has any tasks for you? Maybe you could...sort his paperweights or something."

I scoffed and didn't dignify his remark with a reply. When the street split, I veered right—the opposite direction of the palace.

"Where are we going?" Symon questioned as he followed like the shadow he was.

"The docks."

I ignored the sidelong glance he sent me. Nope. I wouldn't fall for it. *Not getting into that conversation with you right now.*

While Symon waited below, I went up to Zandra's ship. The crew member named Soapy met me at the top of the gangplank. Immediately, he asked, "What'd ye want, kid?"

"I was curious if Zandra was around."

The white-haired sailor with an eye patch crossed his arms. "She's busy."

I peered around him, trying to see if she was somewhere on deck and Soapy was just lying to me. When I didn't see any sign of her, I said, "I'll drop by another time, then."

"Don't ye go around harassin' her now!" he called after me as I left.

"What an odd old man," I muttered.

Symon remained silent as we walked back to the palace.

Once I had changed back into formal clothes, I headed to Rueben's study, planning to smooth things over with him after our last conversation. I paused at the door. Hushed voices came from within.

"The situation is getting worse, Rueben," an unfamiliar voice hissed.

"You don't think I know that? I know it is bad. We—I need

more time to straighten things out and tie up loose ends."

I sucked in a breath.

What...?

"Well, you should do so swiftly. The prince is observant, despite what you think. It won't be long before he notices something is off and realizes you're covering things up."

"Yes." Rueben sighed. "We need to use what little time we have left wisely, before he discovers the truth and everything falls apart. His coronation is only a handful of days from now."

I stumbled back, my mouth going dry.

Discovers the truth? What did he mean?

When I tried to peer through the keyhole, my boot squeaked on the marble floor.

The voices hushed. I froze.

"What was that?" the stranger's voice asked in alarm.

"I will check. You should not be seen if it can be helped."

I dashed away from the door and around the corner. My heart pounded in my chest so loud I was sure everyone in the palace could hear it. I sank against the wall as the conversation rang in my ears. I shook my head, the thoughts forming in my mind despite the screaming denial. Rueben was family. He was my uncle.

But I couldn't deny the conversation I'd overheard.

Was it...was it possible that Rueben, my own uncle, was killing off my family?

My heart twisted, and I slid to the floor. Why *had* Rueben always been so adamant about stopping the search for my sister's murderer? Was he...connected to Devrim in some way?

I grappled with disbelief in my mind, but the more I

thought it over, the more it made sense in that light.

I wrapped my arms around myself as a shiver shook me.

Was anywhere in this palace truly safe? Or had it all been an illusion the entire time?

Was the palace, in fact, the most dangerous place for me to be?

CHAPTER 12

Leo

I FELT STUCK IN PLACE THERE IN THAT HALL.

Despite the terrible possibilities swimming through my mind, I couldn't bring myself to keep walking away. No, I wouldn't. If Rueben really was involved with such things—I needed to know for certain.

Scrambling to my feet and turning sharply, I headed back toward the study. My heartbeat pounded in time with my steps.

As I rounded the corner, Rueben had just slipped out of his office. His gaze landed on me, and I resisted the urge to flinch. I approached him. There was no changing my mind now.

I spoke first. "Who were you meeting with?"

"Who I meet with is none of your concern."

I crossed my arms, not liking how he was dodging my question. "What happened to me needing to be a better crown prince? Wouldn't knowing more about your meetings help with that?"

How much have you been lying to me?

"Not this one. You have other duties to attend to."

"What are you hiding?"

Rueben stiffened, his shoulders rigid. "Enough of this nonsense, Leo. Return to your room if you do not have any studies to keep you preoccupied."

"You're just going to push me out of the way and not answer?" When he tried to step around me, I moved in his way and locked eyes with him.

"Leo—"

Instead of further questions, an altogether different thought slipped out. "You never even asked me if I was okay. You never do."

"That's because I can see for myself that you are fine."

How do you know? A lot of the time I'm not okay. And after this attempt, I was scared. I could've used a pat on the back, or some reassuring words, or—or anything. But you did nothing. Not a single thing.

I didn't dare say any of that out loud.

In the following silence, I wished for Symon's steady presence, but I'd told him to take the next shift off. I wouldn't drag him right back into my drama when it was only more troubles with my uncle.

"Forget it. When it comes to us, things will always be the same." Bitterness edged into my voice. As I turned to get away from the conversation, I muttered, "Do you even care?"

Painful silence rang in the halls. Rueben didn't stop me, or even say anything, as I walked away.

I tried to act like nothing was wrong, even though every-thing was wrong.

The shadows that cut into the corners of the palace grew darker. The secrets clawed deeper than they ever had before.

Rueben's conversation that I'd overheard haunted me. The more I pondered, the more I wondered what Rueben had been doing all along behind my back.

How many occasions, when Rueben had spent time with me—however rare—or simply spoken to me, had he been contemplating ways to get rid of me? Was this why he was so cold? Did he only want more power and control?

The palace was nothing more than a blur, and I only stopped in my room long enough to change into a disguise before escaping the imposing walls, with no bodyguards. I wandered through the city but kept going. The bustle of activity was too much to handle paired with the chaotic mess that churned in my mind. I needed quiet.

I made my way up to a spot I hadn't visited in ages. I'd always come here when things became too much, when I couldn't take anymore. Not even Symon knew of this place.

The top of this particular hill was secluded and sur-rounded by lush forest. From where I stood, the path sprawled down back toward the city. It gave a perfect view of the palace with its tan stone and blue tipped spires.

The teal waters of the inland bay reflected the golden sunlight that adorned everything as it neared sunset. It appeared magnificent, but I knew the truth.

How hollow it all was.

None of it was what it seemed.

It's all lies.

I closed my eyes for a moment. The conversation with Rueben sank in slowly. Deep down, I'd known for a while he didn't care, but it still stung. I had hoped that what I'd thought before was just pessimism.

It had never occurred to me that I would've been right.

A cool breeze rustled the leaves of the trees around me. I stared up at the yellow-pink sky. A hawk soared high above, free from it all. Its call rang out for none to hear but me.

What does it feel like to be that free? To never have to worry about what's below...

In the quietness this far away from everything else, the hollow emptiness within couldn't be ignored. The vastness of it was ready to swallow up everything and left a painful echo in its wake.

A shaky breath escaped me. The emptiness in me was always what had scared me the most. Nothing could ever fill it—if anything, it grew bigger as time passed.

The crunching of footsteps snapped me back to reality.

"Are you following me?" A familiar voice made me whip around.

"Zandra?" I couldn't help but stare at the girl standing there. "What are you doing here?"

"Exploring while I can. What about you?"

"This is a spot where I come to think sometimes. So, if anything, you're following me." My smile fell short. There was nothing to be joyful about when my life was just a hollow shell in a world built on lies.

"What's wrong?"

I turned away so she couldn't see everything written on my face so clearly. "It's nothing you need to be worried about."

"Cass...you don't seem okay."

"That's because I'm not," I admitted with a hollow, rueful laugh.

Her soft touch on my shoulder made me freeze, yet it sent an inexplicable warmth through me at the same time. "Whatever it is, if you need someone to talk to, I'm here to listen."

"Aren't I just the annoying smuggler that bothers you on occasion? Why would you want to listen to any of my problems?"

"Because...sometimes we need someone to listen, even if it's a stranger. And you're not *that* annoying." A hint of teasing traced her words.

Her offer was tempting. Maybe talking to someone detached from the whole situation would be better. I didn't know how much longer I could take it eating away at me from the inside like this. What did it matter if I told her? She didn't know who I was.

Words spilled from me as swift as a river's current.

"I think a family member betrayed me. We'd never gotten along before, but I still never would have thought he'd go this far..." I heaved a sigh. "And I don't know how much longer it can go on before there's nothing left. There's this—this emptiness, and it gets worse. I feel like I'm losing myself. I don't know how much more of me will be left by the time I'm on the other side of it...whatever 'it' even is."

The daunting admission hung in the air. It had long

lingered in the back of my mind, but I'd been too nervous to say it out loud. Too scared that admitting it would make it true.

Zandra soothingly rubbed my shoulder. I swallowed hard. Such a simple gesture...yet it meant so much.

"I'm sorry you've had such a hard time." Her next words weren't what I had been expecting.

"Do you know Adonai, Cass?"

I found a fallen leaf tipped red to stare at. "I know of Him, of course. He created everything. Not much beyond that and a long list of duties people like to tack onto it."

"Adonai's so much more than that, though."

I drew back a step, but not enough to pull away from her comforting touch on my shoulder. "I'm not really up to talking about that right now."

"All right. But any time you'd like, I'd be happy to talk about Adonai with you. Daystrans and Zurinians have very different views on the matter." She gave my shoulder a gentle squeeze. "Regardless, don't give up."

"Why?" The question slipped out before I could stop myself. "Why does it matter if I don't give up?" I hung my head. "What if no one cares if I do?"

"I would care."

I looked up and stared at her. She'd said it so simply with confidence.

"You—you would?"

Zandra rested a hand on her hip. "Is there a reason I can't? So what if I hardly know you—I know you enough. Now don't you dare think it is okay to give up, since you have at least one person who'd care if you did." Her ocean-blue eyes held a rare sincerity I couldn't deny.

Some part of me in the back of my mind warned of the way I was still awkwardly staring, but I couldn't help it.

What does she see in me?

I blinked and shook my head slowly to get out of the daze. "Okay then."

"Good." Zandra smiled. "I should be on my way soon. I can stay longer if you don't want to be alone."

"I should probably head back now." My absence would be noticed soon, and I didn't want to talk to Rueben again so soon after what happened.

"Then see you around, Cass—soon, I'm sure, since we seem to continually run into each other." Her chuckle echoed in my mind even after she'd left.

I stood there for several minutes longer while Zandra's words sank in. I'd gotten a glimpse of a much softer, caring side of the ship captain. Even more surprising—she wasn't afraid of the empty brokenness in me.

"Thank you, Zandra," I whispered. "You don't know how much I needed that."

CHAPTER 13

Zandra

STEAM WAFTED UP AS I SWIRLED THE TEA AROUND with my spoon. Two white and silver teacups along with a matching teapot were placed precisely at the table, just as Marianne had set it up.

My gaze drifted to the empty seat across from me under the palace garden pavilion. Prince Leo had already postponed it a day for vague reasons. Would he even show up this time?

Cass would have made better company...

Unfamiliar bird calls filled the air, and a cool breeze made me regret the choice of my emerald green dress with short sleeves. I shook away the thoughts of the kind smuggler.

From behind me, Galen said, "How long do you intend to wait for this impudent prince?"

I tapped my fingers on the ivory tablecloth. "I'm certainly not waiting all day for him to get around to showing up. If he doesn't come soon, we'll leave." I had better things to do than be subjected to the whims of an irresponsible prince.

After another ten minutes, I made up my mind and pushed my chair out to get up.

"Princess Alexandrina."

I looked up to see Prince Leo. "You're finally here," I stated, a flicker of annoyance slipping into my voice.

He rubbed the back of his neck and slid into the chair across from me. "Er, sorry. I got caught up with some things."

"It's fine." It really wasn't. I didn't like to waste time, but I shoved aside the annoyance best I could. I nearly slipped into speaking with my Zurinian accent, but I caught myself and kept to the bland court tone that I hated. "You are here now."

"Yes..." The prince shifted and took a long drink of his tea. Silence followed. The stiffness between us made every sentence of conversation awkward. I hated it.

I brought the tea up to my lips to try it. A strong floral smell took me aback, and I decidedly set the teacup down. In the short time I'd been in Daystra, it only confirmed my thought that they had the oddest taste in tea. Everything was either bitter, bland, or had overpowering floral flavors that made one feel as if they'd swallowed a garden. I should have packed some tea along with me.

Prince Leo interrupted my thoughts. "Can I be blunt with you?"

I watched him while absently tracing a finger over the smooth silver rim of the teacup. "I didn't take you for a blunt one. Go ahead."

"What are you really doing here?"

My finger stilled. Had he caught on to what I was really

doing? I'd been so careful...

I pasted on a smile and met his calculating eyes. "What do you mean? I'm here to help establish a real treaty between our countries."

"And yet, the timing is so...abrupt."

"What are you implying?"

"Why don't you answer the question?"

I pressed my lips together. He wasn't backing down. *Maybe there is more to this prince after all.*

"Let me be blunt with you then, Prince Leo. I am not thrilled about this arrangement any more than you are—"

"You're the one who suggested it in the first place," he pointed out, his grip around his teacup tightening.

"And I did. Personal preference cannot rule when two countries' fates hang in the balance."

He arched an eyebrow. "A dramatic way to put it, don't you think?"

"At least you should be used to dramatics, I'd wager." I pushed out from the table and stood. "I believe I have another appointment that I cannot be late for. I will be going now."

"Wait." Prince Leo jumped to his feet. He staggered a step, pain rippling across his face.

I stopped in my tracks as he braced a hand against the edge of the table. His face turned two shades paler.

"Are you unwell?"

He grimaced and clutched his middle. "I...I..." The prince let out a hiss of pain and slumped to the ground. He didn't get back up.

"Leo!" The prince's bodyguard sprinted from his post and

knelt beside Prince Leo's motionless body.

The sight of his limp form in a heap on the stone made me shiver. I stifled a gasp as Galen pulled me away from the scene. *Please don't be dead.*

They hurried the prince inside and to his room. I followed from a distance to find out what had happened. When the opportunity arose, I sneaked over and kept an ear pressed to the door, catching muffled bits and pieces of conversation on the other side.

"Poison...in the tea..."

I covered my mouth with a hand. The tea had been poisoned? But I'd nearly drank it...

Thank Adonai for bad tasting Daystran tea.

I leaned more into the door, straining to pick up on more of the hushed conversation.

"It could all be a ruse...get the chance to eliminate him."

Were they talking about the Zurinians? Did they really think we would pull something like this while in such a precarious state of affairs? I furrowed my brow. *What is really going on here?* Was someone trying to frame the Zurinians for this incident?

Footsteps grew closer to the door, and I scrambled back behind a curtain to hide. The man who must have been the royal physician headed down the hall in the opposite direction from where I hid.

Moments later, the prince's bodyguard stepped out. As he passed by my hiding spot, I slipped out and approached him. "Sir Caddel, is it?"

He glanced back at me. "I apologize, but I don't have time

to stop and talk."

"Then I will walk with you." I quickened my pace to keep up with him while Galen followed. "Is the prince all right? What happened?"

"I cannot divulge information to you like this. It's not my place."

"Does that mean he's not all right?"

He clenched a hand at his side. "There are some...delicate circumstances, but you don't need to worry about him. The prince will recover."

"That is good."

I studied his expression rigid with tension. There was something more to this.

Prince Leo might be exasperating to a degree, but the treaty would go to shambles without him. The Daystrans might change their minds and outright refuse an alliance of any kind after this incident.

Sir Caddel stopped in front of a white door with silver embellishments. He knocked before the Steward of Daystra opened the door. They spoke in low voices as the prince's bodyguard explained the situation. Even standing as near as I was, I couldn't make out much of it.

The Steward stepped into the hall and locked the door behind him. "We will handle this matter. Please return to your quarters, Princess Alexandrina."

I gave a small nod of acknowledgement. The two started at a brisk pace down the hall, leaving no room for further conversation. Once I was certain they were gone, I crouched down in front of the door and pulled two pins out of my hair.

"Keep watch," I whispered, inserting the pins into the keyhole.

"What are you doing?" Galen hissed.

"Picking the lock. Takeo taught me how."

"You need to stop spending so much time with the outcast faction. You learn too many questionable things from them."

"What's wrong with befriending my own kind? Everyone else all but considers me one." The lock clicked. I opened the door and slipped inside with Galen.

Leaning back against the shut door, I took in the Steward of Daystra's office. Two of the walls were floor to ceiling bookshelves while the center wall had a large window. The blue curtains were pulled shut, smothering the sunshine.

I went straight for the large mahogany desk in the middle of the room.

"This is unwise," Galen warned. "If we get caught—"

"Then help me search so we get out of here faster."

Looking through the endless papers on the desk dragged on for what felt like hours, though in reality, it hadn't been ten minutes. I blinked hard in the dim light to get the words on paper to clear. How did this man do any work in such a dark room?

Toward the bottom of a pile, the word Andaria, the country that bordered both Daystra and Zuren, snagged my attention. I scanned the report and sucked in a breath. According to this, Hyrans had advanced on Andaria and cut off their communication. Only a few key cities and one territory remained untaken. The Hyran Empire had land to launch their soldiers into the continent now.

There was no way to stop the impending storm.

The moment Andaria fell, war would be upon both Zuren and Daystra far sooner than anyone realized.

I sensed Galen's silent presence coming up behind me. "What did you find?"

"I'll tell you once we're out of here. Help me make sure everything is in order."

We scoured the office, ensuring that all items disturbed were returned to their right order. Lord Rueben had seemed like a particular man; he'd likely notice if anything was amiss.

I crossed the room and pushed a book partway out of the shelf back into it. A mechanical clicking filled the air, and we both froze. A section of the bookcase swung forward. I pulled the secret door open wider. It led into a tunnel engulfed with darkness. Far on the other end, I caught sight of faint lantern light hanging from a wall.

Galen pulled me back before I could plunge into the depths of the secret passageway. A silent argument passed between us, but I wouldn't back down. After a moment, he heaved a sigh. "Let me lead."

The deceivingly long passageway held several twists and turns that left me hard pressed to remember which way we'd come. Water dripped from the ceiling. A cold drop splattered on the back of my neck, sending a shiver through me. Dark shadows shrouded every corner of the tunnels.

Why did the Daystrans have such an intricate passageway network?

When we came to the next lantern, Galen grunted. "Do you remember the way back?"

"No." I bit my lip.

He muttered a curse under his breath and turned to face me. "We—"

"Wait." I held a finger to my lips and strained to hear the faint shuffling.

Muffled footsteps further down the passageway. They were getting closer.

Galen pushed me back around the corner to hide in the darkness. I couldn't see around the corner, but I heard their voices as the two men met under the dim lantern light.

"You're moving faster than expected."

The second man spoke so low it was hard to catch what he said. I tried to peer around the corner, but Galen kept a firm grasp on my arm to keep me in place.

"What are you up to?"

"A strategy's pacing can change. Patience is needed until the right moment."

"You speak of patience, yet you're the one rushing, Byron."

"Timing is crucial. I don't want another mess like the one with the king and queen of Zuren."

My eyes widened, and I lunged forward. Galen pulled me back another step as I struggled against his hold. His hand tightened around my mouth. I wanted to scream at him. Didn't he realize they were people involved with my parents' assassination? They were *right* there, and he wouldn't even let me get a good look at them!

"Don't let emotion lead you," he whispered in a breath.

As quietly spoken as they were, the words were a slap to the face. Galen eased his hold, and I slumped back against the cool stone of the passage, taking in a shaky breath. *He's right.* I couldn't be rash.

When I gathered enough composure to focus on listening again, I'd missed a significant portion of the conversation.

"You all but run the country."

"Precisely, and after this, it will secure matters. Don't demand a meeting with me like this again, Bradford. I don't like to meet out in the open in this manner." Byron's voice held a sharp warning.

Bradford? I recognized that name. One of the Daystran Parliament members...?

"I'd hardly call this out in the open. You're the one so insistent on all the cloak and dagger. But very well, I will use other methods to contact you from now on."

Their receding footsteps echoed in the darkness.

Galen led me along as we hurried after the direction of one. A flash of bright light up ahead indicated he'd exited the passageways.

When we caught up and finally escaped the labyrinth, I looked around for signs of anyone in the palace hall where we now stood.

Not another soul.

My hands curled into fists so tight my nails dug into the palms of my hands. How had he vanished so fast?

Frustration filled each step back to my quarters. I found a place where no one would disturb me and planned to stay there while the knotted up emotions and thoughts tumbled inside.

I braced against the wall and closed my eyes as everything

spun. It had been true after all.

Daystra was behind the deaths of my parents all those years ago—and the murderers were alive and well.

CHAPTER 14

Leo

THE FAMILIAR CEILING ABOVE MY BED GREETED ME.

I groaned, clutching my middle as I eased to an upright position. With still hazy vision, I stared around at the empty room. Where was everyone? What had happened?

Rain beat against the window across from me. The dark grey skies glared back. It had been a sunny day, last I could remember. Not that I remembered much about how I ended up in my room in this state. Going to meet the Zurinian princess was the last moment I could recall. A heavy fog clouded everything else in my mind.

I slid off the edge of my bed and stood—which was a mistake. Fiery pain shot through me, and I lurched forward a step. Scrambling to steady myself, I leaned on the edge of the nightstand table. My whole body ached with a fierce intensity that rivaled the sharp, stabbing pain in my middle.

"Ugh, what is this?"

Everything felt murky and off, as if it didn't quite fit reality.

Am I awake or dreaming...?

I stumbled my way to the door. Eerie silence veiled the halls. For once, when I wanted the palace to be busy, there wasn't a soul in sight. I braced a hand against the walls as I made my way to Cyra's study. Whatever was going on, she would tell me the truth.

Uneasiness washed over me. The palace halls were all out of order, and the rooms weren't as they should be.

By the time I arrived, the pain had worsened to make every step come with a sharp ache. I pushed open the ajar door and stepped into Cyra's study. My blood went cold at the sight of the ransacked room.

Papers, books, and other items from the desk were strewn everywhere, mixed with the toppled chairs. I looked down at the chess piece I nearly stepped on and picked up the black queen.

I brought it over to where she always kept the chess board and froze. Blood stained the black and white board. I covered my mouth with a hand as I caught sight of a trail of blood.

No...no, not again. Not Cyra.

Racing around the corner, I came to a screeching halt. Cyra's still form lay crumpled in a pool of blood.

"No!"

I crashed to my knees at her side, desperate to feel even the faintest signs of a pulse.

But there was no pulse. Cyra was as cold as ice.

"No...I can't lose you." A strangled sob escaped me. "You're the only real family I have left. You can't leave me too."

In the following silence, awful reality sank its claws deeper into me.

It had happened again. First my sister, now Cyra. I couldn't save either of them.

A chasm of emptiness left deep ruts of aching pain in my chest. I wrapped my arms around myself and doubled over. My vision blurred, and the world grew distant, but I hardly cared. Darkness tugged me under, and I didn't fight it.

I can't take this...

✡✡✡

I woke with a start, sucking in shaky, gasping breaths. I looked around wildly, uncertain where I was anymore.

Gentle hands gripped my shoulders. "Calm down, Leo. You're okay."

My vision cleared enough to meet Cyra's blue eyes.

"Cyra," I choked out. "You—you're alive..."

"Of course I am, dear."

"I'm so confused. I don't know what's going on. Everything was so empty, and blood everywhere... I—I saw you dead, but you're here." I rubbed a trembling hand over my face.

"Oh, Leo." Cyra wrapped me in a hug. "It was only a dream from your fever. I'm here."

I crumpled in her hold, clinging to the words.

Only a dream.

She rubbed my back in soothing circles. I still shook, but her comforting gesture and words calmed me. "Deep breaths."

I did as she said. The air filling my lungs helped clear the fog in my mind.

My breath hitched as a fresh wave of pain stabbed through me. Cyra sensed it and gently eased me to be lying down again. "Take it easy."

"Where's Symon?" I noticed his missing presence immediately.

"He's been staying by your side for the last three days. I finally convinced him to get a meal and rest some. I'm sure he will be back soon, nonetheless. We have all been worried."

"What happened?" Grimacing, I pressed a hand to my middle. "This pain...what is it?"

"You were poisoned from the tea you had while meeting the Zurinian princess. The poison was rare, and finding a cure took the royal physician some time... Your system had the poison in it for two days before we were able to get you the closest thing to a cure that we could. That's why you still feel awful, and he said you would continue to as the aftereffects wore off. I'm surprised you woke up just a day after receiving the cure."

I mulled over the information. It hadn't seemed like three days. It had felt like no time at all, while at the same time, it should have been longer than that.

"What of Princess Alexandrina? If it was in the tea..."

"She is well. She did not drink it. Now rest, Leo. You will feel better soon." Cyra stroked my forehead with all the tender care of a mother.

I relaxed and closed my eyes, focusing on the calming motion. Despite this, I couldn't fall asleep. I didn't want to return to the land of dark nightmares that my apparent fever seemed intent to torment me with. Instead, I rested there with my eyes closed, staying awake long after Cyra eventually left.

The stillness gave my mind too much of an opportunity to replay the dream. I shuddered and curled in on myself under the blankets. *Not real.* It was only a bad dream.

The shuffling of someone entering my room acted as a welcomed distraction. I could tell by the way they walked that the footsteps belonged to Symon. The bed creaked as he sat on the edge of it, but I kept my eyes closed and pretended to sleep.

"Lady Cyra said you had woken up for a time. I'm glad the cure is finally working. You're too stubborn to let some poison take you down."

Symon spoke as if it were a comfortable conversation with me. Cyra had said he'd barely left my side in the last three days. Had he talked to me often while I'd been unconscious and fighting the poison? *That stubbornly loyal...*

"Just get better soon. It's strange not having you around."

"Did you miss me?" I cracked an eye open to look at him.

"Leo! You're awake—wait, were you pretending to sleep? You rascal!" He lightly shoved my shoulder.

"What?" A weak laugh escaped me. "I couldn't resist."

"You never change. And fine, yes. I missed you."

"Palace too boring without my stimulating presence to liven things up?"

"Don't push it."

When I attempted to sit up, an aching pain tore through my abdomen, and I grimaced.

"Hey." Symon gently pushed me back down. "Please stay still. You need to keep resting to get well again. You look like death itself."

"Your compliments are boundless, as always." My faint smile vanished when I caught the worried look in his eyes.

I really almost died...

The thought sobered me. I started going over the meeting with Princess Alexandrina in my mind. "Do you know who poisoned me?"

"Not yet. Politics are making it difficult." He ran a hand through his hair. "The tea was from the Daystran side. The Zurinians were the ones who set up the table."

"So it could have been from either side."

"Exactly, and the Zurinians are refusing to let us question any of their people. They say they will investigate their own, and we can do the same with ours."

I frowned. "That does complicate things."

"It is convenient though—almost like the princess knew not to drink the tea. You kept her waiting ten minutes, and she apparently sat there without taking a single sip of it. Even once you arrived, she didn't."

I nodded slowly. It was convenient at best, suspicious at worst.

"Has Brantley been able to find anything out?"

"No, he got pulled away on an assignment—from Lord Rueben," he clarified.

I didn't like the idea of Rueben having Brantley do things. There were plenty of other royal investigators he could have called on. I held back my questions, knowing that was as much as Symon would know about the matter.

"Did Rueben come and see me at all?"

"Once. He asked for the others in the room to leave when he did. He was hard to read."

A weary sigh escaped me. I rubbed my forehead. The headache creeping in did not help the situation. "I'm surprised he even came once..."

A chill ran down my spine followed by a pang as I recalled everything I'd overheard from Rueben's conversation with the unknown man. I shrank down more under the covers. I felt like I was going to be sick, or sicker than I currently was.

Symon rested a hand on my shoulder. "What is it?"

I didn't meet his gaze. Rueben's sharp words still cut deeper than I cared to admit.

"Symon, I...don't know who I can trust anymore."

CHAPTER 15

Leo

THE OVERCAST MORNING SKY MELTED INTO THE churning sea. Grey waves lapped on shore, nipping at the edges of my boots. I ran a hand through the coarse sand as I sat there.

The throbbing pain that seemed to be my new unwelcome companion jolted through me. I grimaced and rubbed my middle. Would this ever quit? Four days had passed since the incident, and it was taking an eternity to recover from the effects of the poison.

The situation within the palace hadn't gotten any better either. Brantley had even made another rare appearance at the palace, apparently reporting back to Rueben. I clenched a fistful of sand as his words replayed in my mind. *"I can't divulge information on this matter. You'll have to speak with Lord Rueben about it. Sorry."*

I still couldn't imagine what Rueben would have Brantley doing, but I didn't like it.

I rested my forehead on my knees as the sea tried in vain to comfort me with its lullaby. "What are you up to, Rueben?" I murmured.

How deep does your betrayal go?

The crunch of sand underfoot alerted me to someone's presence. I didn't bother to look up. Whoever it was would keep walking, and if they decided to cause problems, Symon was nearby.

"Cass?"

My breath caught. I shouldn't have been that surprised. It wasn't too far from the docks and her ship.

I lifted my head to meet her gaze, weakly adjusting my eyeglasses. Blast, the way they constantly fell down on my nose was obnoxious.

"Zandra, hey."

Her gaze flicked over me. "What happened? You don't look well."

"Just getting over being sick. You look tired." I didn't care to explain what kind of sick I was.

"I've had some late nights recently. Why are you out here on a cold, dreary day like this? You do know sick people are supposed to rest and stay warm in order to get better."

"I know it's not the brightest idea, but I...needed to get away."

Zandra crossed her arms and plopped down in front of me. "All right, which squirrel harassed you? I'll go track him down and make the furry imp apologize."

I smothered my traitorous smile with a cough. "Is squirrel harassment common where you come from?"

"Oh, very." She gave a sage nod. "Always need to keep an eye out for those devious balls of fur that harass people."

The laugh slipped out before I fully realized it. I couldn't believe I was *laughing.*

"What? I'm being completely serious." Zandra's face split with the grin she could no longer keep hidden.

"You—" A stab of pain cut the laughter off abruptly, and my breath hitched. I lay back, letting the coolness of the sand seep into my back and arms. With the fresh wave of pain came all the reminders of the problems and threats tied to it back at the palace.

The words she'd said to me during our last conversation cut through the rush of overwhelming thoughts, as bold and determined as she was.

"I would care."

My mind shifted to our previous conversation, but I kept my gaze fixed on the dull grey sky. "You said Zurinians and Daystrans have differing views on Adonai... How?"

Zandra took the invitation to discuss the matter without hesitation. "Daystrans typically put too much emphasis on duty and the rules with what Adonai commands. Zurinians place more emphasis on what Adonai does for us over what we can do for Him."

"Then what does He do besides judge us?"

"Cass." Her voice took on a softer note. "Adonai cares for each one of us personally. He wants us to go to Him and rely on Him for guidance. He wants to support us, but we have to be open enough to let Him."

I shifted, tracing a finger in the cold sand. "But why would

He want to do any of that for us? He doesn't get anything out of it except more trouble. I wouldn't want to bother with people if I were Adonai."

"He still wants us despite everything because we were His to begin with. Like a good Father, He still wants and loves us, even if we are wayward and need correction. Does that make sense?"

The comparison made me think of my own father and how he had still cared about me when I did wrong things.

"When you put it like that, yeah... Your Adonai sounds a lot better than the way that Daystrans view Him."

"He is, though I'm biased. Daystrans tend to lean toward a loveless, cold view of religion."

"I wouldn't argue with you on that." Throughout all the years, lessons, and lectures, never once had anyone made Adonai sound as warm and loving as Zandra did, or compared him to a father. A part of me ached with a longing for it to be true and wondered if this was what could fill the desolate emptiness inside of me.

Don't get ahead of yourself.

I eased myself to be sitting up again and pushed the eyeglasses further up my nose. My gaze found a cracked white shell in the sand to focus on—anything but meeting her eyes. "There's just no reason for someone like Adonai to want me. I'm not very...desirable. I'm never enough."

"Look, whatever or whoever made you feel that way is wrong. You have worth. But even so, you don't have to be enough, Cass. None of us will ever be enough. Nothing prevents you from coming to Him except for your own free will. If you go to Adonai, He won't turn you away."

The splash of waves filled the following silence with a rhythmic lull. I didn't know what to say. I rubbed a thumb over my pointer finger, finding the absence of my familiar ring discomforting. I rarely wore it when I went out in the city.

"Thanks for talking with me, Zandra. You gave me a lot to think over."

"Of course." She stood and offered me a hand. I took it and let her help me up.

She smiled gently. "Take care of yourself, okay, Cass?"

"I'll do my best."

The way back to the palace felt longer than normal, or maybe I walked too slow. I was grateful for a different topic to focus on. Puzzling out things regarding Adonai was much more welcome than the thoughts of guile, betrayal, and lies.

Back in the palace, I slowed to a stop in the middle of one of the corridors. My gaze lingered on the door to Rueben's study. Maybe I had interpreted things wrong. Maybe he didn't feel that way about me, and it was only in my head. I could have misunderstood.

Before I'd fully made up my mind, I crossed the hall and knocked.

"Come in."

I sucked in a slow breath. He was still my uncle.

Turning the cold silver door handle, I stepped in. Rueben stood in front of his desk, organizing a tower of paperwork. He didn't even look up to see who had come in.

I cleared my throat. "A word."

"Leo. I suppose it is good you came when you did. Now I

don't have to track you down to notify you."

"Notify me of what?" An edge crept into my tone.

He always wore such a guarded expression. It was hard to know what he was thinking.

"I am sorry to inform you that your mother won't be coming for your coronation."

"What? What do you mean she isn't coming?"

"The snow came early and blocked the Northern Pass. I know you were looking forward to her visit, as was I." Even as he said it, he didn't look disappointed. Everything was business to Rueben, even when it came to his own sister.

I shook my head in disbelief. "But there are still a few months before it should snow enough to block the pass. It's barely the beginning of autumn."

"You know how unpredictable the snow is in the north. It is not the first time it has come this early. The messenger did receive a letter from her to give to you." He handed me an envelope with the Cassander family seal before returning to his papers.

Without a word, I took it from him and opened it, scanning the contents of the letter.

Dear Leo,

I am sorry I am unable to come. I was so looking forward to seeing you. It's been too long since our last visit. I am sorry I will miss your eighteenth birthday and coronation, but I hope you know how proud I am of you. I know you will be a wonderful ruler. May Adonai bless and guide you.

Love,
Mother

She hadn't written much this time. But then again, my mother's apology letters were always brief, as if she felt too guilty to write more. I wished she had written more, though.

"Now what did you want to speak to me about?"

When Rueben flicked his gaze up again, I got tongue-tied under his scrutiny. I folded the letter back up and grasped for the determination I'd had on first entering his office.

"All—all I asked was that you left Brantley Odran alone and assigned to me while you worked with the other royal investigators, but suddenly, I find out he's off on an assignment you gave him?"

"All royal investigators are at the disposal of the Crown. There were more important matters I needed him for than your irrational obsession with hunting down that assassin."

My grip on my mother's letter tightened, and the paper wrinkled. "What was his assignment?"

"That is confidential. Not all sensitive information can be shared."

"What are you really up to?"

"This again. I don't appreciate the accusations you've been implying as of late. This is no time for fooling around."

"My thoughts exactly." I gave him a pointed look.

Rueben moved around his desk and stepped up to me. I resisted the urge to shrink back a step back as his penetrating gaze locked on me. "What do you think you're going to do?"

"I'm the prince."

All of a sudden, that reason felt weak and meaningless, and he went on to make it painfully clear as to why.

"A negligent prince that no one respects or pays any mind

to. Do you really think anyone would listen to you?"

I opened my mouth to argue but snapped it shut. The realization smacked me hard.

No one listened to me.

Everyone listened to Rueben.

He was the one with all the power. He'd taken all the power, and I'd stood by and let him do it.

I'd been a blasted fool.

Rueben's voice yanked my attention back to him. "Don't start causing trouble, Leo. Cooperate for once in your life. This is not the time to start another rebellious streak."

You mean keep being your pawn.

I stared back. "Don't worry, Rueben. I'll adhere to the schedule, but that doesn't mean I'll stay out of your way."

"What is that supposed to mean?"

"I think you already know." I turned sharply and hurried out of the room. The slam of the door echoed behind me. I didn't have the nerve to speak of what I'd originally intended to. I'd already gotten my answer anyway.

I hadn't even made it back to my room—the closest thing to a sanctuary in this prison of a palace—when Symon caught up to me.

"Leo! There you are. Why in all of Kalmyra would you go off without me? Especially in your current state!" he whisper-hissed.

"I—sorry. I needed to speak with Rueben."

A jolt of pain through my middle made me stagger a step. The frustration in his expression faded into concern. "You're exhausted, aren't you? You shouldn't have been out for so long." Symon slipped a steadying arm around my shoulders. "Let's get you to your room."

I leaned on him as we wound down the winding palace halls. Now that he'd pointed it out, I *was* exhausted. Weariness dragged on my limbs to the point that it felt like I was trudging through mud.

"Couldn't my body just be over this dumb poison already?" I muttered, more to myself than Symon.

He glanced at me and held the door open. "Have you been taking the medicine the royal physician gave you when you're supposed to?"

Oh, blast it all.

"Uh, mostly." I ducked my head and hurried into my room.

"Mostly?" He lightly cuffed my ear. "Leo!"

"Hey, take it easy, will you?" I dropped into the nearest chair, reaching back and rubbing my shoulder. Every muscle decided to tense into tight knots. My body had chosen the wrong day to be angry with me.

I caught Symon watching me out of the corner of my eye. "You had another conversation with Lord Rueben that didn't go well."

"Does the look on my face say it so plainly?"

"Well, yes." Symon moved to be standing in front of me. "There's something I've been meaning to tell you. My provisional two-year term is complete. I applied to be one of your permanent, personal bodyguards. Captain Tesfira passed me. All that's left is for you to approve it."

"Oh." I shifted, caught off guard by the unexpected topic. "You know I'd trust you with my life...but if anything happened to you because of me, I wouldn't be able to live with myself—"

"I've never been more certain of anything in my life, Leo. My purpose is to protect you. Not only are you my best friend, but you're also my king." He bowed, down on one knee as a show of respect. "Please accept my request to serve you."

"I'm not a king," I muttered.

"Soon you will be, whether you like it or not. A few weeks doesn't change that. I know you're just stalling."

I rubbed a hand over the armrest of the chair and tried to think it through, despite the tiredness sinking in. I paused and rolled my eyes when he continued to bow. "Stop bowing. You know it makes me uncomfortable."

"I know. I'll stop bowing when you make a decision."

I huffed. He could talk me into things too easily. "But if you get killed because of me—"

"Leo." Symon waited to continue until I made eye contact with him. "I will protect you. I can't do that if I get killed, so I will stay alive."

I leaned back in the chair, letting out a slow breath. He sounded so sure. The more of the conspiracy we uncovered, the more I realized the lengths they might be willing to go. I had a bad feeling that the conspirators would easily do away with Symon if he got in their way. I hated the danger he was put in simply from wanting to keep me from harm.

"I'm sorry you're getting caught up in all of this."

"Don't you dare apologize. You didn't ask for anyone to try to kill you—well, unless you were trying to fake your death to get out of Parliament meetings. Then you should apologize, but even you aren't *that* reckless."

A faint quirk of a smile crossed over me. "See, aren't you thankful I'm not that extreme?"

"Oh yes. I thank Adonai for that daily." Symon's own smile faded quickly as he refocused on the issues at hand. "Now what's our next step?"

"We need to track down the man with a scar that Heath described and find those two guards colluding with him—"

"Which is a task for Brantley." He shot me a look that said don't-get-any-ideas.

"Fine. I'll pass it on to Brantley." I heaved a sigh. "Then there's the Zurinians. We need to get matters straightened out with them and determine whether they have any hand in this."

"Good. How will we accomplish that?"

My fingers twitched, needing something to fidget with. I grabbed my ring from the table nearby and slipped it on. While rubbing over the smooth metal, I begrudgingly acknowledged the idea.

Once again, it came to dealing with the people I disliked interacting with the most—royals.

"By meeting with Princess Alexandrina again."

CHAPTER 16

Leo

BLANK PAPER STARED BACK AT ME. THE PILE OF crumpled parchment on the desk silently judged me and reminded me of how long I had been at this. I picked the quill back up and dipped it in ink. My hand lingered above the paper, just shy of making a mark on it.

"Blasted crimson, why is this so hard?" I grumbled. It was a simple invitation to the princess to suggest meeting again. How could one little note be so much trouble?

I began writing, sensing Symon peering over my shoulder. "You can do better than that," he commented in regards to my handwriting.

"I just want to be done with this already. The handwriting is good enough."

"A prince could do better."

His critique made my hand slip, and I huffed at the ugly blotch of ink staining the paper. I crumpled it up and tossed it at him. "Quit that. It's hard to focus."

"If you're having such a hard time, I can help you write it." Symon leaned back against the desk as I pulled down a clean paper and attempted it yet again. He started dictating the beginning of a letter. "'My dearest Princess Alexandrina, would you do me the wonder of meeting again so that I can fulfill the desires of my heart and the longing in my soul?'"

I looked up at him and rolled my eyes. "As if!"

He chuckled. "Fine. We'll go for something more realistic. 'Dear pampered royal that I do not wish to meet' or 'to the cause of my most recent social misery.' Or perhaps you prefer something more straightforward like 'dear princess who may have poisoned me.'"

While trying to block out his suggestions, I accidentally started writing the words he dictated. "Symon, shut up!" I grabbed more of the crumpled paper and threw it at his head. "This is not nearly as amusing for the person who has to deal with the situation."

He laughed and ducked the paper projectiles. "Please, you'll laugh over this tomorrow."

"Is that before or after the impending disaster?"

Returning to the paper, I scribbled out the first idea that came to mind. "There. Finally done with that."

Symon rotated the paper around so he could read it over. "That works and keeps it simple."

"Good." I smirked as I eyed the pile of crumpled paper, already making plans to stuff it into Symon's things later to get back at him for making this take longer.

He glanced at me and caught the look on my face. "What is

that for?"

"Nothing." I plucked the note from his hands and slipped it into an envelope. Once I had given the note to a messenger to pass on, I could relax now that my end of it was taken care of.

"Care for a game of chess?"

"You mean care to get beaten by you again?" he remarked, aware of his shortcomings when it came to the game. "I'd prefer sparring."

"Well, we could make it more interesting and—"

A knock on the door interrupted. Symon crossed over to the door and came back a moment later with a small purple envelope in hand. "Your response."

"That was fast." I sat up straighter and took it from him, reading over the contents.

Prince Leo,

I accept your invitation and am available today. After lunch, you may come to the hall outside my quarters and escort me. I look forward to it.

~Princess Alexandrina Veridian

"Now that's some quality handwriting."

"Oh, enough already!" I turned around in the chair and smacked him with the envelope.

"Congratulations. You have a date."

"You're enjoying this too much. Are you trying to de-stress by teasing me? Is that what this is?"

Symon shrugged halfheartedly and changed the topic before I could ask anything further. "Don't forget to take your medicine." He placed the vial from the table into my hand and got a cup for me.

I sighed but didn't argue. I didn't want a pain episode in front of the Zurinian princess. She didn't need to know I had yet to fully recover from the poison.

"Symon, I have an idea, one you won't like."

"On a scale of one to ten, how stupid is it?"

"You'd say it's a ten." I downed the medicine, making a face at the bitter tang. "Princess Alexandrina might be more open and likely to talk about matters if it was only me."

"Let me get this straight. You want to go meet the princess of a foreign country alone when it's entirely possible the Zurinians may have been behind your poisoning?"

"Um, yes?"

"Leo." Symon began then smothered an exasperated sigh. "Can you not use logic with your reckless ideas? It makes it harder to talk you out of them."

"I'd rather know for sure if we can rule out the Zurinians. Besides, even if she's a princess, she's still just a girl. They can't be that scary."

✤ ✤ ✤

Princess Alexandrina already stood out in the hall when I arrived. She wore a pale yellow dress that reminded me of a sunflower petal, and her brown hair was tied back in some complex style as she always seemed to have it.

"Prince Leo." She dipped a curtsey. I bowed in turn.

"Princess Alexandrina, I'm glad you were willing to meet

again." *Because prolonging this social torment is high on my to-do list, apparently.*

"Our last meeting was brief, thanks to the extenuating circumstances. How are you now?"

"Better." I kept a pleasant tone while inwardly cringing at the stiffness.

"I'm glad to hear you are doing better."

We started walking down the halls together. After five minutes, the palace felt more unbearably stuffy than usual. All of a sudden, Princess Alexandrina stopped. "Oh please, for the love of light above, I cannot do this."

I tugged on the collar of my shirt. Had I already managed to offend her?

"What is 'this'?"

"All of it—it's just so awkward!"

I stared at her a moment then dissolved into laughter.

"What's so funny?"

"It *is* so awkward," I agreed. "I'm surprised you actually said it plainly."

"I couldn't stand it for another second. I hate all the formal stuffiness." Princess Alexandrina crossed her arms, the stiff formalness evaporating from her expression.

"And here I thought I was the only royal who hated all the decorum and formalness." I leaned back against the wall, letting my shoulders relax as some of the tension faded. Merely putting it out in the open had knocked down part of the uncomfortable wall that had been almost tangible between us.

An idea came to mind, and I spoke before I could think twice about it. "Would you like to go for a ride? There are some nice paths in the surrounding gated forest within the palace grounds."

"Oh?" Despite her initial surprise at my suggestion, she said, "Yes, I'd like that."

As we headed down to the stables, her guard followed us from a distance. Even when Galen wasn't around, it seemed she always had a shadow.

"Do you want to do something crazy?"

She raised a questioning eyebrow. "What exactly does that mean?"

"Ditching guards and having a break for once."

"That would mean we would be completely alone without any chaperones," she pointed out.

I shrugged a shoulder. "Hey, I'm not the one who wants the marriage alliance. I don't want anything except to relax. If you would rather not, that's fine with me."

Princess Alexandrina thought for a moment. "I suppose we could—if you can keep up."

"Oh, more like if you can keep up." I couldn't help my grin as I whispered, "Let's watch for an opportunity to make our escape."

When four maids carrying tall stacks of dishes emerged through the doors just behind us, temporarily blocking her guard's view, we ran.

"Where are we going?" Princess Alexandrina asked with a laugh as we ran through the palace, probably being the most improper sight to ever tread the halls.

"We're going for a ride, remember?" I slowed to a walk and stopped when I came across the familiar tile on the wall with a chip in it. I pressed my thumb into it, activating the hidden latch that opened the passageway. The sound of stone grating on stone filled the air.

Showing her the secret passages was risky, but maybe the only way to tell who was truly on my side was to give them the chance to betray me. Or maybe, I was just fed up with this uncertainty and ready to take the risk to find out the truth instead of wallowing in uncertainty. I didn't need Rueben to see us like this, either.

I glanced back to see her reaction as a section of the wall swung in to reveal the secret tunnel.

Princess Alexandrina stared in surprise. "I...didn't know your palace had secret passages."

"Well, they wouldn't be secret if you knew about them, now would they? Shall we?" I offered her my arm as I led her into the dark passageway. We didn't use this tunnel as often as the others, so it had no lanterns for light. Not that I needed any. I could navigate most of these passages blindfolded.

She lightly gripped my arm, yet the princess still moved and walked with confidence even in the unfamiliar darkness. "Are there many of these?"

"There are passages interconnected all throughout here. I know them better than I know most of the palace. My sister and I loved to explore them when we were younger."

"What are they for?"

"After the former palace was infiltrated and destroyed, my great-great-something grandfather had this maze of passages built to prevent that from ever happening again. It acts as both an escape route and a defense mechanism to keep intruders from actually getting past the maze—all according to one of the actually interesting lectures a tutor gave once, that is."

Princess Alexandrina's chuckle echoed in the tunnel. "Good to know. It would be easy to get lost in here."

"Lucky thing you have me."

A few twists and turns later, we arrived at what appeared to be a dead end. I pushed in a brick on the wall to my right and the hidden door opened. Princess Alexandrina glanced back at the winding, dark tunnel and then at the stables and inner courtyard that lay before us. "So the rumors are true about you sneaking out."

"Some rumors are so outlandish they're impossible to believe; however, that rumor is one hundred percent accurate, much to Rueben's chagrin."

As we tacked up two horses, I asked, "Do you like riding?"

"I do. The sensation of freedom is almost as good as sailing."

"Ah, I've never been sailing, but you're not the first person I've met who enjoys it."

"What?" She looked at me like I'd been a hermit living under a rock this whole time. "You mean to say you really have never sailed?"

"No, though I find plenty else to do." I mounted my horse. "Now let's go before someone catches us."

I spurred my horse, Seren, on and the two of us raced into the forest within the inner walls, disappearing from the ever watchful eyes of the palace.

Sunlight set the forest aglow. Touches of fiery red, gold, and orange spread through the leaves of the trees around us and proclaimed autumn's approach. Yellow and blue flowers sprang up in the underbrush and lined the forest's path we took.

As our horses slowed to a walk and kept pace with each other, I glanced at Princess Alexandrina. Her face held a sense of awe. "This is amazing," she breathed, leaning her head back as much as possible to take in the canopy of colored leaves. "So this is what true autumn is like."

"You don't get seasons in Zuren?"

"Not really. Zuren has a tropical climate. There is always lush vegetation, but we don't have seasons the way Daystra does."

"Our countries couldn't be more different, even in climate and landscape alone," I mused aloud.

"Different doesn't have to be bad. They are both unique and beautiful in their own ways. There are many flowers here that I have never seen before either."

"Which is your favorite so far?"

She looked around for a moment before pointing to a deep blue star-shaped flower with a white center. "That one. I've never seen a flower that blue before."

"Ah, those are my mother's favorite flowers, genaytians, from the northern region where she grew up. My father had those planted around the palace grounds for her after they got married."

Princess Alexandrina smiled at me. "That's sweet."

I found myself at a loss for words. This was the first time I had seen the Zurinian princess smile genuinely—and at me—and I couldn't deny I found her smile attractive.

Stop it. What are you thinking? What does it matter if she's attractive or not?!

Despite my internal scolding, my thoughts still drifted back to her.

Blast it, Leo! Knock it off.

I shook my head. What was wrong with me?

"This is nice, though." She let out a soft sigh. "Too much has been going on without the chance to relax and think. I'm not very good at remembering to do that. I can get too wrapped up in figuring out a problem."

"In that case, let's forget political talk and negotiations all together. I'll have to show you how to relax more and have some actual fun."

"Fun?" Princess Alexandrina tilted her head in thought, a faint smirk flickering across her face. "What does that word mean, exactly? I have heard mention of it before, but I've never understood the concept."

I chuckled. "I acknowledge that challenge and accept it."

She looked back at me with a smile, and I couldn't help returning it. A comfortable silence settled over us as we followed the winding trail, the songbirds and occasional snort of our horses filling the silence. We continued until we came to a fork in the path and took a left, going down a path Symon and I had ridden on many times.

The sun shone through the forest canopy, its scattered light dancing on the underbrush and lower branches of the trees as the wind gently shook them. Tall pines and deciduous trees filled the forest. The scent of pine and cedar permeated the air.

I risked another glance at her so she wouldn't catch me staring. Princess Alexandrina looked up at the trees with one of the most genuine smiles I'd ever seen. Her joy was contagious, and I soon found myself grinning yet again and feeling more at ease around the Zurinian princess than I had been before.

"If you think the trees are beautiful, wait until you see this." I prompted Seren into a canter, and she followed.

After the next bend in the trail, the river came into view. "Oh!" She slid down from her horse and sprinted to the riverbank, stopping at the edge of the flowing water.

I grinned as I jumped down from my horse and joined her at the riverbank. "This is River Linera, one of the purest rivers in Daystra."

Princess Alexandrina bent down to look at it closer. "It's such a pale blue."

"It originates from the mountains up in the north, and the river ends in the palace grounds. I'll show you."

We followed it downstream for several paces before we came to where the river pooled into a small lake.

"Ohh, this is beautiful."

Crouching at the edge, I dipped my hand into the water. I glanced back at her. "It's nice, if you want to feel the water."

"Why does this feel like a trick?" She crouched down and hesitantly stuck her fingers into the water. "Oh, that is not as cold as I thought it would be."

"What? Were you expecting it to be freezing?"

"I thought you were going to splash me."

I feigned shock. "I cannot believe you would ever think that of me."

"It really wouldn't be that surprising."

Was that a hint of teasing in her voice?

"And the Zurinian princess has no mercy!" I splashed her playfully.

Princess Alexandrina gasped. "I knew it! And the prince of Daystra chooses to make an act of war against Zuren!" She splashed me back.

It turned into an all-out water war as we ran down the bank, laughing and splashing each other. Within five minutes, we were both drenched. I raised my hands, exclaiming, "Truce! I call a truce."

"How do I know your call for a truce is not just a trick?" Princess Alexandrina planted her hands on her hips and squinted at me, even as she smiled. "How do I know you won't turn around and splash me?"

"Oh, well, you'll just have to find out for yourself."

The princess tapped her chin. "Fine. Truce." As her gaze drifted to the water, a more serious tone slipped into her voice. "Our countries have such a complicated history. So much blood has been shed on both sides, whether by obvious means or deceitful ones. More war is not what we want, though. And the longer I have been here, the more I find that Daystra and its people aren't how our elders who fought in the wars described it. I...like this country, and the prince here isn't so bad either."

I stared at her for a long moment. Nobody had ever been so openly honest with me before. Everyone was usually so two-faced, but...she was different. She wasn't like the others.

"The princess of Zuren isn't so bad either. I think it's safe to say neither of us want another war between our countries.

Becoming stronger allies is something that would be good for both sides, if people can get over the past."

"So you do pay attention to politics after all. I was beginning to think you only ran around seeing how long you could irritate your bodyguards and Parliament before they lost their minds."

As she turned around to retrieve her shoes she had left near the horses, I splashed her again. She spun around to face me. "You! What about the truce?"

"Perhaps your insult broke the truce," I teased.

"Oh, you will regret that."

"You're going to have to catch me first!" I broke into a run and beat her back to our horses.

When Princess Alexandrina caught up, she flicked some water from her sleeves at me. "I will get you better later."

"Sure you will," I agreed with a teasing grin. I couldn't remember the last time I'd had this much fun with another royal.

After we had put our shoes back on and mounted our horses once more, Princess Alexandrina said, "Thank you for today. It's been a long time since I had a carefree day like this."

"You mean a *fun* day?"

"Perhaps."

"Well, I'm glad to hear it. Race you back to the palace!"

A laugh escaped me as she took off after me, protesting about my unfair start. The wind rushed past at an exhilarating rate. We galloped all the way back to the inner gates of the palace, not slowing until we had entered the stables again.

"Your Highness!" Galen and Princess Alexandrina's other

bodyguard were both at the stables when we returned.

Galen's face had a look of menace that would have made any man fear for his wellbeing. At that moment, I was glad her bodyguard couldn't attempt to murder me without starting a war with Daystra.

"Please don't run off like that again." He shot me a withering glare before turning back to her. "Are you harmed? Why are you wet?"

What? As if *I* would harm her?

The look he sent me implied he did indeed believe it to be a possibility.

"I'm fine, Galen. We simply went out for a ride and enjoyed ourselves at the river. We didn't leave the palace grounds." She dismounted her horse in one easy, graceful motion.

"I'm sure the fact that you two had no chaperone will arouse plenty of palace gossip," her bodyguard muttered, a look of distaste written all over his face.

I shook my head. "Ah yes, propriety. Imagine the gossip now."

"Someone has to give those gossipers something to talk about, might as well make it something interesting."

A wry grin spread across my face at her words before I quickly smothered it. I dismounted my horse and bowed lightly to her. "I had a pleasant time. I should go. I'm sure I've missed about a hundred boring lectures by now."

As I strode away from the stables, it felt like for the first time in a long while I had some control of my own life. If the Zurinian princess and I put real effort into working things out, maybe we could come up with a different way to secure a treaty where a marriage alliance wouldn't be necessary. Maybe there was a way where I didn't have to be trapped by more expectations.

Acting on a sudden, impulsive idea, I turned around and caught up to the princess and her two bodyguards.

"Prince Leo, is something the matter?"

"Nothing's wrong. I wanted to ask you something." I smoothed out the front of my jacket. "The Founding Day's ball is on the eve of my coronation. I know it is short notice, but I'd like it if you would be my guest at the event."

She smiled. "I accept the invitation and look forward to it."

"Great then."

Determination filled my steps in returning to the palace. It was time to stop allowing Rueben and the others push me around like some pawn with no voice.

CHAPTER 17

Leo

DARKNESS STRETCHED AROUND CORNERS AS TWILIGHT descended on the streets of Maldenia. Orange flickers of lamp-light twisted the shadows and chased them into strange shapes.

I glanced at Brantley. He moved with a natural stealth, used to maneuvering in the cover of darkness in questionable areas to a degree that I was not.

Symon would never agree to letting me set foot in a part of the city like this, and it was why he wouldn't know I had until we'd already returned.

"Wait," my friend said in a breath. He peered around the corner.

"Did we lose him?" I hated the thought of losing the scar-faced guy when Brantley had finally tracked him down.

"No, he's meetin' with two people."

I leaned forward enough to get a glimpse of the burly man

speaking with two others. One looked in our direction, but Brantley yanked me back behind the cover of the building before they saw.

"We need to get closer to hear what they're sayin' first." He led me around the back. We cut through an alleyway with a dubious odor and neared the colluding group.

My fingers pressed against rough stone as we crouched behind a wooden crate to hide. I held my breath, not daring to breathe lest it make me miss important information.

"Now we're outta lot of money, thanks to that no good rat," the one with the scar grumbled.

"Gabriel is the one who went behind our backs and snatched the job up instead of working together and splitting the profit."

"What were you expecting, Ruell?" The other crossed his arms. "And on top of it, the idiot went and got himself caught and turned into a liability. It's no wonder Devrim stopped working with him."

The mention of the name made me go rigid. Brantley gripped my shoulder to keep me in place. I clenched my jaw and fought every instinct within me to confront them right then and there.

"Should we place bets on what day Gabriel will hang?"

Their crude laughs and murmurs of now insignificant conversation faded to the background. Not only was one of them the same scar-faced man the stable master had described, but the other two had to be the Aycill and Ruell mentioned. These were the ones we'd been hunting for.

They were connected to Devrim.

I glanced at Brantley in the dim light. "Come on. What are we waiting for?" I whispered.

"We're outnumbered. While I follow them, go back to the palace and request guards to aid me in apprehendin' them."

That was the smart option. The logical one that followed proper procedure. But it held its own risks.

"What if they catch on to you, and we lose them for good? We have no leads if they get away," I argued.

"Oy, keep your voice down or they'll hear us!" Brantley whisper-hissed. "We need to—"

The wooden crate we'd been hiding behind crashed to smithereens. The three surrounded us.

Blast it all.

"Well, what do we have here?"

I jumped to my feet, reaching for the hilt of my sheathed sword. A force slammed me into the cold, hard cobblestone. I grunted as the wind got knocked out of me.

"What're you doing followin' us?" Scarface, as I decided to call him, questioned. When I didn't immediately answer, he kicked me twice while I was still down. "If you don't talk, you'll die right here and now, scum."

I flicked my gaze over to Brantley who'd gotten pinned to the wall by the other two. In the scuffle, they'd taken our swords.

"Oh? If you wanted me to talk, you should have just said so. I can do plenty of that."

My remark earned me two more kicks. Pain flared in my sides. I smothered my grimace. It was a terrible combination with how sensitive my middle had been from recovering from the poison.

"We know that you trespassed on palace grounds and discussed treason," Brantley stated, only saying as much to distract the guy from beating me up any further.

"And what are you two going to do about it?"

The cold from the cobblestone seeped through and sent a freezing chill down my spine. This was going about as badly as it possibly could.

"The three of you will be arrested for treason, of course," he declared.

The two called Aycill and Ruell both laughed.

"They must be some royal investigators," Aycill remarked, a dangerous glint in his eyes. "I used to be one of those myself. It rarely ends well for individuals in such an occupation. Everyone hates what you really are—spies."

Scarface loomed over me, his blade flashing menacingly in the moonlight. "You gutter rats are going to regret followin' us."

Brantley exchanged a look with me. I shifted, ready to spring to my feet.

"You'll be the ones that will be sorry!" His exclamation distracted Scarface for a brief second and gave me the opportunity to scramble to my feet.

I stepped closer to Brantley who'd manage to break free at the same time. "Tell me," I said, still gasping for breath and ignoring the throbbing pain in my sides. "Where is Devrim?"

"Devrim, eh? What business could you possibly have with him?"

I braced a hand against the wall behind me. "He and I have

something to discuss," I gritted out.

Aycill scoffed. "Not just anybody can meet the best assassin this side of the Halcyon Sea—blast, probably in all of Kalmyra."

"What does it take to get a meeting with him?"

"Nothing you could offer. Unless you had information he wanted—but I doubt you'd have anything Devrim wants. He doesn't do jobs solely for money anymore."

His words sent my thoughts spinning. What exactly did that mean? Was that the case six years ago? If he didn't do it for money back then...why did he do it?

The glint of metal jerked me back to the situation at hand.

"You three conspired to kill the prince. That's treason and valid grounds for imprisonment, at the very least."

The one called Ruell chuckled, his words dripping with smugness. "Perhaps we did, but you won't live to tell anyone about that." Addressing Scarface, he said, "Let's take care of 'em already. We're done wasting time here."

I shifted into a firm stance, preparing for a hard fight as the three armed with swords closed in on us. The pain from the poison's aftereffects and getting roughed up made something as simple as standing difficult. I hated how weak I felt.

If Symon had been with us, he would have stopped me from my own foolishness. I guess he owed me an I-told-you-so, if Brantley and I managed to get out of this predicament alive.

Scarface lunged at me, and I darted to the right to avoid his swing. His slashes were sloppy. *He's not used to a sword.*

"Watch out!"

I ducked, barely heeding Brantley's warning in time as

Aycill's blade sliced the air.

Four additional figures rushed into the decrepit alley. I grimaced. Not more of them...

To my surprise, they attacked the thugs, and the fight swiftly turned to chaos. Snapping my attention back to the one attacking me, I scrambled to avoid his blade. I clenched my jaw as he forced me into a corner.

In the turmoil of confusion, a young woman darted over and blocked his swing. She parried his attack and fended him off. I recognized the ship captain.

"Zandra? What in Kalmyra are you doing here?"

"Thought you might like some help."

I narrowly dodged a jab of someone's blade. "Whatever would make you think that?"

"Oh, you know, the thugs surrounding you and your friend in a dead end alley. Do you often go around weaponless?"

"There were complications."

With the aid of Zandra and her friends, the scales tipped in our favor. A thug suddenly turned and ran. The other two fled in the same direction.

"Blasted crimson, they're getting away!" I started after them.

"Hey!" Zandra fingers dug into my arm, yanking me to a halt. "You're going to run after those guys who nearly killed you just now while you're still weaponless?"

"We can handle it," Brantley cut in and stepped around her. "Come on, every second counts."

I glanced between them. "Sorry, but I need to go." I pulled free of her grasp and took off with Brantley.

I didn't care what it took—another lead would not slip past me.

CHAPTER 18

Zandra

WAS CASS TRYING TO GET HIMSELF KILLED?

I sprinted after him and kept pace. "Wait! Why are you being so reckless? Are you trying to get yourself killed?"

"No time to explain. It's complicated. There's no reason for you to get caught up in this." Cass's breaths came short and wheezing.

Tides, why was he so frustrating?

"Then let us provide you with some support if you're so determined to do something stupid."

"All right," he relented.

They took a turn and went down a street, one that became increasingly more rundown than the rest of the capital. The roofs of the buildings were pocketed with holes, and broken shingles littered the streets. Wooden doors were splintering apart. The cobblestone ground was covered in so much dirt and grime that I almost mistook it for an unpaved road. Most noticeably, not a soul was on the street for more than a few moments. Everyone who stepped out into the night scurried about their business, as if they didn't dare get caught outside.

Kar'el, one of the few bodyguards I trusted, halted in front of me. "Your Highness, they entered the warehouse district. Are you sure it's wise to continue?"

My eyes drifted to the sign hanging on the sides of one of the buildings with a painted black X. This was quite possibly the most dangerous place in the Daystran city I could set foot in. For some annoying reason though, I felt convicted to go after Cass. Even for a smuggler, there weren't any good reasons for him to be in a place like this and chasing those thugs.

"Perhaps not, but I'm going to anyway."

Takeo raised an eyebrow. "You sure? It's the warehouse district. That's not a lovely place in any city, I can tell you that. Are we really getting into trouble over that guy?"

Milo sent the boy a look. "Regardless, we're with you, Captain."

The four of us went with Cass and his apparent friend, Brantley, in the direction the thugs had gone. After searching several streets, his friend came to an abrupt stop at a corner.

"What is it?"

"The two in those cloaks over there. They have the same build and height as Aycill and Ruell, and they keep lookin' over their shoulder as if they're expectin' someone to be followin' them."

I caught sight of the figures he was referring to. It seemed the two men they were after had split off from the other thug.

"We'll go around and cut them off up ahead while Zandra

and her people approach from behind."

I wasn't thrilled with listening to what this Brantley said, but Cass would still do it regardless. He was too reckless for me to walk away with a clear conscience.

Glancing at Cass, I caught a glimpse of a pained expression cross over him. Was it from getting beaten up earlier by that thug? Or was there something else?

We split up and wove through the alleys, careful not to get turned around.

Takeo spoke in a low voice. "Don't you wonder who these guys even are?"

"Probably rival smugglers," Milo reasoned and threw a glance behind us.

I peered around the corner and caught sight of the two thugs in question. Good. We were keeping up with them. "Save the speculation for later. Focus on the task."

When Cass and Brantley cut them off up ahead, we rushed up from behind to surround them.

One still tried to run, but I had been waiting for one of them to try to escape. I dashed to the side and lightly pressed the tip of my saber to his throat. "Surrender."

His gaze flicked to me, then my blade at his throat, as if gauging his chances of escape. In the next moment, he raised his hands in surrender.

The shorter one who hadn't tried to run sneered at Cass. "You're getting yourself into things you don't fully understand, boy."

He glared back at him. "I know enough, traitor."

After the two had been restrained, Brantley addressed us.

"Thanks for your assistance. I admit we did need some in the end."

I nodded briefly. "It was no problem."

He turned to Cass. "Well, I'll bring these scoundrels in now. Ya best be on your way before a certain someone scolds ya to death for all this."

"Your support is absolutely heartwarming."

"What are friends for!" Brantley laughed as he shoved the two captured thugs along.

Speak of scoldings brought Galen to mind. He would not be pleased when he heard of this detour on our excursion. My old friend had been far too uptight since we'd come to Daystra, not that I could blame him.

I looked Cass over but didn't see any serious injuries, although I was sure he had some good bruises after that. "You got a cut on your arm." At first, I didn't realize I had said that out loud.

"Oh?" He brushed a finger along the cut before shrugging. "Must have gotten it in the fight. It's not deep."

Why did Cass brushing his injuries off like that bother me so much?

"I'll be on my way then."

At his words, I asked, "Where are you going now?"

"Probably home. Why?"

"We can escort you back if you'd like, given the fact that you nearly got killed today."

"Are you worried about me?" he asked with a quirk of a tired smile.

Before I could open my mouth to reply, Milo said, "You

look rather exhausted. Why don't you join us for dinner?"

"It's a little early to be eating dinner." I shot him a look. *What do you think you're doing?* Having him over for dinner wasn't necessary. Escorting him back to his home was enough to ensure his safety after such an ordeal. Cass needed to rest, not get into more shenanigans.

"We were on our way to buy food. Besides, the crew is always hungry, no matter the time of day." He turned back to him. "So would you like to join us?"

When Cass's gaze flicked to me, I stared intently at a loose thread on the cuff of my sleeve, avoiding eye contact with him.

Please say no. Say no. It's just one word.

Then the smuggler smiled and said exactly what I was hoping he wouldn't. "I'd love to."

CHAPTER 19

Zandra

BOISTEROUS LAUGHTER FILLED THE LONG TABLE below deck as the crew gathered around and ate. Cass sat at the end, spinning a tale about one of his adventures. He had the group's full attention.

"Ye didn't actually have that many guards chasin' ye, did ye?" Soapy's eyebrow arched.

"Oh yeah, it was a whole group of them all in their shiny blue uniforms!"

Another asked, "How did you get them off your tail then?"

"I jumped out the window, of course!" Cass laughed.

Takeo crossed his arms. "There's no way you could've jumped out the window at that height. You'd have broken your legs!"

"Well, what can I say? I must be lucky. No one will catch me. I'm too fast."

Soapy chuckled and slapped him on the back. "Someone's

gettin' a bit cocky."

"Is it bragging if it's a fact?"

His response elicited another round of laughter from the crew.

I leaned back against the door post, content to remain at the fringes. It was uncanny to watch how well Cass fit in with the others. After a few jokes, he'd gotten them to relax, and they had welcomed him right in, almost as if they recognized him as one of us. The lighthearted atmosphere was a pleasant change of pace.

"Ahh, this boy's got spirit. Captain, let's keep 'im!"

With the tilt of the ship on the waves, I stood straighter to avoid losing my footing. The exclamation caught me off guard.

Could he really be one of us?

But no, it wasn't practical, or logical. When the envoy returned to Zuren, so would my friends on the ship. They had only come in the first place for my sake and let me pose as their ship captain, since none of my outcast friends trusted the traditionalist aristocracy to protect me. As great as Cass might be, it would mean leaving behind his homeland all together to live in a place that disliked his kind. Even if he could get along with the outcasts, he was still Daystran. The bad blood between our countries wouldn't change overnight.

By the time I stopped contemplating the matter, I'd missed the end of his conversation with the crew. I looked up to find Cass right in front of me with that charming, crooked smirk of his.

"Did you hear me? I said thank you for dinner. I had a great time with everyone here."

I smiled. "Oh, I'm glad. You looked like you could use a nice, home cooked meal."

"What? He can't be leaving already! We didn't even get dessert yet!" Takeo objected, his mouth curving downward in a disappointed frown. The crew followed his comment with a clambering agreement that he should stay longer.

Cass's smirk broadened to a full smile. "Dessert?"

Milo stepped over with a small covered picnic basket and thrust it into my arms. "Esme gave me some of the dessert right away. She thought you and Cass might enjoy it while getting some air together? It's rather stuffy and crowded down here."

I fumbled with the basket, sending him a disguised glare. *Milo, quit playing matchmaker—or whatever this is!*

"What? You both could use a friend." He flashed me an innocent smile.

"Uh huh."

"A walk on the beach could be nice," Cass agreed. Whether he was oblivious to Milo's intentions or not, I couldn't be sure.

"Let's go then."

I left the ship with haste and attempted to block out the teasing oooohs from the crew. Cass followed as I led us from the docks down to a path on the beach. I glanced back at the ship not far away, certain that, even from this distance, I could see some of the crew watching us with spyglasses.

Tides, I'd never hear the end of this.

To avert from the silence hanging in the air, I opened the basket to find four sweet rolls inside. "Here." I offered one to him.

"Thanks." Cass took it and tried a bite of the roll. "Mm, this is really good!"

"Milo's wife, Esme, is great at baking." I picked up one of the rolls and bit into it. The flaky pastry mixed with chocolate filling melted in my mouth.

"Does she make all the food for your crew?"

"She rotates with Judah and a few others, but everyone likes Esme's cooking the best."

When I glanced at Cass, he had already eaten most of his roll, and I'd caught him in the act of licking frosting from his fingers. The content expression on his face made me smile at the way something so simple made him happy.

"This must be what heaven tastes like."

I laughed. "Perhaps it is."

A cool breeze brushed over my bare arms and tousled my hair. I shivered. Daystra was much colder than Zuren.

We fell into silence again as we walked along the sandy shoreline. The lapping waves filled the void, a rhythmic lullaby I'd known from a young age. I breathed in the salty air. It didn't feel so awkward now. It was actually kind of...nice.

My gaze drifted to Cass. Things always felt different with him. Something about him that I didn't understand put me at ease in a way no one else had been able to.

His green eyes met mine as he caught me staring. I quickly broke my gaze away, pretending I hadn't been thinking about anything to do with him remotely.

Tides, I take it back. This feels awkward now.

"Why did you get involved back there in the warehouse district? You risked a lot to help me when you didn't know what was going on."

"Oh, well, we were going to buy food at the marketplace, and on our way, we saw you and that friend of yours trailing those guys. We followed you and ended up there."

"But what made you follow in the first place?" he pressed.

I bit my lip, searching for an answer that wouldn't sound strange. "The whole situation appeared shady. It gave me a bad feeling, and...and I didn't want anything to happen to you."

"I probably wouldn't be here if it weren't for you, so thank you—for caring."

"Of course." I averted my gaze to the ground, letting my hair drape down around my face. Strange flutters filled me like rippling water. The coarse yellow sand was so different from the soft white sands of Zuren, upon which I would run barefoot all the time.

After a moment, I looked back at him. Cass had a hand pressed against his side again. Now that I looked closer, there were dark circles under his eyes, and his face seemed a shade paler.

"Did you get injured?" I asked before I could talk myself out of prying. "You keep holding your hand to your side."

Cass glanced down and lowered his hand, as if he hadn't realized he'd been doing it. "Oh. That. Just got a few hits and bruises. It's nothing serious."

I raised a questioning eyebrow. "Right."

Another gust of cold wind blew off from the ocean, and I shivered, wishing I'd taken a coat with me.

"You should have brought a jacket," he said, as if hearing my thoughts. "It'll only get colder."

"I'm not yet used to the weather here."

The wind blew harder and made me shiver. I wrapped my arms around myself. Cass took off his navy coat and draped it across my shoulders. "Here."

I cleared my throat, hyperaware of how his warm hand had brushed against my shoulder for a brief moment. "Oh, um, thank you."

"Next time, remember to take a jacket with you so you don't freeze." Cass turned and stared up at the sky. "Look at those stars. They're beautiful, aren't they?"

I followed his gaze up. In the inky sky, the stars shone especially bright. "You like the stars?"

"Yeah. It can't be that unusual, can it?"

"Well, maybe it is for such an odd smuggler as you, but normally it's not, to my knowledge."

"Know many smugglers?"

"A few."

"Not surprising."

"What's that supposed to mean?" I asked.

He smiled that crooked smirk of his. "Nothing."

We fell into light conversation for a few minutes before Cass said, "I should probably head back. Please thank the crew for the meal and Esme for her dessert; it was some of the best I've had in a long time. And thank you for the company. I had a really nice time."

"Me too." The words slipped out before I could stop them. I didn't know why I felt reluctant to see him leave.

Biting my lip, I contemplated an idea that had wiggled its way to the front of my mind. "Come with me for a minute." Resisting the inclination to overthink things, I grabbed his hand and led him back onto the ship and over to the mast.

"What are we doing?"

"It's a surprise."

"A surprise?" His rich laugh rang in the air and made me smile wider.

I climbed up to the crow's nest and gave Cass a hand to scramble onto the platform with me. After he adjusted to being up that high, he inhaled sharply.

Millions and millions of stars sparkled above us. This high up, the vast night sky felt like an enormous, glittering sea that could lure one into being spellbound for hours.

"This is amazing." He shifted to lean back further. Warmth shot through me when his shoulder brushed against mine.

Breathing in deeply, I stared up at the stars. I didn't want this moment to end. I wanted everything to freeze in place so I could savor each second.

"Oh, look!" He pointed at a certain cluster of stars. "It's the Big Ladle."

"Pfft, that's not what that constellation is called."

Cass grinned. "I know, but my names for the constellations are better than the actual names. See, there's the Tiny Tiger, the Wiggly Willow, and the Grumpy Caterpillar."

I tried to stifle my laugh. "And how did you come up with all these *unique* names?"

"When I was little, I used to stargaze with my mother. We would come up with our own names for the constellations. It's been a long time since we did that together, though..."

He had never mentioned his family before, except when talking about his family's trade. Were his parents alive? Did he have any siblings? If he was alone, did he ever feel lonely?

Cass turned his gaze from the stars to me. When our eyes met, part of me wanted to look away, but another part of me didn't want to. The latter part won.

"What is it?" he asked, tilting his head slightly.

For a moment, I forgot how to breathe. That fluttering feeling came back twice as strong. Then I remembered myself and shook out of the daze. I glanced down at my hands. "I was, uh, wondering...never mind. I shouldn't be nosy."

"Hey, what were you going to say? You can ask me anything."

"I can?"

"Didn't you hear me the first time?"

"Erm, yes." I decided not to meet his eyes directly this time. "I was just wondering about your family, and why it's been a while since you and your mother went stargazing if you liked it so much."

"Oh." A beat of silence passed. "My mother moved back to her old home up in the north after my father and sister both passed away."

I hesitated then reached out. I rested a hand on his arm and squeezed gently, giving what comfort I could. "Cass, I'm so sorry."

"Me too."

Painful regret swam in his eyes along the shores of that hollow ache he tried to hide. "Sometimes I'm lonely, but I'm not all alone. I have someone that fills the void of my mother in a way, and I have somebody that's like a brother to me. And you met Brantley today. He's been a good friend. So I get on well enough most days."

"That's good."

Despite what he said, I didn't miss the strain in his voice or that empty, haunted look. I wanted to chase whatever caused it far away from him. Hearing Cass admit that he felt lonely some days made my heart ache for him. It was hard to imagine him as anything but his happy, charming self.

Cass gave me one of his usual smiles, the deeper glimpse of a more vulnerable part of him vanishing just as quickly as it had come. "Thank you, Zandra. Seeing the stars like this was truly amazing." His expression still held a sense of awe from the sight of the night sky. "It's getting late. I should probably go now."

"Oh." Disappointment I didn't fully comprehend filled me. "I'll see you in a few days, then?"

I hesitated. "I...I'm not sure."

Between Rowan and the other ambassadors planning to push the negotiations forward, along with my own personal investigation, I wasn't sure how much time I'd have. If Daystra ended up coming to a settlement soon—although unlikely—it would mean the negotiations would be finished sooner.

The thought of leaving formed a lump in my throat. When I left, I doubted I would ever see Cass again. And if I did return to Daystra, it would be as the queen through a marriage alliance. Not that being with Prince Leo would be all bad, necessarily.

"There's something I..."

The flapping of sails filled the air. I wasn't sure what I wanted to say, or how I even planned to finish that sentence. A daring part of me wanted to tell him who I really was. That I was the princess of Zuren. But...I was too scared.

Scared that it would change how he saw me.

Why did my identity always end up holding me back both in Zuren and Daystra?

I cleared my throat, but didn't look at him, fearing my resolution would dissolve like sea foam if I did.

"Never mind. You should get going. I didn't realize how late it was. I'll see you soon, I'm sure."

"Thanks again. Goodnight, Zandra."

Cass left without asking about what I'd almost said. I was thankful he hadn't, because I wasn't sure how strong my resolve was at this point to keep such a secret from him. My walls crumbled a little more every time I was with him. Every time he flashed that crooked smirk my way.

I blew out a breath. Cass continually gave me unfamiliar feelings I didn't know what to do with. I knew better, yet I still felt drawn to Cass, even though I shouldn't. It wasn't fair to him or Prince Leo.

Adonai...what am I supposed to do?

A cold, salty wind blew from the ocean, and I hugged the coat tighter around my shoulders. We'd both forgotten about it, and Cass had already left. I'd have to remember to give it back the next time I ran into him.

A slow smile spread across my face as I remembered the moment. Cass had been so considerate and gentle when he'd given it to me.

Leaning back against the mast, I stared up at the stars and sighed. There was so much to think about, some of which I shouldn't be considering at all. Nevertheless, I found myself smiling at the vast sea of stars as I replayed the day in my head, hoping maybe—just maybe, I could stay in today for a little longer and forget about tomorrow.

Chapter 20

Leo

FOR ONCE, THE EMPTINESS DIDN'T CLAW SO DEEP.

The warmth from Zandra and her crew softened the ache. It felt like I could breathe again for the first time in so long, like it was okay to be myself—and they liked who I was. Not the crown prince of Daystra, but just...me.

A small voice in the back of my mind warned me that this feeling wouldn't last—that this couldn't continue—but I didn't want it to fade.

I ignored that voice.

The brilliant night sky shone above me as I strolled down the streets back toward the palace. An unusually warm breeze brushed against my arms. I let out a content sigh and smiled at the thought of Zandra and her crew. Already, I looked forward to seeing them again.

In an instant, the streetlamps all snuffed out around me, leaving the street shrouded in thick darkness. A crash followed by yells shattered the serene atmosphere. My feet headed in the direction of the nearby shouting before I had thought it through.

Outside the Parliament building, a crowd gathered. One man, possibly in his mid-twenties, stood a few steps from the crowd with a lantern in hand.

"When government starts to act for themselves instead of the good of the people—that is when change is needed!" Fiery passion filled his voice. "I won't stand for Parliament's lies any longer. Who is with me?"

The others around me clamored in agreement.

My eyes widened. *Parliament's lies?* What exactly did they mean? I wanted to ask someone about it, but the crowd was far too fixated on the man speaking.

He continued, "And if they are not capable—then down with the current leaders! Make way for someone who can get the job done right."

As the crowd's fervent approval filled my ears, a pit in my stomach formed.

This wasn't just a crowd.

This was a mob.

My blood ran cold as ice. I swallowed hard and had to remind myself that I only looked like a commoner. *Nobody here knows you're the prince.*

Someone in the midst of people lit a torch. I froze at the wicked flames licking the air. It cast a red-orange glow on the faces around me. Of dissatisfied, disgruntled people.

People ready to act.

I scrambled back away from the imminent mayhem. The

tightly packed crowd made it hard to push through. My chest tightened with every breath. I needed to get *out*.

Shouts coming from elsewhere turned everything to chaos as the city guards descended on the crowd. I got shoved left and right like a boat tossed at the mercy of a storm. The force of the mass knocked me down into the hard, gritty cobblestone.

The thunderous pounding of footsteps rang in my ears. I struggled to get back up before I got trampled. I had barely run one block before a black carriage with silver embellishments pulled to a stop in front of my path.

The door swung open. "Get in," a female voice ordered. It sounded familiar, but my mind was too muddled to place it in that moment.

A scream from somewhere behind me drove me into the carriage. I yanked the door shut and turned to see my aunt there.

"Cyra." I slumped down into the grey carriage seat across from her. "Thank goodness."

"Leo, are you hurt?" Her worried eyes searched me for injuries.

"I'm fine, I think. Just shaken." I roughed a hand over my face. "How did you find me?"

"Your bodyguard, Sir Caddel, came to me. He said you had been gone too long, so I promised I'd look for you. I thought you and Caddel were close. Why did you go out without him?"

"Because he wouldn't have liked where I went to look into things..."

"And when did we start going to dangerous, questionable areas that would make even bodyguards wary?"

I internally squirmed under her gaze. "I needed to know the truth. What's really going on and who's pulling the strings behind all of it."

"You mean the ones behind your sister's death?"

"Yes, and the recent assassination attempts. I think the ones behind it are the same people." I clenched and slowly released my hands, willing them not to shake while adrenaline still coursed through me.

"That is..."

"Probably me making connections where there are none and being overly paranoid?" I finished for her.

"No." Cyra shook her head. "It is a real possibility."

I gripped the edge of the seat so tight my knuckles turned white. Somehow, Cyra acknowledging the validity of my theory made it ten times more real.

"What..." I glanced out the carriage window to the darkened streets. "What is happening out there?"

"I tire of the clandestine games everyone's playing. So allow me to be blunt with you." Cyra locked her gaze on me. "You wanted the truth?"

"Yes."

"We're on the verge of war, Leo."

The words slammed hard and repeated in my mind like a relentless hammer in a forge.

"War?" I whispered.

"A few months ago, Hyra and Rin formed a strong alliance. Hyra is making advances to conquer Andaria. From there, they will likely cut off trade with both Zuren and Daystra and then conquer us. Rueben and Parliament were trying to avoid riots and getting the general population in a panic."

The haunting image of the mob filled my mind. "I think they're failing at that, then."

"At first, maybe it was a decent strategy, but now it's downright foolish to try to keep the public unaware about the war." She tsked. "No one will be prepared for it at this rate, at least, as far as the people go."

"Is that why Rueben started using the royal investigators more?"

"I'd assume so, yes. Spies are needed to gather information on the movements of those around us. Rueben didn't trust you with sensitive information."

That explained why Brantley had been so tight-lipped. He really hadn't been able to say anything about the sensitive information when Rueben got involved.

As the revelation tumbled around in my mind, I realized something else. "You knew about it...why didn't you tell me?" I couldn't entirely hide the hurt in my voice. I'd never have thought Cyra to be one of the people who would keep things from me.

"I wanted to, but for a while you were not ready to handle it. Rueben should have tried harder to prepare you, but he's only been putting in the bare minimum effort with you."

"Not the only thing he's been doing," I muttered, wrapping my arms around my sore middle. *I think I'm going to be sick.* I clamped my eyes shut. Would the effects of the poison leave me alone already? And blasted crimson, would this carriage quit being so rocky?

"Leo?" Her hand touched my shoulder. I flicked my eyes

open to meet her calm blue ones.

I answered her unspoken question. "I'm not okay. Why does betrayal hurt so badly?" My voice cracked despite myself.

I shouldn't be that surprised. Rueben had done this with other things in the past. Yet it still felt like a knife in the back. It was different this time—it concerned something much more crucial.

This was imminent *war*.

He'd kept me in the dark about it, even when the Zurinian envoy arrived and the prospect of a marriage alliance was brought up. Was he really determined to usurp me?

The carriage stopped. We had arrived back at the palace, but neither of us moved.

"Leo...I'm sorry," she whispered.

I sat straighter, shoving down the tangled emotions within me. "You have nothing to be sorry about. You're more skilled with strategy and politics. Tell me—how would you go about preventing this war?"

"Well, I would start out by ensuring we have a treaty that will not be broken with Zuren. The Zurinians approached us about making a stronger alliance because we would need each other to survive a war against the empire of Hyra, especially if Rin is providing aid. They weren't wrong. We will need them to survive a war against an empire as big as Hyra." She smoothed out the skirt of her pale blue dress. "If that didn't work, we could attempt an alliance with Nordyn to the south, but we'd have to give up more than we can spare in order to secure such an alliance. Andaria's already made it clear they wish for no alliance with Daystra or Zuren. So..." She trailed off.

"So you would go with the marriage alliance to make the treaty with Zuren happen."

"I am sorry to say it, but yes, I would. After that, I'd work closely with Zuren and prepare for our forces to fight together and reinforce our borders."

"What about Thaylia?" I suggested. "Is there a chance they would side with us this time?—or against us?"

"It's unlikely they would do anything. The cowards are all too pleased with their neutrality to lift a finger to help us or any other country, for that matter. It is entirely possible that Rin would go through our northern border and bring an army to support Hyra, though."

I nodded slowly as I took it all in and tried to ignore the way it felt like everything was tearing at the seams. A long beat of silence passed before I asked, "Is there anything else he hasn't told me?"

"Not that I know of. You may have not heard, but as of this morning, the Zurinians are pushing for us to sign a treaty and conclude the negotiations. I don't believe that is much of a surprise."

"No..." That meant I had little time left if I wanted to act. I forced a small smile to not worry her. "Thank you for filling in the gaps for me, Cyra. I don't know what I'd do without you."

She smiled back sadly. "I will always be here for you, Leo. You have potential to be a wonderful ruler. I hope I get to see you given the chance."

"Me too..."

Quickly, I excused myself and headed inside. I needed to get to my room before I completely crumbled. The more I learned of what was going on, the more I realized how much of a pawn I had become. I hated that more than anything else.

I rushed around the corner of a hall and nearly plowed into Rueben. We stared at each other for a moment, his gaze unusually intense.

A pit formed in my stomach. *No.* I couldn't do this now with him. Not after everything.

"Where have you been?" he demanded.

My shoulders straightened on instinct, as they so often did around him. "I have been out. I had some business to attend to." In an attempt to escape the conversation, I stepped around him, but he blocked my path.

"What business could you possibly have out in the city looking like that? Much less something I'm not aware of?" He shook his head with a sigh. "Do you always have to shirk your duties so obviously in front of everyone? Doesn't it make you feel even the slightest embarrassed?"

I pushed up the eyeglasses on my face and held my tongue. I wasn't sure if I wanted to get into it with him now and give away the fact that I knew he had been withholding information from me.

"What about the Zurinians? You are the crown prince—your coronation is only a week away—what kind of impression are you giving them? They are judging Daystra through what they see here at the palace, and your behavior is not helping."

"As if they had an unbiased opinion of us to begin with? My behavior isn't the reason the Zurinians dislike Daystra. We both know that."

"No, but it is not helping anything either. You keep putting off Princess Alexandrina, and it is making Daystra look bad. Stop shirking your duties and get your act together, Leo. Your decisions do not just impact you anymore—it affects the whole country and everyone in it."

"I know that!"

Rueben's expression turned stony at my outburst. "Do not raise your voice."

I couldn't hold it back anymore, but I no longer cared. "Maybe I wouldn't have such a hard time if you had actually helped me instead of abandoning me to figure everything out on my own!"

"You will not speak like this to me or anyone else. It is rude and unbecoming of the crown prince."

"As if you care about anybody's reputation except your own," I muttered.

"Leonidas Cassander," he warned.

I stared back at him defiantly. "Admit it—you don't want me to rule Daystra. You want to keep ruling the country yourself and make it look like I'm incapable."

His cold gaze didn't stray from me. "What would make you think that?"

"Cyra told me about Hyra and the impending war. You've withheld things from me before, but this is on an entirely different level. At least when I become ruler, I will actually be properly informed about what's going on."

"Don't assign all the blame to me. When Hyra and Rin first formed their alliance, you were informed, but you paid it no attention."

"How was I supposed to come to the conclusion that they

were preparing for war?!"

"You are nearly eighteen. Do I really need to spell everything out for you? It is your own fault for not attending the Parliament meetings, or even bothering to glance at your schedule and follow it for once in your life."

"That's all you ever say to me!" I snapped. "All you ever tell me is how I'm doing it wrong. You don't care about me and never did. The only thing you care about is ensuring I stay your pawn and do whatever you want."

"Your irresponsible and melodramatic conduct is exactly why I don't entrust more to you."

My hands curled into fists. "Keep on thinking whatever you'd like, but I'm not listening to this any longer."

As I stalked down the hall, he shouted after me, "Stop walking away when I'm speaking to you!"

Why? So you can try to murder me? Sorry to disappoint, but I won't be giving you that chance again.

When I finally reached my room, I slammed the door shut with more force than necessary. I hadn't realized Symon was waiting in my room until he hurried over to me.

"Leo, thank Adonai." He gripped me by the shoulders. "I thought something happened to you when you didn't come back by the time Brantley did. Why did you go alone like that? I thought we had agreed you wouldn't..." He trailed off, noticing the look in my eyes. "What's wrong?"

"It's just—I—everything's so—argh!"

I wanted to punch something. Instead, I pulled away from him and started pacing. I tossed the wig off along with the eyeglasses and clenched my hair.

"Take a breath and use your words, Leo."

After taking several deep breaths, I explained all that had happened since I left with Brantley and hunted down Aycill and Ruell, getting caught in the mob, and my argument with Rueben.

When I finished, Symon's tone had taken on a gentler note. "Sit down. You must be exhausted."

Not having the energy to argue, I abandoned my irritated pacing and sank into the nearest chair. My sides protested the movement with a wicked stab of pain. Grimacing, I pressed a hand to my middle. I would not keel over. I was fine, just exhausted and banged up. That was all.

I sensed his watchful eyes on me. "Don't worry so much, Symon."

"When you're like this, it's hard not to."

"Sorry." I rested my head in a hand and let my shoulders slump. When I glanced up again, Symon stood in front of me, holding out the vial with medicine. I took it and gulped down the proper amount. The bitter liquid hit the back of my throat and almost made me gag, but I swallowed it anyway.

"Thanks."

"Tell me what I can do to help."

"I don't know." A weary sigh escaped me, and I pinched the bridge of my nose. "I don't even know what to do with all of this. *If* I even get a chance to decide what I will do about it." I wasn't sure if I meant politically or literally when I said that.

A familiar stubbornness etched into his features. "Don't talk like that, Leo. I'll make sure you get that choice, no matter the paths others may choose to go down. We need to get to the bottom of this, and we can start with questioning the prisoners Brantley brought in."

"Aycill and Ruell. Right."

He looked me over. "But that can wait until tomorrow. You should rest for now."

I pushed to my feet, determined to ignore the physical exhaustion. "I don't need rest. I need answers."

If I rested, I'd stop and think. Things would begin to sink in, and I didn't know if I could handle the onslaught of tangled emotions resurfacing.

"Just please don't let me be stupid and run off without you again," I said.

Symon steadied me with a hand on my shoulder. "You're never getting rid of me, even if I have to tie us together. But at least rest for an hour before we go."

I heaved a sigh. I didn't want to argue with anyone else.

After complying with Symon's request of resting for an hour, we left my room and descended to the dungeons where Aycill and Ruell were being held. Maybe these traitors held the answers we were searching for.

CHAPTER 21

Leo

COLD, STAGNANT AIR WAFTED THROUGH THE DIMLY lit halls of the dungeons. I kept a steady pace, refusing to get distracted from the task at hand. If we could get a name, then this would be worth it.

We soon reached the main hall of the dungeons where Captain Tesfira awaited us. He bowed. "Your Highness, how may I be of assistance?"

"I'm here to speak with the prisoners Aycill and Ruell."

"They are right this way."

Torches lined the long hall of the dungeon. Their orange light flickered on the dark stone, casting strange shadows that seemed to have a life of their own. I sensed the penetrating gazes of the other prisoners on me and kept my eyes forward.

On coming to the cells, I said, "Would you mind giving us a minute to question them alone?"

Captain Tesfira nodded. "Of course. Lemar has remained

silent, and the other two…I wouldn't say they haven't spoken, but it's been nothing useful."

Symon and I continued down to the end of the cell block. Aycill and Ruell were in cells adjacent to each other, not far from Gabriel Lemar's cell. Gabriel scoffed and crossed his arms, saying nothing, while Aycill and Ruell looked surprise.

"Who would have thought the prince himself would come all the way down here?" Ruell raised an eyebrow. His mocking tone grated on my nerves.

"If you answer me truthfully, I will spare you from being executed as traitors." I let my statement hang in the air for a moment. "Who hired you?"

When neither immediately spoke, Symon said, "You can either both die as traitors, or you can cooperate and live. The choice is yours."

Aycill kept a neutral expression in place, but Ruell shifted uncomfortably.

"He was determined not to let anyone see his identity, and he wore a hooded cloak, so it was hard to see what he looked like. He gave us information about the secret passageways."

I stepped closer to the cell bars. "What was his name?"

"We don't work with people's real names. The alias he used was Byron."

"Ruell!" Aycill hissed.

"What? I'm not dying over this! We both know he'd kill us once he knows we've been caught anyway."

From where he lurked in the shadows of his cell, Gabriel remarked, "You worry so much about our employer, but *I'll* be the one to slit your throats before he gets a chance to with the way you're blabbing on."

"Yeah, and some job you did, Lemar," Ruell retorted. "How is it being imprisoned in the dungeon of your target?"

He scowled. "Why you—"

Aycill rubbed his temples. "We'll all be as good as dead if you don't be quiet!"

All three went silent. Gabriel and Ruell glared at one another.

I exchanged a look with Symon. We wouldn't get anything else out of them at this point, not when they could hear each other. I took a moment to look at each of them. "My offer still stands."

As we walked away from their cells, I remarked, "Aren't they the most unique and annoying group of people who have tried to kill me so far?"

Symon didn't respond.

Glancing at him, I noticed the grim determination set in his features.

The flicker of jest I'd only used as cover faded, and my mind went back to the prisoners. While they may not have said much, we had a name now.

Byron.

Could Byron be the key to solving this whole thing after all? He had hired them. And apparently, he was someone with enough power to silence them even if they were in the palace dungeons.

I rubbed my thumb over my father's ring. Was Byron actually a real person? Or could he be an alias Rueben used?

Rueben was incredibly meticulous and careful. If he was

behind this, he wouldn't make the mistake of being seen by the assassins and informants he hired, especially with such a high risk of them getting caught.

Our muffled steps up the winding stairs echoed in the hollow silence. I didn't know what to believe anymore. Unease formed a pit in my stomach. I threw a glance over my shoulder, not able to rid the creeping feeling of the idea that someone was after me. Worse yet, time kept slipping through my fingers like sand in an hourglass.

On rounding a corner of the bustling hall, a servant carrying a large basket filled with shimmering ribbon nearly ran into me. "Forgive me, Your Highness, I did not see you!" She apologized and bowed.

"It's all right. Only a near collision." I offered her a smile so the maid would relax. "What's the basket for?"

"Oh, decorations for the Founding Day's Ball and your coronation, of course."

"Right. I won't keep you any longer then."

After she left, I looked up, catching my first real glance at the decorations strung about. Ribbons of silver and blue snaked around the stairs and draped from the light fixtures and windows. Flowers of white, blue, and gold were ornately placed throughout the hall, boldly pronouncing Daystra's colors.

The entire palace was being lavishly decorated for the Founding Day celebration and the coronation that traditionally followed.

While the palace staff was preparing for the most extravagant event of the year, our enemies were bringing war.

Would there even be a country to rule by the time my coronation came?

CHAPTER 22

Leo

"QUIT BEING FUSSY. I KNOW HOW TO REMAIN UNSEEN." Symon rolled his eyes. "It's my job to shadow you, after all."

"I just want to make sure they don't notice you slinking around."

"Calm down. I won't interfere with your time with your lady friend."

"It's not like that." I ducked under a low-hanging street sign, finding it a good excuse to hide my flush.

Did I have incredibly valid reasons for visiting Zandra and her crew at this time? No. Was I going anyway? Yes.

Everything had spun into a tumult since two days ago, and I still couldn't get my thoughts straight. It all just felt...heavy. I missed the lightness I had felt with Zandra and her crew.

The late afternoon sun sparkled on the light blue waters. I hadn't been to the docks in the daytime as much as at night, but the warm sunlight illuminated the bustling activity.

I wove through the crowds and cut through to the pier I had become more familiar with. The welcomed sight of the *Wanderlust* came into view. A smile tugged on my lips, and I didn't hesitate to make my way up the gangplank and step on board while Symon stayed below.

The deck only had a few scattered crew members going about their day. Zandra wasn't in sight. Had I missed her?

A blur of motion caught the corner of my eye. I yelped as a boy dropped down in front of me from out of nowhere. He dangled upside down from the rigging.

"Cass, you're back!" Takeo grinned.

I dropped my hand that clutched my chest. "Goodness, you startled me. Do you know where Zandra is?"

"Ohh, so you want to spend more time with the Captain? You're not the only one vying for her attention, ya know."

"Huh?"

"Takeo! What nonsense are you prattling on about now?"

I spun around to come face to face with the captain in question as she approached. Her long brown hair shone in the sunlight and fell in gentle waves around her shoulders.

"Zandra, hey."

"Cass, you're back soon. Is everything all right?"

"Everything's great." I flashed a smile, empty as it was.

She gave me a questioning look. Somehow, Zandra saw right through me. "How about a more truthful answer?"

A sigh slipped past my lips. "I'm tired, frustrated, and past my limit in more ways than one. Nothing is all right."

"This conversation got depressing fast," Takeo murmured, dropping down from the rigging.

"Go help Soapy scrub pots and leave us be." Zandra shooed him off. She turned back to me. "Sorry. We can talk, if you want."

"I...don't know." I shrugged a shoulder, at a loss.

I hadn't planned on telling her about any of it. My plan had been to forget everything for a few hours and let myself believe my life as Cass was all there was.

But it wasn't.

No matter how hard I tried to forget—I could only escape the daunting reality for so long.

"Okay," I agreed.

Once we'd stepped over to a more secluded part of the deck near the bow, silence filled the salty air. I rubbed a hand over the smooth wood of the railing. Zandra waited patiently for me to elaborate.

"Everything is crumbling. I don't know what to believe, or how to fix any of it. Blast, I don't know if there is a way to fix things." Resting my elbows on the railing, I let my head sink lower. "It's all so...grim, and emptier than before." *If that's even possible.*

"Close your eyes and take some deep breaths. Listen to the water. That always helps me."

I closed my eyes and breathed in, then out. I focused on the steady cycle of deep breaths and listened to the ocean. Waves slapped against the side of the ship. Salty mist from the spray of the water drifted up to us. Water rolled onto shore while seagulls cried from the docks.

Eventually, a calmness washed over me, but it still didn't reach the deepest part—the part where the hollow ache remained that left everything else restless.

Would I ever find peace?

"I...think I'm wasting my time. This won't change anything." I didn't even know what I meant by that anymore.

"How can I help?"

I glanced at Zandra out of the corner of my eye. "I don't think you can. Can't fix everything, Zandra."

"You're not the first person to tell me that." She huffed, stubbornness in her blue eyes. "Look, I don't know everything that's going on with you, nor do I need to, but I don't want you to be alone. So don't shut people out when they try to help."

"It's not that I don't want your help. I don't even know what direction to go or where to start when it's breaking apart. I'm just...at a loss."

At a loss. Some days it was hard to not feel like my life just consisted of new ways to lose.

"I'm an outcast."

Her statement caught me by surprise. "You are?"

"In Zuren, there's a faction of people made outcasts for going against tradition. They are treated as a lower class for it and don't have the same protections as a normal citizen. A lot of us on this ship are outcasts." She continued, "So I can understand how it feels when everyone is against you and you have to fend for yourself. But you promised you wouldn't give up. Let me help you fix things."

A long moment of silence followed while I thought it over. It couldn't hurt. There wasn't much to lose at this point.

"Do you or your crew know anything about a person named Byron?"

"Byron?" Zandra stared. "Why?"

"He may be involved in some complicated matters. I can't talk about them in detail right now. Don't worry about it, though. I figured you wouldn't know about him."

"I have."

The words made me still. My gaze snapped up to her. "Wait, you do?"

"By chance, I overheard a conversation someone named Byron had in the streets not long ago. He was speaking with a subordinate of some kind. I remember him saying if there were mistakes, he'd make someone else take the fall for it. And...he said that Daystra won't be the same after this. Whatever 'this' was supposed to be."

"Did you get a glimpse of what he looked like?" My grip tightened on the railing.

"Not really. He wore a cloak that concealed his face."

The cold edge in the air cut through me. I hardly paid it any mind.

Byron was real. He wasn't just a ghost.

"Can you show me where this was? Do you remember?"

Zandra nodded. "I can take you there."

"Then let's go." I pushed off from the ship's railing and hurried down the gangplank with her.

✯ ✯ ✯

The shaded alley seemed abandoned at first before we investigated the surrounding area. We searched for traces of Byron or any whisper of him. To my great relief, after arduous searching, we found something better than a whisper—a cloaked figure. While there was a good chance the person might not have anything to do with Byron, there was still the chance that he could be one of his informants. So we followed him.

We wound through so many back alleys and streets, I got disoriented.

Where is he going?

Another figure cutting through an adjoining street caught my attention. He wore all black, and something about the way he moved was...familiar.

I stopped in my tracks.

Could it be?

According to Brantley's information, Devrim was back in Daystra.

The street split off into two opposite paths. The cloaked stranger and the one that was possibly Devrim went down opposite ways.

I threw a glance behind me. I still couldn't catch sight of Symon. There had been no time to discuss anything with him while having Zandra along. I'd hoped he had managed to keep up at the quick winding pace, despite the cloaked stranger's determination to make it hard to follow.

"Cass?" Zandra's voice snapped me back to the moment.

"I—I need to go this way."

Without further explanation, I rushed off in the direction of the other figure, abandoning the cloaked one that could've been an informant for Byron.

I wouldn't lose him.

Despite my confusing change in actions, Zandra followed me anyway. The dark figure snaked through the city. The further we went, the more I grew reoriented.

The man ducked under a bridge, and we scrambled to dart out of view. When I peered around the corner, he had vanished.

Did he just...?

"What?" Zandra frowned. "Where did he go?"

I sprinted over to the bridge and ran my hand over the damp stone. I knew this path. It led to the palace. Pressing in a specific stone, I pulled out a different one at the same time. A mechanical click filled the air before stones grated on each other and a passageway opened.

"This way." Taking her hand, I plunged into the darkness with Zandra.

"Where does this go exactly?" she whispered.

Soft footsteps up ahead silenced us both. We crept after the mysterious stranger.

How had he known the way in? The passageways were kept a secret. Only a handful of people knew of their existence. That fact only spurred me on.

He turned down a passage that led to a dead end, but to my surprise, he slipped into a narrow tunnel that even I hadn't known about. My shoulders scraped against the slick stone. I didn't care to imagine what the stones were coated in.

The man activated an opening and stepped out of the passageway. We followed before it could close again. It took a minute for my eyes to adjust to the dim light instead of the darkness of the tunnel.

What?

Shocked, I surveyed the hall with prison cells lining them. A secret tunnel connected to the palace dungeons?

I hurried down the hall after him, screeching to a halt when he stopped. He drew closer to the cells that held the prisoners Brantley and I had caught before.

At the sight of the approaching figure, Aycill and Ruell both stood.

"Devrim?"

I inhaled sharply, hands clenching tight.

It *was* him.

"Ruell, come closer. I have a message for you."

"Me?"

As he neared, Devrim's chilling voice floated in the air, the haunting threat barely a whisper. "They warned you to keep quiet and be patient, but you didn't listen. You turned into a loose thread and brought this upon yourself."

Metal flashed between them in the dim light.

The sickening realization hit me after Ruell slumped to the ground and lay far too still. Dead. The assassin had just stabbed and killed him.

Devrim dashed to the two other cells with Gabriel and Aycill and swiftly unlocked the doors.

My hand darted to the hilt of my sword, and I started after them.

Blaring lantern light obscured my vision, and a thunder of footsteps drowned out my own thoughts.

"Halt, intruders! You're under arrest."

I whipped around. Palace guards surrounded us.

My stomach clenched. *Not now.*

"No!" I tried to push through an opening to no avail. The guards grabbed a hold of both me and Zandra and stripped us of our weapons. My gaze locked on Devrim with the escaped prisoners further down the dark corridor.

For a single heartbeat, we made eye contact. His cold gaze sent a shiver down my spine. Then he vanished into the night, just as he'd done six years ago.

I thrashed against the guard's hold. "They're getting away! Let go!"

Fighting did nothing. The next thing I knew, they threw me in a cell along with Zandra. I grimaced as my back connected with hard stone.

The resounding slam of the iron door sealed our fates. I sprang to my feet and raced to the door. My hands curled around the frigid metal bars as my chest heaved. My heartbeat pounded in my ears.

I couldn't lose him. Not like this.

The grim hall spread before me with neither guard nor enemy in sight. Adrenaline and anger mixed in a brutal torrent within.

Too late. The mocking words were like a kick to the gut.

I punched the iron bars with each thought ringing in my mind. The pain that rippled through my hand barely registered.

My sister's murderer was here, within reach—and he'd just slipped through my grasp.

CHAPTER 23

Zandra

EVERYTHING HAD HAPPENED SO FAST.

It only registered that we'd been shoved into a jail cell when the slam of the door reverberated in the air.

Cass lunged at the bars, taking out his frustrations on them. They rattled like an old mast of a ship.

"Cass, stop!" When he didn't hear me, I grabbed his arm and yanked him away from the bars. I'd never seen so much anger in him as his gaze snapped to mine. I kept my tone calm as I spoke. "You're going to break your hand if you keep that up."

He pulled free of my grasp and crossed to the other side of the cold, windowless cell. I watched him pace with agitation. What had just happened to fill him with rage like this?

Whatever it was, I didn't like how it affected him. I decided to start with a simpler question. "Where are we?"

"Palace dungeons," he replied shortly.

"What?" I looked around better at the space we were stuck in. "How..." The secret passageway led into the palace. But what did Cass and his situation have to do with the Daystran palace? Or rather, the man he'd been after?

He made no further move to explain. I stepped in front of him, halting his pacing. "Who was that? What is going on?"

Cass averted his eyes and tried to step around me, but I didn't let him.

"We just landed ourselves in the palace dungeons over this. I need to know why. Please."

"I..." He roughed a hand over his face, the one that had bloody knuckles from punching the bars. "It's complicated."

"We have time." I led him over to a corner and sat down with him. Taking his hand, I started dabbing at his bloody knuckles with part of the clean cuff of my sleeve.

"You'll stain your sleeve." His voice didn't hold the anger it had before. It had grown quieter now.

"I don't care." Silence settled over us while I continued cleaning up his hand best I could with the limited resources. I pulled out my handkerchief and used it to bandage his hand. "There, that's better." His hand was unusually cold in mine. I wrapped both of mine around his hurt hand in an effort to warm it up.

A sigh escaped him. He didn't pull his hand away, though. "That guy...he killed my sister."

I stared, shocked. *His sister was murdered?*

"And he got away. Again." Cass's hand started to curl into a fist, but I gently rubbed his hand to keep him relaxed. A long stretch of silence passed before he spoke again, grief lacing his words. "I've been trying to track him down for the last six years. He's been more ghost than assassin. I was beginning to think I'd never be able to find him again."

"Why did he kill your sister?"

"I...I'm not even sure. Devrim is my link to catching the ones who hired him. To getting answers."

That explained his frustration and strange behavior. What had his sister done to get mixed up in matters that would cause someone to send an assassin after her? As much as I wanted to puzzle out the answer, I didn't push him to talk about it in more depth.

His shoulders were tensed, more rigid than a needle, and Cass's eyes remained lowered the whole time.

"Hey," I whispered softly.

Slowly, he dragged his gaze up to meet mine. Inner torture filled his green eyes. I couldn't just sit and watch while he tore himself up on the inside.

Hesitantly, I pulled him into a hug. Cass stiffened at first, but he gradually relaxed. In the silence, his steady breathing became a rhythm I focused on. Being this close stirred up more fluttery sensations like rippling waves within me. But it wasn't entirely unwelcome.

Tides, I didn't even know what to say, but I hoped this helped. Part of me wondered how long it'd been since someone had hugged him.

We stayed like that for a few more moments before he drew back. "Thank you." A calmer expression had replaced his troubled look. Cass slumped back against the stone wall and started rubbing at his shoulder with a hand.

The immovable iron bars stared back at me mockingly. They reminded me of the dilemma I'd managed to get myself into. If we didn't get out of the dungeon soon, my absence would be noticed. While Marianne would cover for me when it came to any diplomatic meetings, Rowan would be concerned, and Galen would be searching every inch of the palace for me. The Founding Day's Ball was only a few days away. I had to escape before then.

I pushed to my feet and went up to the bars. Resting my hands on the frigid, unyielding bars, I scanned the area around our cell.

"What are you doing?"

"First things first, we need to find a way out."

"No one's escaped from this dungeon in over fifty years—well, until today."

"Well then, so can we." I turned back to Cass, lowering my voice. "Could we use the passage that we came in through to escape? Do you remember the way? It was too dark and disorienting for me to make sense of it."

"I remember, and we could use that route. It's a matter of getting out of this." Cass nudged the cell wall with his boot.

I paced the space of the small cell while I ran through possible escape scenarios in my head. Finally, I sat down with a sigh and rubbed at my temples, feeling a headache coming on. "We'll have to wait and try to swipe the keys off a guard."

"By now, they probably won't do another patrol through this block of cells until daybreak. We're the only prisoners in this section and not high on their list."

"I guess we better get comfortable."

More hours passed, and we settled in for the night. We had no choice but to wait for an opportunity in the morning. I tried lying down, but the hard ground poked into my back. I opted for sitting instead and leaned my head against the cold stone the same way Cass did.

It was going to be a long night.

CHAPTER 24

Leo

MOONLIGHT SHONE ON THE EMPTY HALL AS I PADDED down the velvet carpet. A thrill of excitement hastened my steps. Dezaray had promised we would explore more of the passageways tonight.

I barely stifled my laugh of mischievous delight. Sneaking off with my sister was always fun.

When I rounded the corner, I took extra care to be silent so I didn't get caught as I headed to the throne room. Dezaray liked to meet there because it was always empty this time of night and had a good place to act as the starting point for secret passageway explorations.

I wondered what we'd find this time.

The tall gilded doors of the throne room loomed above me. I approached them, my gaze tracing over the gold swirls that seemed to shimmer even in the dark. A strange shiver raced down my spine. I glanced around to make sure no one was watching.

Dez is probably already waiting for me. With that thought, I rested my hand on the cool metal and opened the door slowly for fear of it creaking and alerting others to our late night adventures.

I slipped through and stopped in my tracks. Fear curled tight around my chest.

Toward the back corner of the room, an armed silhouette stood over a form crumpled on the ground. Red dripped off his blade, mixing with the pool of bright crimson that marred the sparkling marble floors.

I staggered back with a cry. "Dez!"

The assassin's gaze snapped to me. His icy eyes met mine. Fear rooted me to the spot. I couldn't move—couldn't breathe.

The darkly dressed figure took steps toward me.

My mind plunged into panic as I wildly sought an escape. *What's happening? What am I supposed to do? He's coming closer! I want my sister! Dez, help!*

I tore myself from the spot and ran. The halls blurred past me as I tried to get away, yet the pounding of footsteps behind me indicated the danger still loomed close.

Catching sight of the adjacent hall, a certain spot there was like a light in the dark. The secret passageways! I dove for that hall and scrambled to activate the hidden mechanism in the wall. My hands shook hard as I traced my fingers over stone. Worry churned in my stomach when nothing happened.

No, no, no, come on! I know this should be here—why isn't it opening?!

I threw a glance over my shoulder, convinced the sound of

my heart slamming against my chest would give me away. My hands only trembled worse.

Gahhh, open! I slammed a fist against the wall. Nothing changed. Why wouldn't it work when I desperately needed it to?

"You'll never escape, Leo."

I whipped around as the assassin pinned me against the wall. Iciness seeped into my back from the cold stone while I uselessly struggled.

"Let me go!" I screamed.

"Your time is finished. Nothing will change that."

The voice was familiar. I peered at his face, and the sight drained the fight right out of me.

"*Rueben?*"

"You should have learned your lesson the first time." His steely eyes didn't waver as he plunged his dagger into me.

Crippling pain washed through me in a dizzying wave. I grappled for breath but found none. My cold hands crept up and clutched my chest where the knife lay embedded. Blood coated my hands as it rushed from the wound.

Rueben yanked the dagger out and stepped back. He didn't so much as flinch.

I slid to the ground, my face contorted in a silent cry of pain. Between ragged breaths, I managed to choke out, "Why—how—could you?"

"It's better for everyone this way."

Any other questions died on my lips as my mind blurred and my vision dimmed. His footsteps grew distant and echoing. Weakness crippled my muscles. I slumped. My hands dropped from the wound, not strong enough to stay there.

No...can't...

Overwhelming pain dragged me into an emptier darkness than I'd ever known.

"No...no...no!"

I woke with a start. My gasping breaths filled the darkness as I gripped my chest.

"Cass! Cass, are you okay?" Her urgent whispers grounded me in reality.

It took me a moment to recognize Zandra's voice and remember where I was. I doubled over and covered my mouth to stifle my single, shocked sob. It had only been a memory mixed with a nightmare.

I swallowed hard and sucked in a deeper breath. "F-fine."

"You don't sound fine..."

With a trembling hand, I wiped the beads of sweat from my forehead. I tried and failed to stop myself from shaking violently.

"J-just a nightmare."

"Sounds like it was a bad nightmare," Zandra said softly.

"It—it was a memory with my sister. It was..." I shivered. Jittery panic rose with every pulse of my heartbeat. The haunting dream threatened to mix with memories of reality. Everything inside twisted tight.

It was a horrible, frightening nightmare that could come true if I wasn't careful.

Fixing my eyes on my clenched fists, I struggled to control the emotions warring inside, the emotions that threatened to tear me apart at times like these.

"I—" My voice cracked. "I would have done anything for her, but I was too late." I closed my eyes as a single tear slipped down my face.

I was always too late.

Often, I had wondered what would have happened if I'd made it to the throne room sooner, even just a minute earlier.

When no immediate reply came, I glanced at her. The nearest lantern out in the hall cast little light, leaving Zandra nothing more but a faint shadow.

"I...feel the same way about my parents."

I could only see the dim outline of her in the dark, but I wished I could've seen her face for a conversation like this. Or maybe it was better that neither of us could see the other clearly. It felt less intimidating to admit the things I never talked about.

"Tides, I know in my head that it's not my fault, but deep down I still go through the ways it could have gone differently. A way they didn't end up dead. But that's the maddening thing about the past. It's the past, and I can't change any of it, no matter how hard I plead with Adonai."

"The past is cruel." My hands clenched tighter. Devrim's appearance taunted me, both then and now. "The only way to get some semblance of peace is to make the ones who did it pay."

Anger and frustration fueled my silent vow. *The next time I see you, Devrim, only one of us will walk away alive.*

"Cass..." Zandra's hand rested on my arm. When had she moved closer?

I ducked my head, uncertain of what she'd think of me. "It's the only way."

"It doesn't have to be."

"I don't see how. I haven't had true peace since that day, not as long as they walk free. Why should the ones behind it continue to live while they stole my sister's life away?"

Raw silence twisted the air. I assumed my words had shut down the conversation.

After several moments, she said, "Justice is one thing. Those who commit crimes deserve to face the consequences. But revenge won't bring you peace, just more emptiness."

"How do you know?" I refused to believe it. If that was true, then nothing would be left. Nothing could make me whole again. There would be no hope.

"Remember what I said about Adonai? He is where we get life—our hope and healing—where we can be filled. Nothing else can substitute for that." Zandra's soft tone left no room for condemnation or judgment.

Deep down, I knew what she said was right. A certain pang always accompanied truth.

"What if—what if I try your way, and it still doesn't get better?"

"That won't happen, not if you're sincere. Don't let doubt and fear leave you stuck in that empty place, Cass." Zandra rubbed my arm in a comforting motion. Her gentleness was a soothing balm in the darkness and pain of haunted memories.

I slouched against the stone. At this point, the chill of the cell had so thoroughly seeped into me, the bitter cold barely registered.

Time crawled on. I lost track of how long we sat there while I grappled with her words. While I tried to determine the truth, and if I was brave enough to accept it.

Daybreak neared. Above, early morning rays filtered down into the cells. I watched the way the sunlight chased away the shadows bit by bit.

Even in complete darkness, light still came again. Night never snuffed it out completely.

The darkness and pain could not reign forever, either.

I finally spoke, worn in more ways than one. "I—I want to try your way."

"Truly?" Zandra sat up straighter, and I could imagine the smile on her face.

"I don't want to live in a desolate world with no hope. It's too...dark." A shudder passed through me. Her hand slipped into mine, and she twined our fingers together. Feeling her hand in mine sent a warmth through me that combated the coldness of the dungeon.

"Then from now on, choose to live in the light."

That's what I wanted. I knew now. It had taken so long to figure out something so simple in the end.

I wanted to live in the light.

CHAPTER 25

Leo

A GUARD'S WHISTLE ECHOED OFF THE HALL AS HE MADE his round. Zandra had kept an eye on the guard rotations, and she was certain this one was the guard that had been on the longest night shift and would be the most worn out. Keys dangled from his belt, their clinking harsh and enticing as he approached. Perfect.

We both stood next to each other at the bars of the cell. As the guard neared, Zandra asked, "Sir, could I have a cup of water please?" Her hoarse voice could have fooled me if I didn't know any better.

A gentle sympathy settled in his features. "Sure, miss. I can get you some." A moment later, the guard came back with a cup of water and handed it to her through the bars.

While Zandra drank it slowly, I slid my hands through the bars and let my arms hang out casually. *Blast.* The keys were on his other side. I wouldn't be able to reach them.

"Hands back in." The guard sent me a reprimanding look. He tried to thwack the back of my hands with his baton, but I yanked them back.

On impulse, I grabbed his baton with both hands and tried to jerk it away.

"You scoundrel!" He struggled with me for a moment before he tore it from my grasp. "Knock it off."

I didn't have enough time to dodge his swing before the guard brought his baton down and smacked my head hard. I stumbled backwards and held a hand to my throbbing head.

Zandra drew his attention back to her as she passed the cup through the bars. "Thank you."

The guard nodded then disappeared down a different hall.

"Are you okay, Cass?"

"Eh, just a knock on the head. I'll be fine." A rueful smile tugged at the corners of my mouth. "Did you get it?"

"My crew has taught me a few useful tricks." She showed me the keys in the palm of her hand before quickly hiding them out of sight again.

We waited until there were no guards in the immediate area before I crouched and started testing keys to find the right one. The first few were too big, and the next couple were too small. I furrowed my brow. There had to be one that fit.

The next key slid into place smoothly and turned with a sweet click. I eased the cell door open, cringing at the creak it made. "Hurry," I whispered.

We slinked down the hall. Our feet crunched with every step despite our best efforts not to make a sound. I became aware of the way our breathing suddenly seemed so loud.

Voices of two guards at a crossway sent us both flat against the crook of the wall. I held my breath as they passed by and continued on. We wound around a few more corners before my gaze landed on the wall that contained the secret passageway we had entered through. It was closed now. We'd have to find a way to activate it.

Zandra and I waited two minutes for the guards on patrol to pass by until all was clear. Sprinting across the open hall, we came to an abrupt halt at the wall. I scanned the stones and ran my hands over them. There would be an irregularity somewhere that would open the secret tunnel.

Stone chafed my palms as I searched for the right one in our small window of time. My heart pounded in my chest. The seconds ticked by like a predator stalking its prey, creeping up and ready to pounce the longer we took.

"They'll come back around any minute," Zandra whisper-hissed. "We need to hide, Cass."

"Just a little longer."

"We're out of time." She grabbed my arm and tugged me away from the wall toward a bend in the path. My hands shook as I followed her. A small part of me nearly laughed at the irony of the situation. I never thought I'd be attempting to escape from my own dungeon.

The two guards on patrol strolled into view from the other end of the hall when we were in the middle of it, completely exposed.

Blasted crimson.

"Halt! Prisoners out of their cell!"

There was no other way to escape. We darted back over to

214

the wall and felt for the activation mechanism as they closed in. My fingers ran over one higher stone with an irregular texture. I pressed it in. It was stiff and resisted at first, but I shoved harder until it clicked.

The stone began to roll open, revealing the passageway we'd used last night. I pushed Zandra forward. "Get in now!"

"Stop them! They're trying to escape!"

I threw a glance at the approaching guards that had doubled in number thanks to the commotion before looking back at the passageway. At the slow rate it opened and closed, they'd catch us before we could get away.

But not if I stopped it and closed it early.

Zandra had only just squeezed through when I slammed my fist into the stone again. My scraped up knuckles smarted with the impact.

"Cass! What are you doing? You won't be able to get in such a narrow space," she called back.

"I know. Get back safe, Zandra."

One of the guards grabbed my shoulder and yanked my hands behind my back. I fought against his hold to stay close enough to the passageway to finish what I needed to tell her. "Two lefts, three rights, then through the narrowest spot and keep straight."

"I'm not leaving you behind!"

"I'll be fine. *Go.*"

More hands grabbed me and forced me to my knees. I didn't quit struggling until I was certain Zandra had gotten far enough that the guards would be unlikely to catch her, even if they figured out how to reopen the passageway.

They dragged me back and locked me in again. I quickly readjusted my wig I used for a disguise that had been twisted about and adjusted the eyeglasses on my face. An eerie silence fell over the place. I sat down alone in the cell. I hoped that stubborn ship captain found her way back.

As much as I took no pleasure in staying in the dungeons, Zandra would have had a harder time getting free. All I had to do was reveal my identity as prince, though the idea of doing so in such a manner left me wary. I didn't want Rueben to find out about this incident.

It hadn't been more than ten minutes of debating my options when footsteps echoed through the silence and halted in front of the cell. I lifted my head.

Recognition flicked across Symon's face. His surprised expression melted into a smirk. I shot him a glare. *Don't.*

He got my silent message and rolled his eyes. "I'll take care of this prisoner myself," he informed the other guards. "It's been decided that he wasn't involved in any treason, and we're to release him."

When Symon unlocked the cell, I stood and mouthed, "*Not a word.*"

I followed him out of the dungeons and back up to my room. As soon as the door was shut, Symon burst out laughing. I yanked off the wig and eyeglasses and crossed my arms. "I know you're busy finding this amusing and all, but we have more important things to do."

"You—you got captured by your own guards while sneaking around?" He clutched his sides. "I've been looking everywhere for you. I was worried something happened after we got separated. I didn't even think to check the dungeons of your own palace!"

I let out a frustrated grunt. Symon would never let me live this incident down. "Yeah, yeah, enough already."

"What about the other prisoner that had been with you? From what I gathered, it sounded like you two were working together...?"

I narrowed my eyes at his implication. "I'm not that idiotic! I wouldn't let some criminal escape just so I could save face." Begrudgingly, I explained, "It was Zandra. She was in the cell with me."

"Oh? So you spent the night in the dungeons with your lady friend?" Symon bit the edge of his lip. He was enjoying this far too much.

"Shut up and quit smirking like that. She got through the passageway and is hopefully back at her ship now. I should probably check on her later today to let her know I'm not still stuck in there. Otherwise, she might try to sneak back in or storm the palace—something crazy like that."

He scoffed. "Like she would storm the palace."

"Zandra's the kind of person that would run head on with an entire army if it stood in her way." A wry smile spread across my face at the thought.

"Sounds like you two stubborn idiots are perfect for each other."

"I'm sorry, where were you? Oh right, wandering around wondering where I was and if anything had happened to me." I shot back, hoping to steer the conversation away from Zandra.

"What? I'm supposed to read your mind these days?"

"In this case, yes."

"Please, Leo. There are at least fifteen instances I could name where your rash actions left you in a predicament."

I opened my mouth to argue but, after a moment's consideration, instead admitted, "You're right."

He stopped and looked at me. "I think I heard you wrong. It sounded like you just said I was right?"

"No, you heard correctly." I rubbed the back of my neck. "You *are* right. I've been a reckless and lousy crown prince."

"Wow...who would have thought? A night of imprisonment really does change a person."

I wrestled with the temptation to smack him. "I'm being serious."

The run in with Devrim had brought a gravity with it, and my conversation with Zandra about Adonai had made me take a good look at myself. I had wasted too much time running from the things of the past that haunted me. Maybe if I'd been more diligent in my duties, if I had shown others that I had the capability to be a ruler they could count on, maybe Rueben wouldn't be trying to get rid of me.

If I had been a good crown prince in the first place, there would be no reason for anyone to dethrone me. Maybe my own recklessness had brought everything to this point. I had no one to blame for this mess but myself.

"Don't be so surprised." I crossed the room to my dresser and slid my father's ring back on. The familiar sensation of it brought comfort. "And...there is something else. We ended up in the dungeons because I was after Devrim."

"What? Are you sure it was Devrim? Here?"

"I saw him kill one of them," I breathed in a whisper, shaking off the new memories lurking in the back of my mind. My hands curled into fists. "He broke Gabriel and Aycill out of prison, and they got away. I know it was him."

I sensed the way Symon went rigid with alarm. He shifted to stand a few paces closer behind me. "What's the plan now then? Do you intend to hunt Devrim down?"

"As much as I'd like to, Daystra's facing the possibility of war—a war we can't win. There's no time to fool around. He will receive justice for his crimes in due time."

"You sound more level headed about it. That's good."

"I want to be a ruler the people of Daystra can be proud of, someone they can rely on." When I glanced back at Symon, he had a satisfied look on his face. "What?"

"Oh, nothing. I've just been waiting for you to come to this point for a long time. It's good to finally hear it."

I rolled my eyes. "You always have to be right, don't you?"

"I told you, it's part of my job description."

"Right, your job as my personal secretary."

He gave my shoulder a light shove. "I'm no secretary. Someone has to keep you alive."

"Uh huh." Turning, I grabbed a bundle of fresh clothes and headed into the other room while he remained there. "I'm going to change and take a bath. Once I'm finished, we can head to my first lecture of the day."

Symon said, "See, now I know you're impersonating the prince! The Prince Leo I know would never say that."

"Har, har." I closed the door and let out a breath. My gaze drifted down to my bandaged hand, and I slowly unwrapped it.

Starting from now on, things would be different. I would attend all the lectures and Parliament meetings I was expected to; I would do what I was supposed to; I would listen and better understand the political aspect of things, even if it wasn't my favorite topic.

Starting now, I would be a crown prince my father and sister would be proud of.

CHAPTER 26

Leo

THE LECTURES AND MEETINGS THAT DAY WENT better than I had expected. Apparently, when I focused more intently, things weren't as boring as they seemed at first glance.

To my relief, the meeting that morning with Princess Alexandrina went incredibly well. She was open to working out a treaty that didn't need a marriage alliance. She had agreed that there were other ways to strengthen an alliance between Daystra and Zuren that did not involve matrimony.

Everything began to feel like it might finally work out. Even Rueben seemed mildly impressed by the unusual effort I was putting in.

I worked hard to finish the last of my duties for the day before I went out to see Zandra. When she caught sight of me coming up the gangplank, she exclaimed, "Cass! You made it!"

"Hey, you sound like you didn't think I could."

She planted a hand on her hip. "I'm just glad I don't have to break into that place to haul your slow hide out."

"Oh, *I'm* slow? You're the one who took your sweet time getting into that passageway!"

Zandra scoffed and shook her head. "You're completely ridiculous, you know that?"

"So are you, Captain." I grinned when she rolled her eyes. Why was teasing her such fun? "Want to take a walk on the beach?"

"Any reason why it can't be here?"

"Well, it can be here, if you want your entire crew eavesdropping." I gestured to a few of her crew members that were obviously spying on us from the crow's nest and several others who pretended to be busy while watching. Symon had also made a point of wanting me to remain in places he could shadow me.

"On second thought, that may be best." Zandra grabbed her satchel and slung it over her shoulder before striding over to the gangplank. "Are we going? Or do you have a tea party to attend first?"

"Nah, I had my fill of tea parties in the dungeons." I jogged ahead, unable to resist teasing her. "Come on, Zandra. Don't be so slow!"

"Why you!"

I laughed as she ran to catch up with me.

When we reached the beach, we both slowed to a walk. The further we went, the quieter the background noise of the docks became. Our muffled footsteps in the sand and the gentle lapping of the waves filled my ears. It was as if we had slipped away to our own world where it was only the two of us. The sun grew more golden as it escaped into the horizon, chased by the various colors of a vibrant sunset.

I broke the silence that had settled over us. "You know what I've always wondered?"

"How you can be so annoying yet thoughtful at the same time?" Zandra said. "Yes, I do wonder that from time to time."

"Ha ha—waaaiit, did you just say I'm thoughtful?"

"No."

"I think you did." I smirked. "Just admit it."

"Never," she replied, a mischievous glint in her eyes. "So what have you always wondered?"

I didn't want to break the lighthearted mood with the heavy thought I'd been about to share. I'd rather make her laugh. I stopped walking and lowered my voice. "Do you want to know a secret?"

Zandra shot me a questioning look. "What?"

I leaned closer. "This is supposedly a state secret, so you didn't hear it from me, but I've heard that Daystran princes *melt* when they get wet."

She had been listening closely until hearing the last part. "You're so ridiculous!" She shoved me back with a laugh.

"I know. You're welcome." I gave a mock bow. "Ready to provide you with entertainment whenever you please, milady."

Zandra threw her head back, and her sweet laughter filled the air. I smiled wider.

We strolled down the beach together in enjoyable conversation. The ocean turned calm, and deep colors of orange and soft pink painted the evening sky.

"The sunset's beautiful, isn't it?"

Zandra's gaze focused on the sunset, but I looked at her. In that moment, she was far more beautiful than any sunset. "It really is."

A breeze picked up and blew between us, making her shiver. I was about to tease her about stealing my jackets when she said, "Don't worry. I came prepared this time." Zandra took out a jacket from her satchel and put it on—my jacket. "I was going to give this back to you. That's why I brought it with me."

"You can keep it."

"Why? So you have an excuse to see me?" Her blue eyes danced with a teasing mischief that made my heartbeat quicken.

"I don't need my jacket as an excuse to see you. I have a much better excuse."

"What's that?"

"Because..." In a breath, the words spilled from me before I could change my mind. "I love you."

CHAPTER 27

Zandra

THE WORDS HUNG IN THE AIR. I STARED AT CASS, AT A loss for any coherent words. I hadn't expected him to say anything along those lines, and I was too stunned to sort through the confusion of emotions his declaration stirred within me.

Cass smiled at me again. "You don't have to say anything. I just wanted to tell you."

We continued our walk on the beach in silence. Every time I thought of those three words he had said, the fluttery feelings stirred. I glanced at Cass, only to find his gaze on me. I quickly fixed my eyes on the ground instead.

This all felt surreal. Was I dreaming right now? If so, I couldn't decide if this was one of the best dreams I'd ever had, or my worst nightmare.

How can I give him an answer? How can I promise him anything?

My mind went back to the most recent meeting with Prince Leo. I'd been pleasantly surprised when he'd suggested another way to go about forming a strong alliance without a marriage—one that had solid potential to work. It might even go better than the original plans, since both our peoples were not completely satisfied with the current solution, given our history. It seemed the Daystran prince was finally acting like the ruler he was.

Prince Leo would soon be king of Daystra, and I knew him well enough by now to deem that he would not double-cross Zuren. He would keep his word with any alliance or treaty we made.

As selfish as it was of me to indulge in his suggestion, the thought of having even the slightest chance of things turning out the way I'd begun to secretly hope encouraged me—maybe even made me a bit reckless.

Logic warned me that it was unlikely to work out with someone like Cass, but my heart told me to trust and listen to him, despite the slim chances. I wanted a love like my parents had, not an empty love tied to duty.

I didn't want to fight my feelings any longer. I wanted to be with him, even if it was a fragile fantasy that might shatter all too soon. For the next few moments at least, I could live in that fantasy.

Reaching out, I grabbed his hand. I couldn't read his expression as he stopped and looked at me, let alone imagine what went through his head then.

Gathering my courage, I met his gaze. "I...I love you too."

He gave me one of the sweetest smiles I had ever seen, one

that made my heart flutter and left me breathless. When I saw the way he looked at me—as if he were looking at something unspeakably precious—I knew I couldn't give him false hope. I cared about him too much to knowingly hurt him.

I added hastily, "But I'm not sure how long I will be staying in Daystra, so—"

Cass wrapped me in a gentle hug, catching me off guard. "I don't care."

At first, I stood there stiffly, too surprised to do anything; then slowly, I moved to return his embrace. I hugged him tighter, soaking in his warmth. I didn't know how this would all work out in the end, but I knew that I wanted him to be by my side. He made me feel more. He made the whole world so much more vibrant.

I love you.

I wanted to tell him that every day. I wanted to make him smile and laugh. I never wanted Cass to feel trapped in the grief, loneliness, and darkness I had glimpsed before—I knew all too well what that felt like. I wanted him to live each moment of his life knowing someone cared about him. That he mattered.

Cass stepped back, taking his warmth with him. I couldn't deny there was a part of me disappointed it ended so soon.

"Was that okay?"

I smiled. "Yes, more than okay."

He leaned in closer. My heart stuttered, forgetting how to beat properly. "That's good to hear." His soft voice held so much care. He lingered there for a moment, and I became convinced I'd forgotten how to breathe. Then Cass drew away.

"I should get going."

"Do you have to?" I instantly ducked my head. *Did I just say that out loud?*

He chuckled and smiled that crooked smirk of his. "Believe me, I don't want to, but I'm trying to be more responsible these days. Do you want me to walk back with you to your ship?"

"No, that's all right."

"I might be busy for the next few days, but I'll be back," he promised.

"I'll be waiting."

I remained alone on the beach while I watched him walk away. I hugged his coat tighter around my shoulders. All those doubts and reasons I had continually reminded myself of for not getting too close seemed...trivial now.

Now that I knew what it felt like to be loved by him.

A smile spread across my face. Even if circumstances were still a complicated mess, I didn't regret coming along with the envoy to Daystra—far from it.

CHAPTER 28

Leo

THE SUN SHONE BRIGHTLY OVERHEAD WITH LARGE puffy clouds dotting the cerulean sky. For today and today only, I'd forget the palace, politics, and conspiracies. It had only been four days since we'd admitted our feelings for each other, but every moment since then with Zandra had been amazing.

A mischievous grin spread across my face as I caught sight of Zandra standing at the previously agreed upon meeting place of a street corner. When she had her back turned, I sneaked up on her.

Upon looking back to find me right in front of her, she jumped. "Cass!"

I laughed. "Surprise."

"You rascal." She shifted the straw basket that preoccupied her arms.

"What's in the basket?"

"Esme, Milo's wife, made us a picnic lunch, for wherever it

is you want to take me?"

"You'll see. Some things are better left as a surprise." I winked and linked arms with her, leading Zandra off.

We left the city and hiked into the surrounding forest. The deeper we walked, the more the pine trees towered over the path. Their green boughs glowed in the afternoon light and waved in the breeze. Out here, summer still lingered.

A soft sigh escaped me. The heaviness that had weighed on my shoulders for so long finally began to ease as of late. The empty ache didn't have the sharp pang it usually did; it had begun to dull.

My gaze drifted to Zandra, and I smiled.

She gave my hand a gentle squeeze. "What is it?"

"I'm just happy. This is one of my favorite places. I don't get out here often."

The forest thinned as the ground gave way to more hills. We neared the top of a hill where a large boulder sat. "Let's get to the top!" I scrambled up the smaller rocks to climb onto the boulder, periodically pausing to help Zandra up after me.

We came to the peak of the boulder where a grand view stretched out before us. Sprawling green hills rolled on for as far as the eye could see until they greeted the mountains in the distance.

I rubbed my thumb over my father's ring, which I'd chosen to keep with me this time when I went out into Maldenia. The glimpse of the mountains reminded me of my mother. She wouldn't even be here for my birthday today. In the past, she'd at least been able to make it for this day. Yet on the birthday I really could have used her presence the most, she didn't come.

I'd always had bad luck. Mother was never there when I really needed her.

"It's nice to have your company. This is when I would spend the day with my mother, but...she isn't visiting me this year."

"Oh? Is it a special occasion in Daystra?"

Even though my birthday was two days before Founding Day, the date coronations were held, to most it was nothing but another day.

I shrugged. "Just my birthday."

"Your birthday is important." She poked my shoulder. "How old are you then?"

"Eighteen." At my answer, an amused smile flitted across her face. I cocked my head. "What's that look for?"

"I'm a year older than you, in that case."

"What? You're messing with me."

"I'm not." Zandra plopped down on the boulder, and I followed suit. "We will make this day a good one since it's your birthday."

"Don't you know? Having you makes it a good day."

"You sweet charmer."

"But you love me anyway." A wry grin split my face.

Zandra opened the basket between us, but I didn't miss her slight blush. "How about we eat?"

We munched on the sandwiches and sliced fruits in the basket and ate until we had our fill. After a time of sitting in comfortable silence while we stared out at the scenery, she asked, "What is your mother like? If you don't mind me asking."

"Well, she is generous and kind. Mother liked to get me

nice things when I was younger, but all I ever really wanted was her. She was often busy." I rubbed my hand over the rough rock underneath us. "Sometimes, I wondered if she used business as an excuse to avoid me later, after my father and sister died. If I was too painful of a living memory for her to face."

Zandra squeezed my shoulder. "That must have been hard."

"It was...still is." I couldn't stand the depressing turn the conversation had taken. I pushed to my feet and stepped back to the edge of the boulder.

"What are you doing?"

"Going down, of course."

She frowned. "You can't jump that far."

"Watch." I turned and slid halfway down the rock and pushed off from it. For a single moment, I was weightless before gravity took over. I landed on the ground below, but I did so with an unbalanced footing that sent me tumbling down the grassy hill all the way to the bottom.

"Cass!" Racing footsteps accompanied her yell. "Cass, are you hurt?" Zandra stood over me.

I feigned a moan as I dragged myself to sit up. "The hill broke more than just my fall."

Her brow creased with concern as she knelt next to me. "Where—"

With a smirk, I tugged her into a hug. As she realized I'd only faked it, she muttered, "You are a rascal."

My smile widened. "This is nice."

She shoved me back half-heartedly and sat up straighter.

"I ought to smack you for such a trick."

"I was only playing around."

Colorful wildflowers surrounded us in the long grass. I picked a yellow one and tucked it behind her ear. "You make the flowers look prettier." My hand lingered there, her warm cheek against my fingertips.

Her eyes met mine, and the rest of the world faded into the background again. An eternal moment passed between us.

She's so wonderful...

The snap of a stick broke the moment. We both pulled back and glanced around for the source. I groaned inwardly. *Symon, you've got to be kidding me. Of all the times you choose to not be a stealthy bodyguard?!*

I cleared my throat. "Must have been an animal."

"Yeah, an animal."

The awkwardness in the air was almost tangible. I struggled to bring up another topic to regain the easy flow of conversation. The rumbling of thunder drew my gaze upward. Grey skies clouded over what had been a sunny day. Rain trickled down and swiftly became a downpour.

"Tides," Zandra said. "When did this storm roll in?"

We both scrambled to our feet. I grabbed her hand and ran with her to escape the rain. Large puddles formed along the path. As we came across a particularly big one, I stomped in it.

She laughed. "Hey! You'll get me all wet."

"So? We're already wet!" I jumped in another one and splashed us both.

"Oh, is that how it is?" Zandra beat me to the next puddle and stomped into it hard, sending a spray of water at me. We laughed as we ran along, splashing each other in puddles the entire way back.

✡✡✡

When we arrived at the outskirts of Maldenia, we veered off into a street filled with shops. The rain still fell, but it didn't ruin our time. We darted from eave to eave to avoid the rain while we perused the window displays. The warmth from the shops' lights melted away the cold darkness of the streets.

Zandra stopped in front of a dress shop that had a blue dress which faded into a rich purple on display at the window. She stared at it with interest. "That dress is beautiful. I've never seen anything like it."

"Are you thinking of getting it?" I wondered.

She shook her head and chuckled. "Where would I ever wear such a thing? Come on."

We continued our stroll down the street in pleasant conversation. After a while, a pebble smacked into the back of my shoulder. I threw a glance back to see who'd thrown it and shot Symon an annoyed look.

"What was that?"

I turned back to her. "Oh nothing. The street kids must be feisty today and in the mood to toss rocks." Even with the rain, a sweet aroma filled the street we stepped onto. "Whatever that is, it smells good."

"I think it's coming from that shop with the red roof." Zandra steered us in that direction.

We entered the bakery. The warm interior was a welcome

change. Caramel, nutmeg, and other spices I didn't know the name of permeated the air. The light chatter of customers muffled the patter of rain pouring into the streets outside.

"Pick something. I'll get you one for your birthday."

"If that's what you want." I scanned the racks of freshly baked rolls and loaves of bread before deciding. "The one with the frosting there."

"A sweet roll. I'm so surprised," she teased, having figured out my attraction to sweet things already.

I grinned impishly. "I like what I like."

While Zandra went over to the counter to purchase the food, Symon sneaked up behind me and whispered in my ear. "Are you almost done?"

"Blasted crimson!" I whipped around to face him, keeping my tone a hushed whisper. "I told you not to do that. And no, we are getting something to eat now."

"It's been hours. I agreed to letting you go out and keep away from the palace for the day, but I didn't realize it meant I'd be subjected to watching you two flirt."

"Jealous?" I smirked.

"Goodness, no. I just have no desire to watch you two."

He made a face, and I poked him in the ribs. "Oh yeah, and thanks by the way for making it so awkward earlier! Here I thought bodyguards were supposed to be *stealthy*, not stepping on sticks."

He flushed. "I was trying to look away. You two seemed like..."

"Let's just leave it there," I quickly said, not needing to hear him finish that sentence. "I don't want to talk about this topic with my best friend any more than you do."

"Good. So you'll be done soon?"

"It's my birthday, and it's the one day I can do as I want."

Symon sighed in exasperation. "Consider me putting up with this as your birthday gift."

"Thank you. Now go before she sees you." I pushed him out the shop door before the discussion could continue. Right as I turned around, Zandra came over.

"Who were you talking to?"

"Oh, uhm." I thought for a moment for the best cover, glad he'd been wearing commoner clothes. "Just some obnoxious cousin I ran into. Don't mind him."

"Okay, well, I found out they also sold tea here. I ordered some along with the rolls."

"Sounds great."

We sat across from each other at one of the small tables in the corner of the shop. Our soaked clothes made puddles form underneath us. Rain pattered on the window, but the warmth of the bakery along with the steaming tea had driven off the chill. I rubbed at my wet eyeglasses with the back of my sleeve. These things could be annoying, though.

The sweet rolls distracted me, and I bit into one, savoring every bite of cinnamon and vanilla. I glanced up to see Zandra watching me with a smile. "What?" I wiped at my face.

"Nothing. I hope you had a happy birthday, Cass."

I smiled back. "It was happy, thanks to you. The best day I've had in a long time."

And I truly meant that.

CHAPTER 29

Leo

EVERYTHING HAD GROWN SO MUCH MORE VIVID since Zandra had come along. Things finally felt like they were getting better. Every time I thought of her, a smile spread across my face. I'd never been so excited to see someone again before. Even my heart beat faster at the thought of her.

Though reluctant, I tried to push aside all thoughts of Zandra and focus on the present. Parliament had called for an emergency meeting. Significant news had reached the palace—that much I knew. I just didn't know what yet.

Upon arriving at Parliament with Rueben, the meeting quickly commenced. Lord Alan addressed the assembly. "My fellow Daystrans, while this news may be shocking, I will be blunt, as I believe swift action on our part is the best course."

He took a moment to look around the room. Some nodded along in agreement, while others eyed him with uncertainty.

"News reached us this morning. A skirmish broke out on

the border, and there were significant casualties."

"Hyra is attacking?" one member asked in surprise.

"No, not Hyra. Our border we share with Zuren."

My head snapped up. *What?*

The room went from tense silence to shocked murmurings and whispers.

"Information was leaked by an unknown individual, and the news spread about the possible alliance with Zuren. It is unclear who or how it started, but the skirmish held many casualties for both sides. One could accurately describe it as a massacre."

Another member shouted, "It was a trick all along to get our guard down!"

More gasped murmurings followed. I sat back in shock, my vision going out of focus.

No. It can't be.

Lord Alan continued, "There is no evidence that the Zurinians purposefully set this up. It took place in a non-critical area, but the impact adds more gravity to the treaty. I know many are undecided on their stance in regards to the Zurinian-Daystran alliance, but we need it now more than ever. We will not be able to fend off border skirmishes with Zuren while dealing with Hyra attempting to invade at the same time. We need to put aside our prejudices and old grudges and work with them. It is the only way we can survive as a country and remain sovereign."

"How can we be sure the alliance will hold steady amid all the turmoil? Is this not proof that it will not work?" Lord Wellington pointed out.

One of the Parliament members that I'd never gotten along with, Lord Thompson, spoke up. "Marriage is the best kind of unity to settle issues such as these. The prince has made a valiant effort to work something out with the Zurinians, but that method will no longer suffice. It now depends on his willingness to enter into an arranged marriage, if we want this alliance to give us a real chance at peace." He flicked his gaze my way, and I clenched my jaw. *You rat.*

I sensed the way all eyes turned to me, but it was Rueben who asked the question.

"Well, Prince Leo, are you willing to enter into a marriage alliance with Princess Alexandrina?"

A long pause followed as I internally debated. Everything was happening too fast. I wanted time to think, but there was none. If I didn't speak soon, I'd likely lose the remainder of Parliament's support and any glimmer of respect they had for me.

All my doubts and frustrations reared their head, tempting me to slip back into my old patterns of recklessness.

No.

That's not who I am anymore. That's not who I want to be anymore.

I made eye contact with Rueben and answered for all of Parliament to hear, even if it killed me on the inside. "Yes. We should proceed with the marriage alliance with Zuren."

Everyone returned their attention back to the discussion of details. The rest of the Parliament meeting passed in a daze. With the repercussions sinking in and everything it would mean, I was too preoccupied to listen.

I rested my forehead against my fist, suddenly light-headed. I wanted to hit something. Why did it have to be now of all times? Why did it have to be right after Zandra and I had confessed our true feelings?

Why did everyone good in my life get taken away?

Adonai, why...

The world could be so cruel.

After the meeting finished, Rueben stopped me before I could hurry off to my room. "Leo, about the alliance. I know you were working on a way around the arranged marriage, but—"

"I know," I said, not needing to hear it all over again. "What about Parliament? Not everyone agreed with this method in the first place."

His shoulders noticeably relaxed, as if he'd been expecting me to cause trouble. "Don't be concerned about Parliament. Everyone is aware of the gravity of the situation. Even if there are complications, I have enough connections that we can sway the vote in favor of the alliance if I use a few favors. Thank you for doing your part. I have noticed your recent dedication and effort you've been putting in, and I hope it continues. I am...proud of you."

I could only stare at him, at a loss for words. Rueben had never once in my whole life told me that he was proud of me, or anything close to it.

He cleared his throat and shifted a half step back. "In that case, there is much to do. I will see you later."

Still not comprehending the words I had heard, I nodded absently. Rueben departed, and I continued on to my room where I changed into my disguise. With a pang, I realized this would probably be the last time I ventured into Maldenia as Cass.

I was so lost in my own thoughts that I didn't realize Symon had stopped in front of me in the passageway until I ran into him. "Oh, sorry."

"You're not okay, are you?"

I tore a hand through my hair. "There's no other way. I have to go say goodbye to Zandra...for good."

"Are you going to tell her the truth of your identity?" I knew what his underlying question was. *Are you going to hold onto her or let her go?*

"It's better if she thinks I'm going somewhere far away." Every fiber of my being screamed at me not to do this, but I didn't have a choice. "The Founding Day's Ball is tomorrow night, and my coronation is the day after. I can't put it off."

I'd put off even acknowledging my upcoming coronation for long enough. I wished I didn't have to face so many facets of reality all at once.

I didn't move yet, though. I was stuck in place as I stared down at my hands. How could I do this to Zandra? She would hate me for it, and I wouldn't blame her.

"I'm going with you," Symon stated. "Let me know if I can help with anything."

A rueful smile tugged at the corners of my mouth. "You're always helping me out. Thank you for that. This is one thing I have to do on my own."

We left the palace together. I dragged my feet and took longer than necessary to get to the docks. Part of me hoped

Zandra wasn't there, and that I wouldn't have to do this.

To my dismay, she was there.

She smiled when she saw me. "What brings you here so late?"

"Uhm." I glanced at one of her crew nearby. "Can we talk? Alone."

Zandra led me up to the helm of her ship, picking up on my mood. "What's wrong?"

I stopped myself from sighing. I hated myself for what I was about to say, especially so soon after our last conversation. "I—I came to say goodbye."

Guilt slammed into me like a ton of bricks at the stricken look on her face. "What do you mean?" She lowered her voice. "Are you in trouble?"

"No. Recently, I..." I couldn't bring myself to meet her gaze as I lied to her face. "It's because of my business. I need to relocate, and it's far away from here."

"Oh." Zandra turned from me to stare out at the sea. "When do you leave?"

"Tomorrow morning. I wanted to tell you before I left. You deserve to know."

Painful silence stretched on until she asked the question I'd been dreading. "What about us?"

"I don't want to leave. There's a part of me that wants to say 'forget it' to my responsibilities and go with you, wherever it is."

That wasn't what I'd meant to say. Running away wasn't the noblest of choices, but in this moment with her standing right there, I wasn't sure if I could let go. And my heart couldn't bear another lie.

She looked just as uncertain as she stared down at her boots. "You can't abandon your responsibilities, and neither can I."

"If it were only me that it impacted, I would give it all up for you without a second thought. But...it would be selfish of me. I have people counting on me. I...have to leave."

"I understand." Her words filled me with relief and dread at the same time.

We both stared out at the dark expanse of ocean. I knew that no matter how desperately I wanted this, it wouldn't—couldn't work. She was a commoner from Zuren, and I was the prince of Daystra. And right now, Daystra needed as many allies as possible for this war, which meant I had to marry for the good of my people, not my heart.

I would have given anything to not be a prince in that moment. I'd never wanted it more. It hurt, more than I ever thought possible. This whole thing tore at me so much, especially the part where I knew I couldn't do a single thing to change it.

I had to force my next words out. "I guess this is goodbye."

Zandra would sail on to her next adventure, while my alias Cass would disappear, and I would return to being just Prince Leo.

"I don't want to say goodbye." Her voice was thick, as if it was just as hard for her to say it.

"Neither do I."

She hugged me tightly. I sucked in a deep breath, trying to get air into my suffocating lungs. This would be the last time I ever saw her—that thought alone was almost enough to shatter my resolve. Her grip felt almost desperate, as though she'd realized the same thing.

The sweet scent of jasmine filled my nose. I held her close as she leaned her head onto my shoulder. "I still love you," I whispered. I didn't want to hear it back; I only needed her to know that.

Eventually, we both let go, reluctantly. "Wait here for a minute." Zandra went below deck and came back a moment later. She handed me a bundle. "Your coat."

I shook my head. Maybe I should take it and sever any remaining ties between us, but I couldn't. "Keep it."

"You sure? It's a nice coat."

"I'm sure. It looks better on you."

Zandra nodded, clutching the jacket to herself. "Stay safe and watch your back. That tongue of yours is bound to get you into trouble."

"Excuse me, but you're the one with the sharp tongue." Our eyes met, and we shared a sad smile. "I'll never forget you, Zandra. You changed my whole world. You're so amazing and special. Don't forget it."

She rubbed her eyes and tried to conceal a sniffle. "The same goes for you. I will never forget you, Cass."

For a breathless moment, we stared at each other, as if trying to communicate everything that was left unsaid between us. After another beat of silence, I made myself tear my gaze away from her and forced my legs to walk, to leave the only girl I had ever loved.

I stopped at the gangplank leading off her ship. I wanted to look back at her one more time—for the last time—but I knew if I did, I wouldn't be able to leave.

Closing my eyes, I drew in a breath. *I'm so sorry. You don't know how much I wished things were different.*

With my next step, a burning pain tore through me. I clutched my side as I stumbled. *Not this again.* I'd thought I was finally over this. I had been more consistent in general with taking the medicine, and it hadn't bothered me in a while.

"Cass!" Zandra raced to my side in the blink of an eye. "What's wrong?"

"It's—nothing," I grunted out. I just needed to sit for a second and it would pass, but I wouldn't rest here. I couldn't.

I tried to take another step, and my legs gave out. Zandra steadied me, preventing me from collapsing. "This is not nothing! Just rest here for a moment, and I can fetch Esme from below deck. She's a good healer. Whatever is wrong, I'm sure she can help you."

"No." I shook my head, wishing I hadn't when it brought on a dizzy spell.

"Cass!" Tears welled in her eyes as she looked at me.

"It's better if I leave. Don't worry about me, I'll be fine. I'm sorry for causing you so much trouble."

"Please don't leave like this. Not like this."

"I'm sorry." Gritting my teeth, I stood straighter and lifted her hand off of my arm. I walked away, leaving her and the ship behind. My sides ached, but the pain in my chest was worse, and it wasn't from any injury that could be treated.

I'd said goodbye to Zandra, and I would never see her again. I just hoped I hadn't hurt her too much. I never wanted to hurt her, ever.

Concern wrinkled Symon's expression as he steadied me when I rejoined him. He gripped my shoulders, keeping me upright more than my own legs were at the moment. "Leo, what happened?"

Grimacing, I gritted out, "I think—I forgot to take the medicine yesterday and today."

He cursed under his breath. "The blasted aftereffects of the poison are taking a long time to subside."

I nodded weakly, pushing the eyeglasses further up my nose. The edges of my vision dimmed, and I clenched my jaw. *Stay awake.* I leaned against Symon as we made our way back to the palace. He kept shooting me worried glances. On arriving, he sent for the physician while helping me to my room.

I stifled a groan as I crashed onto my bed. Blast all the poison in Kalmyra. This wasn't what I needed on top of everything else right now.

The physician came and gave me the same bitter tonic as before but in a stronger concentration, and I drank it. After an hour or so, the pain in my sides gradually lessened to only a dull ache—the same dull ache I was getting used to living with.

Symon eyed me warily, as if I would break at any moment. "Are you sure you're all right now?"

I slid off the edge of my bed. "I'm fine."

He frowned. He didn't believe me.

"I'm fine now, Symon. Really. The physician gave me a new vial of that tonic. I promise I'll keep it with me and follow his instructions better this time."

"If you say so." He followed right behind me when I left my room. "Where are you going now?"

The dull throbbing pain crept over me again for a moment. I subtly braced a hand on the wall. "I need to speak with Princess Alexandrina."

"You're really going forward with it then?" Disbelief rang in his voice. I could hardly believe it myself.

"I don't have a choice... I never did."

Even though it was the truth, it still stung.

Princess Alexandrina wasn't in her quarters. Her maid nervously informed me that the princess had gone to the palace gardens for some air. Although it was tempting to use that as an excuse to delay the inevitable, I steeled myself and headed to the gardens.

The princess of Zuren walked at a leisurely pace with her bodyguard, Galen, following a few paces behind. However, as I approached her, there was something about her that just felt...off.

"Princess Alexandrina."

She turned around to face me. "Oh, Prince Leo. Hello." Her smile wasn't the same as before. It seemed forced.

"I was hoping to have a word with you."

She nodded and gestured for me to walk with her. "I'm assuming this is about the recent news concerning our countries?"

"Yes." I cleared my throat, pushing back the urge to change my mind. I had to do this. For both the country and for my father and sister. "At the original treaty negotiations, you mentioned the possibility of a marriage alliance between

Daystra and Zuren."

"I remember well," she said slowly.

Keeping my gaze forward on the path ahead, I focused on the conversation instead of the ache that only dug deeper into me. "After further consideration, Parliament and I both believe it would be a good idea to move forward with marriage arrangements. I know I avoided you and made things harder at first, and I am sorry for that. I wasn't trying to be rude. At the time, I wasn't interested in marrying anyone."

"I came here not exactly wanting to suggest it in the first place, even if it had been my idea, originally," Princess Alexandrina admitted. "When I first met you—well, I wasn't very fond of the idea of an arranged marriage with a reckless prince who ran around the palace duping his guards."

"Fair enough." I couldn't help my smirk despite everything. "But you don't know how fun it is until you try it yourself."

Galen spoke from behind us. "Her Highness will not be attempting to rid herself of her guards. Again. Not as long as I am here."

"Don't worry, Galen. He was only joking."

I stopped walking and dragged my gaze from the stone path to her face. "My coronation is in two days." I took a deep breath, refusing to think about Zandra and how much I already missed her. "In light of the situation and our positions, I would like to propose an alliance between Daystra and Zuren through marriage. Between us."

"Right." Her response wasn't the reaction I'd expected. She didn't sound pleased—the opposite of it. She seemed stiffer than usual, and she kept avoiding eye contact. "If you don't mind me asking...was there someone else you cared for at one time? I only ask because I know that look—I understand that look."

I shuffled from foot to foot, taken by surprise. Had she experienced lost love too?

"To be honest, there...was someone, but it wouldn't work out, no matter how much I wanted it."

"I'm sorry."

Raw silence followed. I didn't want to be standing here, doing this, any longer. "What is your answer?"

"Yes." Princess Alexandrina's words came rushed. "I accept your proposal. I look forward to Daystra and Zuren's future alliance."

I made myself respond, "As do I."

After a beat of silence, I excused myself. I needed to get somewhere I could breathe before I screamed or suffocated—it would be one of the two.

By the time I reached the roof of one of the towers, darkness had fallen. I leaned over the edge, gulping in as much air as I could. First I had to break things off with the girl I loved, and then I had to go and propose to someone I didn't truly love, all within one day.

Thick, dark clouds covered the sky, leaving it empty of stars. Of all the nights there had to be no stars...

I rubbed my hands on the smooth stone, trying to distract myself from the turmoil of my thoughts. In the courtyards of the palace below me, torches sparked to life as night set in. The random bursts of flame made it appear as if the palace had caught fire. A bitter part of me wished it would. *Let it all burn.*

A tiny part of me wanted to take one of those torches and start the blaze myself... Thankfully, a more sensible part of me chided that such stupidity wouldn't solve anything.

I habitually twisted the ring on my pointer finger. With a shake of my head, I murmured to myself. "Get through the next few days, then it will get easier."

"It will."

I glanced back to see Cyra. "Oh, hi."

She smiled sadly as she came to stand beside me. "I wanted to check on you. Today had to be rough. How did things go with Princess Alexandrina?"

I blew out a breath. "Well, she agreed that we should move forward with the marriage alliance."

"I am sorry, Leo. I knew how much you were hoping things would work out differently."

"I knew the chances were slim..." But I'd gone and gotten my hopes up anyway. I roughed a hand over my face. In a matter of hours, everything had fallen apart.

"I want to congratulate you and at the same time tell you I'm sorry. I understand not being able to be with the one you truly love because of politics."

Something about the sorrow in her voice pulled me from my own moping. "It sounds like you speak from experience."

"Unfortunately, I do." She rubbed her hands together slowly, staring down at the palace below. "It was a long time ago, but I fell in love. I wanted to marry him so badly. Everyone disapproved because he came from a country we were enemies with."

"The king's sister marrying someone from an enemy

country—I can see why no one would like that. Still, it should be your choice."

"They don't care about our own feelings or preferences, only what suits them best. It didn't matter to me, though. I would have run away with him in a heartbeat, and I wouldn't have cared where we went."

"What happened?" I'd never heard this story before.

"My brother—your father—caught me sneaking out to run away with the man I loved. He wouldn't allow me to leave and disappear into the night." Her tone grew softer. "I wasn't very happy with your father for many years after, although I eventually came to terms with it. In the end, I understand why he did what he did."

I shook my head. "That's nice that you understand, because I don't."

"You will find your perspective changes with time. But I decided if I couldn't be with the man I loved, then I would not marry anyone. You, of course, don't have that luxury. At least Princess Alexandrina seems nice."

"She is very kind and has turned out to be a good friend," I agreed.

I knew that I could build a good, lasting friendship with Princess Alexandrina, and that we would get along well with each other. Maybe if we both wanted it badly enough, it could develop into something more—but I wasn't ready to think about that possibility yet. It was too soon.

"She's just not...*her.*"

"We don't always get what we want in life, Leo. We can only do our best to hold onto what we care most dearly about and forge a path ahead."

She spoke with such conviction and certainty. I hoped to feel those things again one day. My recent decisions had left me feeling more than a little unsure of myself.

I leaned against the balustrade. "Was—was my father nervous before his coronation?"

"Oh, he wouldn't show it, but he was more nervous than you, I think. Don't worry too much. You will do great, Leo. You will be a wonderful and just ruler."

I met her gaze. "Thank you for all your support over the years. I don't know if you realize how much it's meant to me. I wouldn't be at this point without you."

"Watching you grow into the person you are now has been a privilege. Don't ever let anyone break that spirit of yours, no matter what." Cyra patted my arm. "I should retire for the night. Remember, you will do great."

"Wait, I have to know. What happened to him?"

Her smile turned rueful. "I don't really know, and I don't think he knows what happened to me either."

Cyra descended the winding stairs, leaving me to mull over our conversation. If nothing else, at least things hadn't ended as severely with Zandra as they had for Cyra. That would have been terrible. At least I knew Zandra was safe, and that she would get to live a free and adventurous life, even if I couldn't.

"At least she's free," I whispered to myself, determination washing away my feelings of reluctance. That one thought would get me through the coming days.

CHAPTER 30

Zandra

I TUGGED THE COMB THROUGH MY LONG, WAVY brown hair, as if overfocusing on doing my hair would make me forget about Cass and our conversation the other day. How he was leaving—had left.

A storm of emotions churned within and threatened to snap me from the inside, but I would not let them rule me, no matter how much it hurt. My eyes burned and my chest ached. I tugged harder when I hit a tangle in my hair.

I knew it would have to end. The likelihood of that fragile fantasy turning to reality had the odds stacked against it painfully high.

But that didn't change the way I felt.

"Oh, Your Highness, please be gentle with your hair!" Marianne rushed over and slid the comb out of my hands. "Allow me, since you seem to be impatient with it today?"

I swallowed back a sigh and stared at her reflection in the

mirror. "Go ahead."

"Thank you. I want it to look spectacular for the Founding Day's Ball this evening." Her pleasant chatter while she did my hair only worked to distract my mind for so long.

Somehow, Cass had managed to slip past my walls and gotten me to care, despite everything I knew. I couldn't afford to care about someone like him when I came along with the envoy, and yet I did.

I'd never cared for anyone the way I did for him. It was a breathtaking, startling feeling—terrifying, even. The kind of feeling that made me want to sacrifice things I shouldn't if it meant I could be with him.

The price to obtain that fantasy was too high, though. Too many lives were at stake. I wouldn't abandon my brothers, my country—everyone—for my own heart.

Part of me had been glad Cass ended it before I did. I still couldn't decide if that was worse or better. He could go on with his life, at least. His memories of me would fade with time, and I'd hope and pray his heart healed along with it.

Marianne finished with the crown braid that wound around my head and wove purple flowers into it. I gripped the edge of my chair. My heart pounded at an unsteady rhythm. The flowers reminded me of being in that field with Cass. I closed my eyes and took in a slow breath to steady myself.

I'd told him I understood, and I did. It's not as if I wasn't about to do the same thing. But my heart wasn't as easy to convince as my mind.

A lump formed in my throat. There was so much I wished I could have told him. So much I should have said but never did.

The aching pain wrapped tight around my chest. None of this would have hurt so badly if I hadn't seen the hollow resignation in his eyes, if he hadn't told me he didn't want to go...and if he hadn't been injured.

Now my last memory of Cass would be of the way he had almost collapsed, crippled by deep pain. He had held his side like that before. Whatever was wrong, it must have been a reoccurring injury, or one that had never healed all the way.

Every time I thought of Cass now, I would worry whether he was okay and had gotten the help he needed. We hadn't even known each other for long, but I couldn't imagine never seeing him again. That bothersome, charming street smuggler, of all people. Except...he was more than that. So much more.

I leaned back against the chair, letting my shoulders droop for a moment. My hand felt cool as I rested my forehead in it. I needed to pull myself together and focus on fixing the matters at hand. It was the reason I had so hastily agreed to Prince Leo's suggestion of moving forward with the marriage alliance, even if being tied into a relationship with someone else after everything with Cass would be hard.

There was so much I had wanted to tell him, everything he meant to me—but I hadn't. The words had stuck in my throat. I hadn't managed to get them out before he left. Now I'd never get the chance.

Cass was gone, and he was never coming back.

The harsh reality echoed in my mind. *Tides, stop thinking about him.*

Marianne patted my arm, gently pulling me out of my thoughts. "Your Highness, is something the matter?"

"Nothing to be concerned about." I stood abruptly and headed into the large closet. Focus. I needed to focus on preparing for the ball in a few hours.

The dress I'd chosen had three-quarter sleeves draping elegantly from the arms, and the top half was a deep blue that faded into a rich purple at the skirt. It even had hidden pockets—something I planned to make good use of. It was the same dress I'd seen when I'd been out in the city with Cass.

He'll never get to see me in it... I wonder what he would've said if he had.

"How beautiful," Marianne commented upon catching up to me. "It will certainly make a statement tonight."

"It will." I looked over it, trailing a hand down the silky fabric. The blue of Daystra paired with the purple of Zuren. The two colors together displayed a kind of unity that would jar everyone there, along with the announcement of my engagement to Prince Leo.

I'm really doing this.

I picked up the half blue and purple masquerade mask with sleek curves that had been made to go with my dress. I'd been informed that the Founding Day's Ball had long ago turned into a masquerade ball. *How ironic.* Even on an important day like this, people still played games.

Some played with cards and wagers at upper class parties.

Others played with lives.

My hand curled around the mask. War loomed closer with every passing day, yet in many ways, this ball would be a battle of its own.

✡✡✡

Gold, silver, and blue embellishments covered nearly every inch and spare corner of the ballroom. Blue silk banners lined the stairway railings and glittering white decorations wound around in the chandeliers that lit the room. Flowering walls of white cascaded down in various places.

I stood for a beat of silence at the top of the stairs. No one had noticed me, and I hadn't been announced yet. Squaring my shoulders, I adjusted the masquerade mask to ensure it stayed in place. *Here we go.*

Prince Leo stepped through the double doors. I turned to face him. He wore a black suit with silver buttons and stitching, along with a silver and blue masquerade mask. I couldn't deny he looked rather handsome tonight.

His stunned expression as he met my eyes wasn't what I had expected. What could have shocked him so much? The dress?

"Prince Leo." I dipped a small curtsy. "Are you well?"

"I—I'm fine." Whatever was on his mind, he didn't speak of it. "Shall we?"

I nodded and turned to face the party. Polite conversation and light laughter echoed through the air as people mingled. It stopped the moment the announcement echoed through the ballroom.

"Crown Prince Leonidas Cassander and Princess Alexandrina Veridian, the princess of Zuren and betrothed to the prince."

I could have heard a pin dropping in the following silence. I caught the sneers and glares some people sent my way. My favorite was the startled expressions as they took in my dress that had a combination of Zuren's *and* Daystra's colors.

I kept a pleasant smile pasted on, glad for the masquerade mask that acted like a second wall of protection. Everyone could act how they wanted without consequences by using the masks to conceal themselves—something I was not entirely fond of.

As we descended the stairs, I leaned closer to tell him, "This is the first masquerade ball I've ever attended."

"Well then, I'll make sure you have a good time. You look stunning, by the way," Prince Leo added, seeming almost flustered. But in the next moment, he was back to his normal self.

"Thank you. You look quite good yourself."

I flicked my gaze up at the crowd of people who were pretending not to watch us. I was the first Zurinian royal to attend a Daystran social event like this since before the White Sand Wars. Needless to say, my presence drew attention.

Prince Leo extended his hand to me as we stopped in the middle of the ballroom. "Ready?"

It was tradition that the royalty and any guests of honor dance first, along with the higher-ranking nobility, to officially start the night off—that tradition was the same between Daystra and Zuren, at least.

The music began to play, and I took his hand. It was warm in mine. As people around us began to dance, my pleasant demeanor faltered. "I have no idea how this dance goes. I only ever learned one traditional Daystran dance," I admitted in a whisper. People overhearing I didn't know the fundamental Daystran dances would only give them more of an excuse to mock Zuren. I flicked my gaze at the others around us in an attempt to mimic the dance on the spot.

He kept his voice low enough so only I could hear. "Hey, don't worry about it, just follow my lead."

When he said that, I found myself not hesitating to trust him. As Prince Leo swept me through the steps of a Daystran waltz, my mind was split between trying to keep up with the movements of the dance and trying to ignore how distracting it was to be this close to him.

Since when had his physical proximity ever affected me?

I smiled nervously. "On a scale of one to ten, how bad of a dancing partner am I? Honestly."

The corners of his mouth quirked upward. "You're the only person I've danced with besides my dancing tutor, so I think we're doing pretty well, all things considered."

The nerves faded from my smile. He could have fooled me.

"When I visit Zuren one day, maybe you will have to show me some of your Zurinian dances."

"Oh?" I leaned forward an inch. "I didn't know you had any plans to visit my country after the negotiations were finished."

"What can I say? I once met someone from there who made me intrigued to see Zuren for myself."

"Whoever it is, I'm glad they could persuade you. I look forward to it."

There came a part in the dance where he twirled me. When Prince Leo pulled me back to him, I realized how close we were—closer than before. I struggled to keep my footing, and it wasn't because I didn't know the dance.

Our eyes met. I'd never realized before how green his eyes were. The ballroom and people around us faded away, and for a timeless moment I felt entranced in those green eyes.

Cass came to mind, and I broke my gaze away, feeling breathless. Even my knees felt weak. *What am I doing? What's wrong with me?*

I cleared my throat. "I think I need some air."

"Of course."

Another song started, and we eased our way toward the other end of the room, in the direction of one of the balconies. However, a noble wearing a black and gold mask with sharp features stopped us. He reminded me of a vulture.

"Prince Leonidas, I did not expect you to be attending this year, nor would I have imagined you would choose to invite the Zurinian princess."

"Lord Thompson, as much as I would like to converse with you, I am preoccupied with my guest."

"I see. Well, when you do have time, I look forward to finding out how you managed to get past your shortcomings and finally decided to take an interest in the country's affairs and act like a crown prince. Or shall I refer my question to Lord Rueben instead?" A smirk flitted across his face with the remark.

Prince Leo appeared unfazed by his words, but his grip on my hand tightened. "I will be sure to let him know to schedule some time for you then."

"Everyone is watching to see how you handle matters with

the Zurinians. I hope we see positive results, or perhaps they will see what we expected from the start—a failure. The only problem is that this time, if you fail, we will all reap the consequences."

Shocked, I stared at Lord Thompson. This noble would dare to say something like this to his prince's face?

"Yes, well, people will see things whichever way they please, regardless of what actually happens."

Prince Leo began to pull me along, but I planted my feet firmly and looked at Lord Thompson, not able to let it be. "Parliament member or not, you ought to be respectful to the prince."

"Respect?" He said it as if there was something funny about the word when it came to the prince.

I clenched my jaw. I hated people that acted as if they could be as rude as they wanted and do anything they pleased. I said, "Apologies, I seemed to have forgotten that your vocabulary may not include that word. Last I recalled, Parliament has as much, if not more, bearing on the survival of your country. The real question is if you and your colleagues will do your part, or if you will fail and bring Daystra to ruin."

With that, I spun on my heels and strode to the balcony with Prince Leo, confidence in every step so no one would question us. When we finally made it out onto the balcony, I breathed in the fresh air, relieved to not be stuck in that stuffy ballroom any longer.

The wind gently glided over my skin. The night air had a chill to it, but between my longer dress and the stuttering, warm feeling from being so close to Prince Leo while dancing, the cold didn't bother me like it usually did.

"I can't believe you said that to Lord Thompson." A wry grin split the prince's face.

"He had it coming for acting that way. I hope I didn't make things worse between you and Lord Thompson."

"Eh." He shrugged a shoulder. "Don't give it a second thought. That guy has always been a pain. Nothing I do will change that."

"Where would we be without the noble brats in the world?" I remarked dryly.

"We would have much less to be annoyed about."

When he smirked, I tilted my head as I looked at him. A strong sense of déjà vu washed over me. When Prince Leo smirked like that, it reminded me of someone.

It reminded me of...

Cass.

A sharp intake of breath followed the thought. There were aspects of both of them that were alike, now that I paid closer attention. Prince Leo did sneak out into the city often, but what would the crown prince of Daystra be doing traipsing around as a smuggler?

Although, Cass never had said he was one. I'd assumed, and he had never corrected or confirmed it.

Stop considering these wild ideas. I clenched a handful of the folds of my skirt.

I only saw Cass in Prince Leo because I missed him. And yet...my mind tumbled through the comparisons faster than I could keep up with.

The two had never been in the same place at the same

time. In fact, the timing eerily aligned with events. Even Cass's sudden departure matched the time right before Prince Leo approached me about the marriage alliance.

He laughed when he noticed me staring and touched his cheek. "Is there something on my face?"

Even their laughs were similar.

"Oh. It's nothing." I shook my head. No. There were aspects of them that weren't alike at all.

While they could both be reckless, Cass couldn't be more charming and carefree, unlike the prince. Not to mention, Prince Leo had black hair while Cass had brown and wore eyeglasses! They couldn't be the same person. They just happened to look alike and have similar personalities. That had to be it.

I dropped my gaze and froze as I recognized the silver ring with dark etchings on his finger. I swallowed and did my best to sound casual. "What is that ring, by the way? You wear it often."

"Oh, this?" He glanced at it. "It's my father's ring."

"I—I see."

Prince Leo had worn this ring all along. I'd never paid it much mind before. But now that I studied it—Cass had worn that same ring on the last day I'd seen him.

It was the late Daystran king's ring passed onto his son. It would be impossible for a commoner like Cass to have something like that, unless...

My hand clenched the silky fabric of my skirt tighter. I couldn't believe...after everything...

Cass and Prince Leo were one and the same.

I wanted to laugh and scream at the same time. How had I not realized it sooner?

Tearing my gaze away from the ring, I met his eyes. A rush of overwhelming feelings hit all at once. Words got stuck in my throat as I grew flustered. How was I to tell him that I was Zandra? Would he still love me if he knew the truth?

He stared back, and his brow furrowed. Something akin to recognition flickered in his expression. What was he thinking about? It seemed like he was on the verge of saying something himself.

Prince Leo—Cass—held out his hand to me. "Shall we go back inside?"

His question threw me off, not at all what I'd been expecting. It took a moment before I got an answer out. "I...you can go ahead. I'll meet you back in there. I need a minute to gather myself."

"Take your time. I promise you won't be missing anything interesting." He winked before slipping through the doors.

"Wait—" The words died on my lips as he vanished into the crowd inside.

I rubbed my forehead. For a few minutes, I closed my eyes and gathered myself. Why was I hesitating now? It was Cass!

The thought of him drove me forward and back inside. I needed to talk to him and tell him everything. To my great frustration, I couldn't find Prince Leo in the sea of dancing pairs.

A whisper of gossip caught my attention. The Steward of Daystra had disappeared from the Founding Day's party all of a sudden, and so had the prince.

No...something's wrong.

I pushed my way through the crowd, acting as polite as possible while inwardly groaning at how long it took. Just when I'd almost maneuvered through the crowd, a man stepped directly in my path. He wore a white suit that matched his white and blue mask.

"Pardon my intrusion. I was hoping to have a dance with you, Your Highness?"

"Oh, I am preoccupied at the moment, Lord..." I trailed off, not knowing his name.

"Lord Bradford," he supplied with a chuckle. "My apologies for not starting with introductions."

I stilled. *Lord Bradford.* The Parliament member knew something about my parents' assassination—that much I'd discerned from overhearing him in that passageway with Byron.

When he offered me his arm, I didn't hesitate to accept. This might be my only chance to speak with him. As we slid into a dance, I could focus more on our conversation after going through the motions of it once already with the prince.

"You've made quite a stir," Lord Bradford commented. "I can't decide if there's more talk of your marriage alliance with the prince, or your color choice of dress and what it implies."

"Well, I hope I don't make too much of a mess for you, like the one with my parents."

His shoulders stiffened, but his empty smile remained in place. "Whatever do you mean by that, Your Highness?"

"Why don't you tell me?" I countered. When the dance drew us closer, I whispered in his ear. "You have knowledge about my parents' murderers—I'd very much like to know what that is."

"I don't know where you have heard such rumors, but you are mistaken. Why would I have anything to do with the late king and queen of Zuren?"

"I'm not mistaken. I heard you one night speaking to a gentleman named Byron in a passageway."

As the dance ended, his pleasant smile faded into a serious, calculating expression.

"If you choose to ignore me, I'll make sure word of this spreads faster than any wildfire you could put out." I gestured to the room around me. "I wonder how badly that would damage your position and the negotiations."

Lord Bradford's eyes narrowed. "What do you want?"

"To talk to Byron."

"You are a brazen girl."

"So I've been told. What shall it be?"

"You want to meet him? Fine then." He flicked his hand in a gesture to follow him.

The halls he led me down grew narrow and dim. I'd never been through this part of the Daystran palace before. Lord Bradford's muttering to himself about how it was Byron's mess to deal with faintly echoed back to me. My fingers brushed over my knife hidden in my dress's secret pocket, reassuring me that I was ready for any surprises.

I expected a secret passageway to be our next turn, but instead, the noble brought me to a plain wooden door. "In here." Lord Bradford slid out a key from his pocket and unlocked the door. He stepped ahead of me and entered. The door slowly swung open enough for me to follow.

I kept a hand within easy reach of my concealed weapon as I stepped in.

Time to catch this traitor.

The room had several crates and wrapped objects and seemed to be used for storage. I sucked in a sharp breath at the sight of a figure crumpled on the ground, far too still.

I'd found the Steward of Daystra.

No...

Then what had happened to Prince Leo? What had they done to him?

"Why have you brought her here?" a voice snapped.

"She started figuring things out. You deal with her. She is your problem."

I whipped around to face the voices and froze. "You? You can't be serious that this is—that you're this Byron?"

Rowan stared back at me levelly. "It was an alias that served its purpose."

Despite being a friend of mine and my family's for several years, I didn't recognize the man standing before me. The man who'd been the chief advisor for so long no longer looked the same. Not when Rowan had that cold, hard edge in his gaze. Whatever he and his cohorts were about to do, he didn't have any doubts or remorse.

My hands curled into fists. "How could you, Rowan? How could you be involved in such a thing?"

"Do not let your anger overrule your rationality."

"Rationality? You want to talk about who's being rational right now? We came here to work out a better treaty with

Daystra so we could survive this coming war. Even if it meant sacrificing myself in a marriage alliance, I was willing to do it for Zuren. Now I find you conspiring with others—and the Steward of Daystra here on the floor like this... What have you done?"

He brushed past me and closed the door softly. At some point, Lord Bradford had slipped out without me noticing. I tensed for a moment and reached for my knife, uncertain what he would do next.

Rowan turned back to me. "Don't act rashly. There is a reason for all of this. You want to know why I'm aiding these Daystrans in their plot to dethrone their prince?"

I locked my gaze on him, the fight in me ready to ignite in a moment's notice. "Enlighten me."

"The Daystrans murdered King Arden and Queen Julianna. You came here to find out who sent the assassins that killed your parents. Well, I know who it was." A beat of silence passed before he said, "The late King Leonidas."

The words slammed me like a tidal wave. I leaned a hand on the wall to steady myself—to prove this wasn't some twisted dream.

"What?"

"The Daystran king believed if he could eliminate the Zurinian royal family, he would be able to conquer Zuren. I did not intend for you to find out this way."

Raw silence hung in the air as I processed the information. Prince Leo's father had my parents killed...

"Wait, did you have a hand in King Leonidas's death?" I didn't know for certain how the late Daystran king had even died, but the look in Rowan's eyes was answer enough. "You did, didn't you? Which meant you've known who was behind my parents' deaths for years, yet you never told me or my brothers."

"Timing is a sensitive matter. You and your brothers were not ready for it."

I clenched and unclenched my hand. The anger rose within my chest, rapid as boiling water. "You betrayed us all. Why?"

Rowan's face was unreadable. "It is complicated, and it's not necessary for you to know."

"Traitor." I glared and slipped my hand to my hidden knife. My fingers curled over the smooth, cool hilt. "Creating more wrongs doesn't make what happened to my parents any better. You will face justice for your crimes, Rowan. I won't let this go."

"You do not get to make that choice."

I rushed at him, but he darted out the door and slammed it in my face. I lunged for the door handle. A frustrated grunt escaped me on finding it already locked. "Rowan! Let me out of here!"

His short reply came in one irritated breath on the other side of the door. "Stay out of it."

"There's no way I will," I growled. "Stop this before it's too late."

"It is already too late, Princess Alexandrina. What has been set in motion cannot be undone now."

The clack of his footsteps on marble grew distant as he walked away.

"No! Don't you realize you're dooming us all?!" I banged on the door hard. I needed to escape this room and find Prince Leo before they got to him and—

I tried to shut the horrible thought down, but my mind finished it anyway.

Before they killed him.

CHAPTER 31

Leo

I KNEW THOSE EYES.

When Princess Alexandrina had her mask up, it made her eyes more noticeable—blue eyes that felt so familiar. They belonged to the wrong person, though.

And that dress. It was the same one she had liked. I'd met them at around the same time, but there were instances I had been with Zandra while the princess was clearly elsewhere at meetings.

How could someone like Zandra and Princess Alexandrina be the same?

I pushed through the crowd to a secluded corner and leaned back against the wall. The throbbing pain grew sharper. I smothered my grimace and made sure no one else could see before I took out the glass vial from the physician. Only a small amount of the remedy remained.

Had I already taken most of it in such a short amount of

time? I shoved it back into my pocket. It would be better to save it for later than run out now.

I pushed off from the wall and straightened. I needed to find Cyra and talk about these matters with her. She had perspective that I lacked when it came to Zandra.

Symon rejoined me in the hall. "Your Highness." He spoke in his more formal tone as he did when we were around others. "Where are you going?"

"To speak with Cyra. Have you seen her?"

"Last I saw she was speaking with one of the Zurinians from the envoy over that way."

I veered off in the direction he pointed out, scanning the crowd of masked people for my aunt. A swish of blue and dark hair caught my eye before the figure stepped through the white flower wall decorations.

Quickening my pace, I followed her. I came to an abrupt stop at the empty hall before us. I glanced back at Symon. "Did you see where she went?"

He studied the hall. "There are only one set of doors down this hall. She probably kept going."

My gaze landed on the doors I'd avoided like the plague itself for the longest time. I was drawn to them before I could think too much and found myself in front of the intricate gilded doors.

Seeming to pick up on my mood, he spoke quieter. "You're really going to enter the throne room?"

"Yes." I clenched my jaw. Even if it meant I missed Cyra, I needed to face that room and those memories before I had to stand there for my coronation tomorrow. If I waited any longer, I'd lose my nerve.

I rested my hand on the cool handle, knowing the vivid memories this would force to the surface. Then I squared my shoulders and pushed open one of the tall doors. The creaking hinges echoed in the silence. I stiffened as I took in the throne room. It was the same as it had been all those years ago.

The tall floor to ceiling windows on both sides of the hall allowed the moonlight to flood the room, and a few torches lined the walls for additional light, most likely lit because of the cleaning and preparation for tomorrow. A velvet carpet red as blood led up to the throne that stood erect in the center of the room.

The throne itself shimmered. The legendary lunarium throne was rumored to remain white only for the true heir and turn black if the wrong heir sat upon it. Deep within me, I'd always feared that when my coronation came, and I sat on the throne, it would turn black.

I shoved those fears away as my gaze drifted to the floor in the back right corner. The marble shimmered in the moonlight, clean and polished, but I still remembered what it looked like when it was stained with blood—my sister's blood.

Time stopped as I walked down the long velvet carpet and past the throne. Flashbacks of Dezaray lying there with an assassin standing over her with a bloody blade filled my mind. I remembered the way he turned a fraction of an inch when the doors had opened and I had stumbled upon the incident. How he'd vanished before I could even yell for help. When I had run to her limp form, shaking her, frantic and panicked.

Years later, I couldn't forget the way her slick blood had

stained my hands. Most of all, I remembered the sickening moment I realized she wouldn't wake up again.

My stomach lurched, and I held a hand to my throbbing side. I took a step, and the pain turned sharper than it had been before. I grimaced. *Why now?*

"Leo, are you okay?" Symon moved in front of me and frowned. "Again?"

"I have what the physician gave me." I dug in my pocket and took out the small vial of bitter-tasting tonic. "I don't know why the stronger concentration of it still can't get rid of this."

"Hold on." He snatched the vial from me and examined it closer. "I don't know about this. The physician keeps giving it to you, and it only seems to make your symptoms go away temporarily. He's the palace physician, for Kalmyra's sake. He should know how to cure you by now, regardless of how uncommon the poison might be."

"What are you saying?" I tried not to sound as out of breath as I felt.

"I'm saying that it might not be a bad idea to get a second opinion."

I struggled to focus on his implications. "You think the physician is giving me the wrong remedy?"

"I don't like the way the remedy never works, even after all this time. I know he's been the royal physician for the last twenty-five years, but when we don't know who inside the palace is plotting against you... I don't want to risk it and trust that he's on our side because of how long he's served the royal family."

My legs gave out, and I collapsed. The burning pain spread

like wildfire on the inside.

"Leo!"

"Blast," I muttered, clutching my sides as I hunched over. I'd never been this ill in my life. Something felt so...*wrong.*

I'd been so stupid to never suspect the royal physician in the first place.

"Can you wait here for a moment? I'll get the physician's apprentice. He might not be any better, but maybe he knows nothing of what his master has been doing."

"Just go—and don't take long."

Symon raced off to fetch the physician's apprentice, leaving me alone in the throne room. A bitter laugh escaped me as I realized I was on the ground in the same spot Dezaray had died.

I had underestimated the people who wanted me dead. I had underestimated Rueben. I thought that by becoming more responsible and taking on my duties as I should, he would be satisfied and stop this nonsense.

An odd sound drew my attention. For a moment, I thought I started imagining voices, but they weren't in my head. They sounded close, but still faint and muffled enough that I couldn't quite make out who the voices belonged to. They had to be in the secret passageway.

I dragged myself across the marble floor over to the wall and listened. Even this close, the voices echoed in a strange, distant kind of way.

"Are you sure it will take effect tonight?"

"Yes. The partial cure only works for so long before the poison will overtake his system again."

"And you're sure this is the real cure? That it will save him?"

Something about one of the voices felt so...familiar.

"Yes, I have given you the proper antidote. As long as he drinks that, he won't die."

"Are you sure they haven't suspected anything by now?"

"They have trusted me for the last twenty-five years. They never suspected me six years ago with the king. You have nothing to worry about."

The room became cold as ice. *Six years ago with the king?*

Was he really saying...my father had not died of an illness, but from being poisoned?

"They never suspected you that you know of, at least. If things don't go as planned, you are to tell them that the person who ordered you to do this was the Steward of Daystra. I don't care what they do to you. I can promise it will be ten times worse if you betray me. Do we have an understanding?"

"Don't underestimate my desire to see the day the steward is ousted from this palace."

All this time, I'd been focusing on the wrong person. Rueben had been framed. I had been so blind and believed what they wanted me to.

"Head down another passageway so we aren't seen together. Rueben is always watching."

Darkness edged at the corners of my vision. My hands clenched into fists. The traitors were right on the other side of that wall. I tried to get to my feet, only to take a few steps and stumble to the ground again. *Blasted crimson!*

A shuffling and clicking snapped my attention up to the

wall. Someone was leaving the secret passage. My breath caught. In a matter of seconds, I would find myself face to face with one of the people behind all of this.

The passageway door swung inwards, and the person stepped out into the light of the throne room, allowing me to finally see their identity. Even with the masquerade mask, I recognized her.

Cyra.

CHAPTER 32

Leo

IT...COULDN'T BE.

Why—*why* did it have to be her out of everyone in the palace?

As her gaze snapped to me and our eyes met, I said her name in a breathless whisper. "Cyra."

A flicker of uncertainty crossed over Cyra. I'd caught her off guard. Her expression shifted to concern as she hurried over and knelt in front of me.

"Leo." Cyra's gentle hands steadied my shoulders and kept me upright. I wanted to jerk away from her, but the wave of pain from my middle made me slump forward into her arms instead.

"Easy. Focus on breathing." Her calm voice filled my ears. I didn't move, half between relaxing in the hug and pulling away after what I'd heard.

How could she be like this when she was the one who'd

caused it? Cyra acted the same as I'd always known her. Caring, gentle, concerned for me—how much of that had been the real her?

"How could you?" The whispered words held the pained betrayal I couldn't hide. "Tell me that I'm mistaken. That it isn't true."

Silence dragged on.

Cyra slid her blue mask down and cast it aside. "So you did overhear. I've kept it from you for long enough."

I scraped together enough energy to push away from her. I staggered to my feet and braced against the wall.

"You...poisoned me?"

"Yes, and I have the real cure." She slipped out a glass vial containing a dark green liquid.

My gaze locked on it. When she didn't immediately give the vial to me, it cemented the reality of her betrayal.

"Are you going to let me die?"

Her voice turned even and neutral. "That depends on what you choose. You have two options. Either you establish me as Steward and we can rule together—you focus on the aspects of kingship you'd like while I handle the rest—or you choose to fight and force me to do something I will have no pleasure in doing."

Her cold ultimatum sent a chill down my spine. I flicked my gaze back at the shimmering seat in the center of the room. I'd never hated that blasted throne more.

"*That's* what this is about? I thought you had no desire to rule."

"I have other reasons besides power to want the throne.

Not that I don't mind the revenge on my half-brother in the process."

"My father?"

"He ridiculed and tormented me throughout our childhood. Those whispered rumors you've heard are not wrong. Leonidas was a cruel and ruthless individual. He made my life miserable, all because of who my mother was. He always feared that I would take the throne and his position from him, and it drove him to be even crueler to me. Now I'll make his own twisted fears come true, even if he isn't here to see it."

The information about my father tumbled in my head, and I didn't know what to believe. I knew Cyra was only my father's half-sister and that some judged her for it, but it had never mattered to me. I'd assumed it wouldn't have mattered to my father, either.

"I'm sorry if my father treated you like that, but I don't— you know I never cared about that."

Her expression softened. "I know. That is why it's taken me so long to enact this part of the plan. You are one of only two people in all of Kalmyra who never acted differently with me because I am illegitimate. I will always be grateful for that, which is why I'm giving you a choice right now."

I winced as another stab of pain hit me, reminding of what she'd done while my mind reeled with revelations.

"I—I considered you a mentor and a friend—more of a mother than my own. I trusted you!"

The anger of betrayal lent me strength. I pushed off from the wall and lunged for the cure in her hands. Cyra sidestepped me. Staggering, I turned sharply and lunged again.

I pinned her arm to the wall. "Was it you? Did you have Dezaray killed?"

She grunted and tried to wrench her arm free from my grasp. "It wasn't in my original plans. She saw something she shouldn't have."

A fresh wave of shock and betrayal slammed me. The one I'd been after all this time was the person who'd been the closest to me. My sister's killer had been right in front of me, but I'd been too blind to realize it.

Cyra yanked free of me while I snagged the bottom half of the vial and held on tight. My chest heaved. With every breath pain pulsed through my middle. I refused to let go of the cure that my life depended on.

"How can you do this to me? And my sister? Even if my father wronged you, what did we ever do?"

"It has to do with far more than you are willing to understand."

In our struggle to get the cure from the other's grasp, the vial slipped from both our hands. The echo of shattering glass bounced through the room as the vial broke into a hundred scattered pieces. The cure drained into a small puddle on the marble floor.

"No! You foolish boy." Cyra's face twisted in frustration. "You let your own rashness seal your fate. I gave you a choice for a reason!"

I stumbled back. The world spun, and this time it wasn't from the poison.

I'm...going to die.

I shook my head hard to clear the dizziness and feverishly looked around. A weapon. I needed something to defend myself.

All that was within reach was the shattered glass. I dove for the biggest shard and swiped it up off the ground. Before Cyra had a chance to counter, I pressed the sharp edge to her neck.

She held my stare unflinchingly. "Will you end me just like this?"

"I should, after everything you've done."

Despite my words, the idea of killing her made me falter. In that moment of hesitation, the great doors opened behind me. I threw a glance over my shoulder. A group of seven armed soldiers filed in.

"Lieutenant Blaine, punctual as always," Cyra calmly greeted the head soldier of the unit. She didn't seem alarmed about the glass shard still at her throat. "It's time."

He dipped his head in a nod of acknowledgement. "Men, surround him."

One grabbed a hold of me and jerked my arms behind my back. My eyes widened as the palace guards surrounded us. "How?"

"You're the one who put me in charge of recruiting and assigning palace guards," she pointed out. "I admit, Tesfira was somewhat of a hindrance throughout the years, but I have taken care of him now."

Taken care of him? What exactly did that mean?

Symon, I remembered. He would be returning soon. What would Cyra do if he walked in on all of this? Would she just kill him? I clenched my jaw, struggling against the hold of the guard.

"I have already sent guards to apprehend Rueben for attempting to assassinate the crown prince. He is guilty of treason, regardless of what happens here."

I narrowed my eyes. "So you're pinning this all on him? Because, as long as he walks free, he will fight against you ruling Daystra in any capacity."

She smiled in satisfaction. "You really are more perceptive than Rueben gives you credit for."

Memories flashed through my mind, and I shook my head in an attempt to dislodge them. How had it come to this?

As I dragged my gaze up to meet hers again, I realized I didn't know the person standing before me at all. I wasn't sure if she was bluffing or serious when she spoke of killing people, even me.

"Did all those years mean nothing to you? Were you pretending from the start? Were you only ever using me?" I desperately wanted to cling to any flicker of truth to prove that it hadn't all been a lie.

"This was the plan from the start, Leo. I can't stop this now for any fondness I may feel toward you. We have come too far."

I gritted my teeth as a wave of lightheadedness washed over me.

All this time, Cyra had been using me, just like everyone else. That's all I had ever been my entire life—a pawn.

CHAPTER 33

Zandra

I PULLED OUT THE HAIRPINS SECURING MY HAIR AND let it fall down around my shoulders. I crouched down and started fiddling with the door lock. Thank Adonai the outcasts had taught me the basics of lock-picking.

I bit the side of my cheek as I worked on the finicky lock. *Come on.* It took several tries before a click sounded. I tried the door handle and let out the breath I had been holding when it turned smoothly.

A moan from across the room made me stop short. I crossed over to the Steward and knelt down. "Lord Rueben." I shook his shoulder. He didn't seem conscious. They must have drugged him.

I grabbed him by the arm and dragged him over to the door. I grunted at his weight, nearly tripping on the hem of my dress several times in the process. I missed my ship captain dresses that were more suited for activity.

I don't have time for this. I left the Steward lying on the ground just outside the door. A servant would find him soon enough and he'd get help.

The halls blurred by as I raced down the winding turns. Where could he be? On coming near the ballroom again, I met Galen out in the halls.

"Galen!" I skidded to a stop.

"What's wrong?"

"He—I—Rowan is involved in treason, and he knew all along who killed my parents—a-and Prince Leo's in trouble. He needs my help. I need to find him. There's no time."

Galen didn't ask for further details. "I go where you go."

Every footfall pounded in my ears. I scanned the halls for a sign—anything. Up ahead, I caught sight of the prince's body-guard turning down a different hall. "Sir Caddel!" We caught up to him within seconds.

"Princess Alexandrina, whatever it is will have to wait. The prince—"

"The prince is in danger," I said. "The conspirators are making their move. Do you know where he is?"

"Blasted crimson. He's in the throne room."

The three of us sprinted through the palace. My thoughts raced like the wind in a ship's sail.

What if we didn't make it in time? What if I was too late after all? What if he was dead and I'd never be able to tell him once more that I loved him?

When we came to the tall, intricately carved doors that led to the throne room, we stopped. Galen held a finger to his lips before he eased the door open a crack.

Prince Leo stood on the far side of the throne room, backed into a corner. My heart thudded in my chest at the sight of him, my Cass, still alive, but a pit formed in my stomach as I took in his plight.

"So this is what it's come to?" His gaze was locked solely on the woman he was addressing. Her raven hair fell in waves, stopping just past her shoulders. This must be who Rowan was working with—Lady Cyra, the prince's aunt. Several guards circled them, but they made no move to arrest her. These guards had allied with her.

"There is time left. You can still choose."

When Cass glanced back at the guards for a moment, I caught the indecision and confusion that flitted across his face. He was backed into a corner and didn't know how to get out. He faced his aunt again, his hand moving to a phantom hilt of where his sword should be but wasn't.

Sir Caddel's hand flew to the hilt of his own sword, and he took a step forward.

"Wait." Galen stopped us. "We need a plan. If we hold off until they move the prince, it will be easier to intercept them."

"I'm afraid that won't be happening."

I snapped around and scowled at Rowan. The sight of the traitor made my blood boil. "Galen, get the prince to safety. I will handle him."

"Your Highness—"

"That's an order."

If we didn't do something now, we'd lose. We were out of time to think.

Galen thrust his sword into my grasp. "Then fight as I

taught you."

We split off, and I went for Rowan. He evaded my slashes one after another. I grunted. How was he so fast? And when had he learned any fighting skills?

The further down the corridor we got, the more frustrated I became. I couldn't even touch him.

"The prince is going to die. You can't save him."

"Just watch me."

I slashed and landed a solid kick to the back of his knee. Rowan stumbled a few steps, and I took the opportunity and advanced. "I told you. You wouldn't get away with this."

He flicked his gaze to the wall right to the side of us. In an instant, he lunged and smashed in a stone. A secret passageway opened. Rowan dashed inside.

I sprinted after him into the pitch blackness. *You're not getting away.* I faltered as my eyes still needed time to adjust to the drastic change in lightning.

A kick to my knee made my leg buckle. In one swift motion, he twisted my arm and yanked the sword out of my grasp. Rowan pinned me back against the rigid stone.

I tensed my shoulders and sucked in a breath. The blade's cold steel pressed against my neck. I didn't dare move.

"You underestimate the lengths I'm willing to go." The hard edge in his voice sent a chill crawling down my spine.

Mildew tinged the air, as repulsive as the traitor before me.

"You're right. I did underestimate you." My heart pounded in my chest in the dark silence. I slid my hand to the hidden dagger and clenched the smooth handle. I would not let Rowan end the prince. "But you made a miscalculation, too."

I sliced his wrist and snatched my sword from his grasp. Nothing but air met my blade. Retreating footsteps echoed in the tunnel.

Tides. I'd never be able to keep up with him in this dark maze of passageways.

"Coward!" My yell reverberated in the dark tunnel. "This isn't over!"

CHAPTER 34

Leo

"TIME IS UP. IT'S YOUR MOVE, LEO."

The irony wasn't lost on me. The familiar words when we played a game of chess held a bitter context now.

"What? Still indecisive?"

I glared. "I hate you for what you did, but that hate is not so great that I don't want to live."

"Survival is always a good motivator, but how do I know you mean it? That you're not only saying what I want to hear?"

I kept a neutral expression to mask my frustration. Cyra knew me too well. I needed more time. "Can you guarantee you have more of the cure?" I countered.

"I know the source. I can get more of it before you run out of time."

She wasn't bluffing. She wouldn't be this confident and straightforward otherwise.

"I have one condition. If I agree, you don't touch my

friends. They stay out of harm's way."

"Very well—but if you break our deal, they will be the ones to pay the price. That should give you enough incentive to keep your word." She extended her hand for me to shake and complete the deal.

I clenched my jaw. I would never forget her face in that moment. Cyra wore the same expression of pleasure and satisfaction she did when she was about to win a challenging chess game.

Taking in a breath, I tried to disguise how much the throbbing pain in my side bothered me. I stepped up to her and slowly reached out my hand to shake hers.

"Politics is just a global game of chess, my dear Leo." Cyra cupped my chin, cold triumph in her eyes. "And I just eliminated your king."

I glared even as I wanted to shrink back from her touch, but her grip on my hand tightened. She leaned in a fraction. "And I'm no fool, Leo—take him to the dungeons for now," she ordered.

I wrenched free of her and raced for the doors. It might be my one chance. I dodged the guards that chased me and closed in.

My sides smarted with pain and made me crash to the ground halfway. A groan slipped out as I hit the marble floors. The world tilted sideways.

No, can't pass out.

Two guards pulled me to my feet and dragged me along. I took one last glance back at Cyra in the throne room. I didn't know what I'd been expecting to see—remorse? Guilt? Pity?

But her face held none of those. Only a cool, collected expression that stood as unyielding as a stone wall.

The four guards escorting me closed the doors, blocking my view. Their boots echoed like a march of doom. The desolate palace halls remained empty of activity. Everyone else was too preoccupied with the Founding Day's Ball. Each marching step closer to the dungeon further sealed my fate.

On rounding the corner, one of the guards grabbed my arm and gruffly pushed me along. I grunted in annoyance at the fifth guard who had joined at some point. I opened my mouth to make a retort until I saw his face.

Symon. I almost said his name out loud but held my tongue.

He gave my arm a squeeze in silent reply. By the look in his eyes, he had some kind of plan.

We approached the hall that connected to the dungeons and came around the bend. Galen, Princess Alexandrina's chief bodyguard, ambushed the guards. A second figure came up from behind and joined the fight.

In the attack, Symon yanked me back out of the fray. "Come on." He slipped an arm around me for support.

"Wait..." The other one fighting the guards looked like Zandra and she fought like her, but she wore Alexandrina's dress.

"There's no time." He pulled me along, and we ducked into an adjacent hall. I leaned on Symon when we took a small break. "Leo, are you okay?"

I didn't know how to answer that. A new round of throbbing pain made me gasp. I nearly slid to the floor, but I clutched his arm instead. "Let's just focus on getting out of here."

The others rejoined us, and I stopped short at the sight of her. "Zandra." The name slipped out before I could stop myself.

Her blue eyes widened at the name. She slid her purple masquerade mask down. "Cass?"

A ghost of a smile spread across my face. "Yes."

Princess Alexandrina and Zandra are the same person. There was so much I wanted to ask, so much more I wanted to say, but time pressed down on us and stole any chances for further conversation.

The four of us hurried into the closest passage and shut the door behind us.

"They can still follow us," Symon said. "Which passageway should we take? What will they least expect?"

I didn't hesitate to answer. Cyra may know me well, but I knew her too. "Cyra doesn't know that I have knowledge about the dungeon passageway. From the sounds of it, Rueben and the others are being kept in the dungeons."

"Then we'll head there. Lead the way." He shifted to better support me as we continued. "And remind me never to leave you alone again. You get into too much trouble on your own."

"You know how hard I try," I managed to grit out. With every step through the winding passageways, pain jolted through my sides and made it hard to breathe. I nearly cried out, but I bit down hard on my tongue. The metallic tang of blood filled my mouth.

We used the interconnecting passageways to get down to the dungeons and avoid patrolling guards. Upon stepping out of the tunnel that opened in front of one of the main dungeon halls, I winced and braced a hand against the wall.

"Cass!" Zandra gripped my shoulder, throwing worried glances between me and the passage behind us.

"I'll be fine," I gritted out. I couldn't tell them that without the antidote, Cyra had all but killed me already, even if it wasn't by her own hands. It would only distract them when we needed to focus on fleeing. At any moment, pursuing guards might find us. I shoved down the pain and ignored it the best I could.

My gaze snagged on a figure in a cell that we passed, and I stopped. Rueben sat in the front corner, his ankles and wrists chained.

"Uncle Rueben..." I whispered as I crouched down on the other side of the bars. A pang of guilt washed over me. If we had worked together from the start instead of being in constant conflict, would everything still have come to this point?

"Leo?" He rasped, his voice hoarse. He looked at me with a dazed expression. What had they done to him?

"We'll get you free."

"No, you need to get out of here. This is Cyra's insurance. She has the key for these chains on her... You can't get me out."

I bit my lip. Indecision left me stuck to the spot. "I—I don't know if I can leave you here. Who knows what they might do to you?"

Rueben reached through the bars and gripped my arm. "If you're caught here, there's no chance for any of us. Don't worry about me. I can deal with Cyra."

A guard's shout echoed from further down the dungeons. We were out of time.

Words rushed from me in a tangled mix. "I'm sorry for— everything. There's so much I should have done differently and—"

"You are not the only one. Now be that spirited boy who has a talent for sneaking out and escape while you still can."

The thundering footsteps of the guards sounded closer with every passing moment.

"Run, Leo!" Rueben urged.

Symon pulled me to my feet. "We have to go."

I tore myself away from the cell and ran down the hall with the others. Dread formed a pit in my stomach. Please don't let it be the last time I see him.

We raced to the wall that held the entrance to the escape tunnel. Thankfully, this time the mechanism gave way without trouble. As the passage began to open, the guards caught up and surrounded us.

"Surrender," one of them ordered.

I caught the look Symon and Galen exchanged before they ushered both me and Zandra into the cold passageway.

"What are you doing?" She tried to step back out of the passageway, but it started to close again. "Galen! I won't let you sacrifice yourself just so we can escape!"

Her bodyguard flicked his gaze back at us before he drew his sword. "Get back to Zuren and warn your brothers. We do not know the extent of Rowan's treachery, and there is still a war coming."

Symon stepped in front of Zandra and blocked the opening

for her to slip out. "If we don't go now, we'll lose our chance and what he did will be for nothing."

The sounds of fighting and the guards' sneering voices filtered through from the other side of the wall. I cringed. I hated leaving more people behind.

She grunted and tried to move around him. "Get out of my way."

"Zandra." I grabbed her hand. "I'm sorry, but...we have to go, like Symon said. Galen can only hold them off for so long."

Dust crumbled from the ceiling as the passageway door sealed shut.

Even in the faint light, I knew that determined look of resolve. "Fine. Let's go."

Aware that the guards wouldn't be far behind, we hurried through the winding tunnels as fast as I could lead the way. A cold draft curled around me. I shivered. Had it always been this chilly down in these passages?

Water droplets from condensation on the ceiling dripped onto the back of my neck. I barely swallowed back my yelp of surprise. Jittery adrenaline did nothing to help my focus.

We continued through the small, labyrinthine passage. Finally, I halted and rested my hands on my knees and took deep breaths. With each inhale, pain radiated through me.

"Are you doing all right?" I didn't have to look up to know Symon was hovering over me, worried. "Are the side effects from the poison getting worse?"

Zandra gasped. "What?"

Despite our circumstances, I couldn't help but smile a little. Even now, she still cared. "It's—a long story."

Symon threw a glance over his shoulder. "We need to escape the palace. They won't stop searching until they find us. Nowhere in Daystra is safe as long as Cyra's in control. We need to get somewhere out of her reach."

"Zuren is our only option."

We both looked at Zandra. She said, "My brothers will protect you if you take refuge in our country—or at least, I will convince them to."

"Even then, we probably wouldn't be safe for long." I straightened and leaned back against the frigid stone with a grimace. "Not when Cyra has Zurinians on her side."

Zandra's expression turned stormy, and she muttered about traitors under her breath.

"Right now, Zuren's still our best chance for refuge," Symon reasoned.

Shouts echoed from further down the dark tunnel. I bit back a groan at the prospect of more running. We weaved through the passageways in a twisted, winding route. My knowledge of them gave a much needed advantage in order to avoid the guard's patrols flooding into the labyrinth.

We rounded a bend, and I crumpled to the ground in a heap.

"Leo!"

The stony ceiling above me spun and felt like it would never stop spinning. "I..."

Zandra and Symon helped ease me up to rest against the gritty tunnel wall.

"I'm sorry. I'm so sorry..."

I had believed a lie for the last six years.

All this time, I'd thought Cyra had been the one on my side, the one trying to help me, and that Rueben had been the one against me—the power hungry one. But I had been wrong. So wrong.

She was the one behind my sister's death.

I clamped my eyes shut, partly from the pain and dizziness, partly from the violent storm of emotions warring inside of me. "Cyra's taken the throne, the palace, and imprisoned everyone in it who would be against her—and it's all my fault."

Cyra had deceived me from the beginning. She had twisted my perception to suit her plans. I had been her perfect little pawn, doing whatever she wanted whenever she chose, all while letting me think I decided on my own.

I should have seen it coming. I should have realized what Cyra had been doing all along. Instead, I'd been irresponsible and reckless and let her go on doing whatever she pleased with little, if any, opposition.

I'm such a fool.

Zandra rested a hand on my shoulder. "It's not all your fault."

As memories filled my mind of all the time Cyra and I had spent together, I shook my head slowly, regretting it when the world tilted again. "Every time...I always end up being a pawn that does exactly what they want."

Was that what I was destined to be for the rest of my life, however long—or short—that might be? Was I always going to be trapped as someone's pawn?

"Leo." Symon gave my shoulder a gentle shake. He waited until I looked at him. "If you really don't want to be a pawn, then get up and fight it. If you want to fight Cyra, we need to get to the border and take temporary refuge in Zuren."

The plain statement of reality stung, but it was also what I needed to hear. After a moment, I nodded. I rallied my strength before getting to my feet again.

Zandra and Symon exchanged a worried look when I took a step and couldn't hide my grimace. "We'll be able to rest once we get to the border," she promised. "We just have to get to the border."

The border. It felt so close and yet so far.

I clenched my jaw in determination. "Right."

The muffled echo of our footsteps melted into the distant chaos of guards hunting for us. Evading them proved to be difficult, and hours drained away in the cold, damp tunnels.

I didn't know how or when I might face Cyra again. But I did know this: she was wrong if she thought I would bow down to her and not fight back.

A month ago, she would have been right, and I probably would've let her have the throne—but not anymore. Things were different. *I* was different now.

I would never be anyone's pawn again.

EPILOGUE

Cyra

PHANTOM MEMORIES HANUTED ME AS I WALKED down the long halls to the throne room. But I was no longer a child, and my half-brother wasn't here to torment me and make me feel less than worthy. He was long gone.

Even though he might not be here to see this, taking the thing he had loved most from him— just as he had done to me all those years ago—was so satisfying.

I entered the throne room with Rowan, clasping his hand in mine and leaning into him. After all this time, after everything, we could finally be together. No one would separate us.

"I've wanted to tell you this for so long," I said slowly. "I love you. You are the only one I have ever loved."

"I loved you all those years ago, and I still do. Nothing will ever change the fact that I love you, Cyra."

Rowan pressed a kiss to my forehead, and I closed my eyes, wanting to remember this moment forever.

In that moment I knew. It was all worth it. All the horrible things I had endured in my life, nearly two decades of being separated from him, the excruciatingly lengthy season of planning and patiently waiting—it was all worth it, because it led me to this moment.

We continued walking together. "Things went rather well, although not entirely according to plan." My gaze drifted to Rowan's bandaged wrist. I'd been relieved the royal physician had been able to tend his wound swiftly, at least.

I hadn't considered that Leo might leave Rueben and the others down in the dungeon and flee without them. I had expected him to confront me again and end things then and there, one way or another.

"While the poison in him might kill him soon, it can't be counted on. He could still find a remedy. I will send the best mercenaries after them, and the loose ends will be tied up," Rowan reassured me.

"Leo can be unpredictable."

I approached the throne, almost touching it but not quite. I knew the legends about lunarium and hadn't decided if I wanted to test the validity of those myths yet. "If my brother could see me now, oh, how he would regret all of those things he said and did to me—how he tore us apart."

"He's not a problem anymore, love."

"You're right." I smiled. "We can finally be together now."

The memories and words of my father, step family, and all those who mocked me and thought I would never amount to anything taunted me as I stared at the tall lunarium throne. I had spent so much time as a child staring at this shimmering seat, wondering what it would be like to sit on it.

"It's only the beginning."

To the flames with the legends. I sat on the throne and held my breath for a second.

Immediately, it turned cold beneath my hands and crackled like splitting ice. Startled, I leapt off the throne and watched as the clear crystal turned inky black, spreading from center out until the throne resembled obsidian. The cracking sound echoed off the walls until it at last fell silent.

So the legends about lunarium weren't only a myth. A part of me was angry. Everything in my life always had to be against me, even this forsaken hunk of mineral.

But I couldn't care less whether some mineral thought I was right for the throne or not. With this, no one would be able to hurt me anymore or lord their power over me.

A triumphant smile spread across my face as I settled back onto my throne and looked to Rowan.

"It's good to be queen."

ACKNOWLEDGMENTS

So much goes into the creation of a book, from the first spark of an idea to the physical book held in your hands. Years of work went into *Gilded Crown*, but I couldn't have done this alone.

Above all else, I want to thank my Lord and Savior for giving me the gift of this story and the means to carry it out. This book wouldn't exist without Him.

A special thanks to my beta readers: Kathryn, Courtney, Nora, Ella, Sienna, Lydia, Heather, Grace, Avie, Bethani, Nicole, and Paige. Thank you so much for taking the time to read over my story and give feedback on it!

A special thanks to my editor, Selina R. Gonzalez. This book wouldn't be what it is without your help, feedback, and expertise! (She's also an amazing author. If you like fairytale retellings, go check out her books!)

A huge thank you to Laura Hollingsworth who designed such a stunning book cover, along with my world map and character art. You have this incredible way of peeking into my head and creating what I imagined, but ten times better. Thank you so much for all the lovely artwork!

A big thanks to my family for all the support they've given me from the very beginning. I know not every writer gets support like that, and I'm grateful I have you guys as family. Thank you for cheering me on and encouraging my writing for all these years. A special thanks to my mom for helping me walk through these stages and figuring things out. I appreciate you so much. And thanks to my brother Jacob for always being my reliable logistics guy! (You keep my fight scenes realistic, even if I get grumpy for having to rewrite scenes because of it, lol).

To my cousins, Aila, Bella, and Kaija, who were there from the start. Thanks for listening to me ramble on about my writing and helping me brainstorm ideas, and for answering those random texts at the most random of times. You guys are the best. Thanks for always being there for me, both as my "first fans" and as my honorary sisters.

Hannah—you'll always be my writing partner in crime. Thanks for adoring my characters even when I felt like strangling them, encouraging me, and reminding me of what I was working toward during the harder times.

Thank you so much to Kathryn, my brainstorming buddy who is practically the other half of my brain, for helping me out with the extra detailed editing in the final stages (you save my sanity—or what's left of it—hurray!). Likewise, thank you to Nora for helping me out with the proof reading.

Heather, Hannah, Kathryn, and Isadora—you are such special friends, and the best I could ask for. Thank you for all your enthusiasm for my writing. Thank you for never letting me give up, for helping me work out all the crazy trouble the problem child (Leo) threw my way, and for always being ready to jump into brainstorming, or simply listening when I needed it. I couldn't have asked for better writer friends to support me on this journey. You know I'm not one short on words, but I'll stop there before the acknowledgements turns into its own novel. Needless to say, you guys mean the world to me.

A special thanks to the Young Writers Workshop. I've learned so much there, and it has fostered such a beautiful writing community that I'm grateful to be a part of.

And last but certainly not least, I want to thank you, my readers! Thank you for taking a chance on Leo and his story. Without you, I would have no reason to write. My ultimate goal as a writer is to touch the lives of my readers, and I hope I was able to accomplish that with this story in some way. I hope Leo and his crazy shenanigins made you laugh, and that beyond that, you could connect with them and their story on a deeper level. Never forget, no matter how dark things around you may seem—there is always hope.

~Natalie

About the Author

Natalie Nordby is a fantasy author who writes epic stories filled with adventure, twists, intrigue, and clean romance. She lives in the forests of Northern Minnesota where she first discovered the magic of imagination and her passion for storytelling. Through her stories, she desires for others to know they are not alone, and that even in the darkness, there is still hope.

When not traipsing through fantastical worlds with her characters, Natalie enjoys the violin, archery, studying foreign languages, and searching for epic music for her writing.

You can find Natalie on Instagram @bookenthusiast_97 where she's happy to chat about books, travel, tales of adventure, and anything in between.

Keep up to date on all of Natalie's publishing news by joining her newsletter.

www.natalienordby.com

✡✡✡

Please Leave a Review!

Thank you for reading! Reviews help authors and future readers so much. If you enjoyed this story, please consider taking the time to leave a review on Amazon or Goodreads! I would greatly appreciate it.

~Natalie

KINGDOMS OF KALMYRA

SHATTERED THRONE

Book Two currently in development

www.ingramcontent.com/pod-product-compliance
Lightning Source LLC
Chambersburg PA
CBHW010532100726
47903CB00011B/2984